Reception

Reception

L.M.VINCENT

BUNBURY PRESS
MANCHESTER, MA

PART ONE

You are invited to a pre-nuptial Reception
honoring the upcoming marriage of
Melissa Lynne Manning to Rodney Evan Schoenlieber,
on Friday evening, March 13, 1981
at the home of Margaret Manning . . .

Monday, February 16, 1981, 10 A.M.

Blair Brackman held the invitation in his hand. It had been a bitch to even pull out, the crème-colored stock jammed so snugly in its shiny gold-lined envelope.

The text was a flowery cursive, like the message in a Hallmark card, until the bottom, where the type face changed into an upright and all capitalized font that conveyed imminent danger, like warning swimmers of a riptide.

SHUSH!!! IT'S A SURPRISE!!!
DON'T TELL A SOUL!!!

Blair, for one, was certainly surprised. And he of all people should have known about it. Perplexed, he absently tapped the card against his office desk and rubbed his forehead with his free hand. He couldn't recall ever having seen an embossed invitation that employed a succession of three exclamation points, and three times in a row at that. Clearly this was the handiwork of Meg Manning, unleashed and unsupervised, he thought. No question about it. Otherwise he would have known.

Naturally Blair already knew everything else about the upcoming nuptials, and more about the intended groom Rod Schoenlieber than he cared to. At the thought of such an understatement, Blair even managed a half-hearted chuckle to himself. The ceremony itself, as he had been informed early in the planning stages, was a relatively informal gathering for close family only—mainly consisting of the Schoenlieber clan from out of state—in the smallest of the banquet rooms in Crown Center. No bridal shower, no bachelor party, no luncheon at the club for the bridge group and Meg Manning's society friends. Melissa had insisted, and she told Blair as much repeatedly. She had also told him that this state of affairs had irked her mother beyond belief, which he had surmised before she even said a word.

"She'll get over it," Blair told her at the time. He was able to come across as philosophical, even optimistic, though he himself was in great psychological pain at the time, as he tended to be during Melissa's therapy sessions. He had become gradually more adept at disguising his distress, which he attributed to the acting class he took as an elective at the University of Missouri.

Since Freddy Herzmark's mother had cancelled the twelve-year-old's session because it conflicted with an orthodontist appointment—clearly Freddy's teeth were more important than his anger issues and intermittent bed-wetting—Blair had an empty fifty minute slot. He glanced at his schedule book for that Monday morning, confirming that the next scheduled session, unfortunately, was with the dreaded Dickie Rawlings. But for the next forty-seven minutes, Blair had time to think things over, delve into the insidious thoughts that beckoned to him the instant he saw the invitation.

Two words came into his head and remained there. "LAST CHANCE." A warning, and an urgent one, repeating itself as an inner voice Mobius strip. The little shin-dig of Meg Manning's possibly represented the last, and only remaining chance, of saving Melissa Manning from herself.

Blair continued to tap the invitation against the desk top, in sequences of three taps, just like the exclamation points. Then he picked up the empty envelope and looked it over, half expecting to see the words "LAST CHANCE" written on the front. Only then did he notice for the first time—perhaps because he had been so distracted and irritated by the use of a "Love" stamp—that the envelope was addressed to his old office, one that he hadn't occupied for nearly two years, although in the same building. Fortunately the mailman knew him, and had delivered it anyway to the correct box. How close had he come to missing out on his "Last Chance"?

Frankly, up until then he had made scant progress with Melissa. He kept waiting for the light bulb to go off in her head and often wondered if the cord was even plugged in. She had shown surprisingly little insight about her tendency to choose the wrong men for herself. He had helped her disengage from Mitch Harrington more than two years before and had tried to put the brakes on the affair with Rod. Not overtly, of course. But Melissa had a blind spot and seemed incapable of breaking the pattern on her own, despite his subtle but probing guidance. He had done his best, and could not be faulted for lack of motivation, but in blue moods he saw her lack of progress as his own professional failure.

Now a new opportunity presented itself. And, as a last ditch effort—his own last chance—he would resort to unconventional means. He would free himself of professional constraints and do more talking than listening for a change. Blair made the decision then and there, tapping the envelope on his desk in an increasing crescendo that ceased only when the card escaped his grip and he was forced to retrieve it from the floor.

Blair Brackman, outside of his usual office hours, would attend Meg Manning's little pre-wedding get-together and do what was necessary: he would break up the damn wedding.

※

Indeed, the party had been the brainchild of Margaret Manning: a pre-wedding reception in honor of the upcoming nuptials of daughter Melissa Manning—she had disposed of her previous married name of Harrington—to a total unknown by the name of Rod Schoenlieber. Rod was not a local Kansas City boy, but from a small town in Iowa, the name of which—being a small town in Iowa—was of no consequence and thus difficult to remember for non-Iowans. The idea for a party occurred to Meg a short time after Reagan's inauguration at the end of January; likely watching all those fancy inaugural balls had given her inspiration. After all, for her to be cut completely out of entertaining for her daughter's wedding was beyond humiliating, it was downright un-American.

In theory, the concept was to introduce Rod to Melissa's old friends, both for the purpose of getting to know them and to make him feel more comfortable in her circle, him being from Iowa and all. Melissa, of course, had a broad and sophisticated collection of friends, none of whom were likely to have much in common with Rod. Rod was a salesman for the telephone company, a fact that Meg had difficulty revealing to her bridge and golf friends. She would hastily brush off the question as if her future son-in-law's employment were of no consequence compared to the happiness of her eldest daughter.

"He has an important position with a large multinational," she would say when pressed, with a quick whisk of her right hand, adding preemptively, "He's originally from Iowa, but went to college in Bloomington."

When the subject of the wedding itself came up, she had another standard response.

"Fortunately it's only going to be a *small* wedding. And I couldn't be happier with that—I went through all that hoopla with Melissa the *first* time!" she would jovially confess, doing her damndest to disguise her embarrassment. "Why, I practically had to *beg* her to spare me the aggravation and all that money!"

And then she would tell them all she was arranging a small reception before the wedding, because she needed to do *something*, but that none of them should be upset about not being invited because only an intimate group of Melissa's closest friends and contemporaries were included. Melissa had *insisted* on that, Meg would go on to say, feigning remorse.

More accurately, Melissa had insisted that her mother refrain from hosting an event of any kind, but Meg refused to take the admonitions seriously. Melissa, her fickle daughter, couldn't truly feel that way at all. She wasn't really serious.

"I *am* serious, Mom!" Melissa had repeated, increasing the volume with each volley.

"I know, dear."

"I'm not just saying that, Mom! I'm *really* serious!"

"Of course you are, dear."

"Promise me you won't do anything, Mother!"

Meg bore the expression of indulgent motherhood. Who knew a daughter better than her own mother? Melissa simply didn't want to impose, put her dear Mother out, especially this being the second go-round. The poor kid was embarrassed. Hadn't Melissa just let it slip that Rod would be in town for a meeting the end of the second week in March? She just *happened* to mention that?

"Promise, Mom!"

"I promise, dear," said Meg, holding back a wink.

But whom to invite?

Wednesday, February 11, 1981, 5:00 P.M.

"What party, Mom?" Val Manning had dropped by her mother's apartment off Brush Creek Boulevard shortly after the end of the school day, a ritual mid-week visit under the meagerest of pretenses. She taught Social Studies to eight and ninth graders at Meadowbrook Junior High and, despite homework to grade, refused to sacrifice precious week-end time for such filial visits. She was single, after all, and deserved a life.

Since Melissa was, at best, reliably unreliable—and in fairness frequently on the road on business—Val had assumed the responsibility for checking in on Mom, especially since their father, Meg's ex Charlie, lived on the West coast with Sheila, his second wife of ten years. Of course, at this point in Meg's advanced middle age, any "looking after" was little more than assuaging Val's own guilt. Meg golfed, played mahjong, was in a bridge group and a book club, and seldom lunched in. Ora Lee still came in twice a week and would cook magnificent dinners in advance and package them neatly in the freezer in zip-lock bags, identified and dated. Money wasn't a problem. If Meg had any problems to speak of, they were First World ones.

"You heard from your father, lately?" Meg asked, ignoring her daughter's question. She had just returned from the beauty parlor, and her freshly auburn-dyed hair was in a stiff bouffante, which she patted with her fingertips as if it were hot.

"No . . . and *what* party?" Val turned back to the sink. She made sweeps around the drain with a dry sponge—a meaningless gesture, of course, but she wanted to seem helpful. The sink was spotless. Ora Lee had seen to that on Tuesday, and apparently Meg hadn't even run the tap since.

"Who said anything about a party?" Meg asked innocently. "And don't bother with the sink, darling . . . Ora Lee was just here yesterday."

"You said something about a party. Just a minute ago." With restraint, Val replaced the sponge on the counter, now the only thing out of place in the apartment. The urge to throw it across the room, or better yet, at her mother, began to manifest itself as a slow burn along Val's cheeks and forehead.

"I simply asked if you were sure to be available on the second Friday evening in March."

"To help with the party." Val closed her eyes and took a deep breath before continuing. "I hope you're having a get together for the bridge ladies, Mom . . ."

Meg fluffed the firm upholstered pillows on the white leather Florence Knoll couch. She gave one a final slap.

"You know how much Melissa wants a party for the wedding! No engagement party, no actual wedding ceremony that outsiders can attend . . . why, the poor thing's hardly able to mark the occasion with lunch at Winstead's . . ."

"Because that's the way she *wants* it! Mom, no! Melissa doesn't want a party! She made that emphatically clear!"

"That's nonsense." Meg plopped down on the sofa. "Of course she wants a party, she's just saying that she doesn't. You know Melissa . . ."

Val could only roll her eyes.

"Mel doesn't know a thing about this, does she?" After the long, exerting roll, Val's fatigued eyes needed to take a long rest. They closed.

"Of course not, dear . . . what kind of surprise would that be?"

∽∞∽

Mother and daughter sat on the sofa, a comfortable space between, both pretending to be casual and relaxed. They held tea cups, and if refills were necessary, the entire pot—under a Mondrian-inspired quilted cozy—was within easy reach on the Noguchi glass-topped coffee table. The remaining hot water and floating jasmine flowers would be wasted, though, poured down the sink. Val wasn't a fan of jasmine, and Meg already took natural diuretics for leg swelling—that her doctor was unable to detect—and didn't want to be up half the night peeing.

The interrogation was in progress and at a dead end. Val had deemed it essential to discover the names on the guest list, although it was too late to do anything about it, since Meg already sent out the professionally-printed invitations.

"There's no point in even discussing it anymore, Val, dear . . ." Meg said at the outset, hoping to avoid the entire conversation. "I already mailed them out. And I used those special 'Love' stamps."

"But the *list* . . . surely you must have the *list* somewhere."

"I already told you, Val dear, I must have thrown it out. Maybe Ora Lee did."

"And where did you get the addresses again?"

"I told you. I was rummaging through the bureau drawers, cleaning things out, and came across that old address book of Melissa's. And what luck that was! As soon as I came across it, I knew the whole surprise party thing was meant to be."

"And the old address book . . ."

"I told you, Val, don't you ever listen? I must have thrown it out. I was cleaning things out, remember? Maybe Ora Lee threw it out."

Ora Lee was a convenient alibi for Meg, who was renowned for absent-mindedness. In situations like this, Ora Lee was always the dog blamed for the unavowed fart.

Striving to appear calm, Val deliberately set her cup on the coffee table, and then frantically searched every drawer of the bureau in her mother's bedroom with the thoroughness of a member of the narcotics squad. She had nothing to show for her efforts except a puncture on the tip of her right index finger from a swiping encounter with a golf tee.

The fact that the address book was out-of-date gave Val the most cause for concern. Melissa went to great lengths to keep the details of her private life beyond reach of her mother's obsessive, controlling tendencies. Meg strived to be in the loop. She assumed that all of her daughters' friends viewed her as a fascinating and with-it peer, worthy of friendship independent of their relationships with her daughters. "All your friends just *love* me," she said to both of them since grade school. For all Val knew, her mother might have invited Melissa's eighth grade class from the Barstow School to the upcoming festivities.

Val accepted that her mother had no more information to give, without perhaps, the use of hypnosis. Had the session been an actual torture session—were Meg Manning swollen and bloodied, with broken bones and torn off fingernails—she would have just started making up names. She wasn't lying, she honestly didn't have a clue. The slate had been wiped clean. Meg never paid much attention to names, anyway, and it wasn't surprising that after a fortnight's interval, she couldn't come up with more than a couple of names from the list, other than the obvious one of hostess—she had mailed herself one of the embossed invitations—and Val, whose omission from the mailing list, Meg claimed, had been an oversight.

Val sighed.

"Okay, Mom, just one more time. Deirdre Rehnquist . . ."

"Yes, of course, I remember Deedra. She and Mel were such great friends at Barstow . . . and did I mention her husband, that Italian fellow?"

"Greek, Mom. He's Greek. John Palopolus."

"Yes, that was it. Always seemed like a funny name for an Italian."

"Greek, Mom. And they're divorced now."

"What a shame."

"And not exactly on the best of terms."

"Well," said Meg, with the finger-wagging tone of voice, "divorces happen all the time, and people have to be adult enough to get over themselves."

Val didn't think this was a good time to protest or bring up the sticky subject of her father Charlie and Sheila. It was hard to pass up such a great opportunity, expose her mother's complete hypocrisy, but there'd be other opportunities—things could wait until the next time her father's alimony check was late, Meg leaving multiple messages for her lawyer Harry Bernstein.

Meg sipped her tea and sat back, balancing the cup close to her body. The homeopathic dose of stimulant possibly jogged her memory.

"And I mentioned Sylvia and Harry's son, right?"

"Blair?" Val's shoulders tensed.

"Yes. Blair. He used to date Melissa in high school, remember? Sweet boy."

Val chewed at her lower lip and aimlessly looked around the room, shifting her eyes as if she were watching the progress of an imaginary cockroach traversing the carpeting.

"You remember him, don't you? He went out with Melissa a few times in high school?"

"High school was a long time ago, Mom," Val finally said.

"Well! And you tell me I have problems with *my* memory . . ." Meg leaned forward and set down the teacup before rising.

"Stay put," she said, inching her way around the edge of the table, "I have to pee."

Val took the bundled teapot to the kitchen counter, lifted off the cozy, and poured the contents into the sink. Blair Brackman was on the list. A bit odd, inviting Melissa's therapist to her engagement party; but then, her mother didn't know about the therapy. Maybe he'd decline, recuse himself for professional reasons. Her feelings were a jumble. On the positive side, depending on who had made the cut and who had the courage to show up, the availablity of psychological help could be beneficial, even necessary. And personally, she had kind of a thing for him.

Three or four hydrated, puffy jasmine flowers didn't make their way down the drain. Valerie Manning looked at them scornfully and reached for the sponge on the counter.

Saturday, February 14, 1981, 12 *noon*

Rebecca Harvey whistled silently over the top of the steaming cup of black coffee. Her lips, well coated in the pink shade of an impatiens and with a shimmering, glossy finish, formed a seductive moue. Rebecca was a seductive woman, tall, full-bodied, with burnt umber eyes and a strong but straight nose that people envied.

She wore her dark hair down and parted in the middle, in homage to the Peggy Lipton of yore and her own hippie college days at Mizzou. Frequently she would brush the hair away from her eyes, first one side, then the other, with the third and fourth fingers of the respective hand, as the need arose. Those, in themselves, were seductive gestures, avoidable with the judicious use of bobby pins, which Rebecca would sooner die than employ.

Sometimes, knocking it out of the sensuality park, Rebecca would slowly pass her outspread fingers through her hair from forehead to the crown of her head. She would freeze at the top of the gesture—head tilted back, elbow aimed ahead—eyes unfocused. And with her hair fully and tightly held back, the full expanse of her forehead was exposed. The revelation, not generally noted by women, had the effect of sudden, unexpected full-frontal nudity for a male—a liquored-up co-ed in Fort Lauderdale lifting her tank top to reveal pendulant breasts. And that was just Rebecca's forehead.

That Rebecca did not have a girl-next-door persona only added to her appeal. Striking and attractive, without question, but there was a particular hardness to her features, the strong jawline and a prominent brow, enhanced by her athletic, loose-arm swinging, aggressive stride. Rebecca was not one to emanate wholesome; rather, she impressed many as being provocative, with just a touch of bad girl, a tad unseemly as marriage material. But in a good way, of course, and first impressions could deceive. Her voice, in keeping with her demeanor, was a husky, sensual come-hither contralto, like Bizet's Carmen. And like Carmen, she was a heavy smoker, which did nothing to tip her more toward the Sandra Dee side of the scale.

These signals were not consciously sent, the gestures were no more than habits nowadays, hold-overs from her late teens and twenties, when she had been boy-obsessed and borne the reputation of being pretty easy. Of course, in those days, promiscuity didn't carry all that much of a stigma—at least not in college—and Rebecca, with her intelligence and brutal honesty, was well-liked by most girls as well as those young men who hadn't had sex with her. She had been a bit mercenary in those days, though, over-sexualized and searching for something, and when she discovered that it wasn't really worth looking for in the manner that she had adopted—being groped and groping back—it was too late. Her daughter Beatrice was now eight years old, and had just been dropped off at her dance class at the nearby Westport Ballet School.

The coffee was still too hot. She set it down on the dark-wooded bar table and took a drag from her cigarette. Courteously, she twisted her mouth before blowing the smoke out; the swirling triangle flowed in a rapid stream ninety-degrees to the usual trajectory. John Palopolus, sitting across from her, did the same, scrunching his face as if he had a nose itch.

John and Rebecca were long-time friends, their smoking mannerisms conveying mutual respect. They manifested such courtesy to few others. Rebecca, more than most, had made many men's eyes sting from cigarette smoke aggressively steered. This non-verbal communication was universally understood, and guaranteed against unwelcome advances. Rebecca wasn't interested in screwing around anymore, despite initial impressions, and hadn't been for quite some time. As far as sex went, she was less of a male-hater than male-adverse. Besides, as a working single mother, she had better, more important things to do.

"So . . . when did you get the invitation?" John asked, crunching out his cigarette with several good puffs left, as he used to do when money hadn't been an issue. The question was a pointless one, her answer irrelevant, serving no other purpose than resuming the conversation.

"Yesterday's mail," Rebecca said.

"Me too."

"Really odd, her mother doing that."

"I'm sure Melissa will be absolutely mortified."

They were at the New Stanley Bar that Saturday afternoon. Over the past several weeks, at Rebecca's initiation, the two had made the late morning rendevouz a standing date. That Bea had her ballet class nearby was only a pretext. "I have to be hanging around by myself, anyway," she had told him then. "Why don't you keep me company? You can walk from your place, and you don't even have to change your underwear. No pressure." She was grateful to resume her old relationship with him. No surprise, during his marriage to Deirdre, Rebecca had been pretty much pushed out of his life.

She was worried about him. Since Deirdre had left, John had gone progressively downhill—reclusive, depressed, drinking and smoking too much. He had lost his column at the *Kansas City Star* after missing multiple deadlines due to emotional tremors from the split and hadn't pursued any freelance work to speak of. Rebecca had never known a time when John didn't have at least two or three writing projects on the fire.

Money was also becoming an issue. John hadn't exactly mooched off Deirdre, but he was careless with money—typically forgetting to carry his wallet—and Deirdre could always be relied on to bring out the credit card linked to her trust fund. Plus the liquor cabinet was always well-stocked, since Deirdre was a well-practiced imbiber herself. Without an accounting, and generally with his head in the clouds researching and writing, John hadn't been aware of how much he spent on the incidentals—or necessities—of Johnny Walker and Chesterfields. The knowledge came as a shock, an unanticipated dousing of ice water.

John had Doonesbury-esque bags under his eyes in the best of times, but Rebecca now saw that his eyes were puffy, the bags dark-lined, like double shiners. He had never been the well-coiffed type, with his pudgy, putty-like face, hair that had started thinning before any of his peers, and a physique that was precociously flabby. His body, like the Rome of past, had expanded its borders without retaining its conquests. Previously, he would survey himself in the mirror and pledge to go on a diet. He had been with Deirdre then, and wanted to have a better physique for her sake. Now he just stared at his reflection, wondering how he could look like such an ape below the neck when the hair on his head was so rapidly thinning. Still, at over six feet, his heft made him physically imposing.

There simply wasn't much point in modeling himself after the GQ fraternity types, but neither did John harbor any such interests. At Princeton he had been known for his slovenliness and train-wreck of a dormitory room in Witherspoon, occassionally as a loose cannon behaviorwise, but also for his intellect. Equally facile at math and science as he was with history, philosophy, or government, Palopolus was remarkably well-read, insightful, and articulate. He was one of a handful of undergraduates who had a personal relationship with professors, routinely visiting them during their office hours just to chat. Mentally, he had the fitness of a triathelete. After graduation, he had taken a free ride for a master's degree at the University of Missouri School of Journalism, returning to the Kansas City fold as a conquering hero.

"And who the hell else did she invite?" Rebecca again. "It's not as if she's exactly up to date with Melissa's current social set."

"Nor are we. Have you even met the guy? I haven't." John took a sip of his first Scotch of the day and stared down into it as he swirled the glass.

"I haven't either." Rebecca made a slight involuntary movement of her lips. "It's like . . . it's like . . . she's hiding the guy or something."

"Once burned, twice shy," said John. He said it again, this second time clearly in reference to himself.

"Will you go with me?" Rebecca, with an expectant look, gave her coffee another small sip before replacing the cup.

John continued to look down into his drink.

"Not sure I'll be able to make it."

"Bullshit, John. You have to get out. You're becoming a burnt out case."

"I *am* a burnt out case."

"Fuck you and your wallowing, John. For Christ's sake . . ."

Palopolus looked up at her, his eyes watery. "How do we know Deirdre wasn't invited? I'm not going if she's gonna be there! No way in hell. Undoubtedly with some guy she's met, to torment me and show everyone how great she's doing. 'Your assignment: Compare and Contrast.' Fuck it."

"I haven't run into her lately, John. Not that I care to. Maybe she's out of town."

Rebecca had never understood them as a couple. Not their dating to begin with, let alone them getting married, and not just because of the personal animosity she harbored against Deirdre Rehnquist. Rebecca had always considered Deirdre a selfish, spoiled bitch, although admittedly one in an attractive package. Before college, she had only known her remotely through Cotillion. Deirdre was a private school girl, attending Barstow. Even as a public school kid at relatively affluent Shawnee Mission East, Rebecca didn't travel in the same circles. And worse, she often dated more of the disreputable older boys, borderline hoods.

For a few moments Rebecca and John didn't converse, each lost in their own reveries about Deirdre, distinct but both unpleasant.

At Missouri, John Palopolus had been Rebecca's intellectual soul mate for most of her junior and senior years until she was forced to drop out. He had been dependable, supportive and non-judgmental, leading her back to a relatively safe harbor as she navigated the chaotic waters of her life. A few years older and in the master's program, he had been her graduate T.A. in a journalism course, Radio-Television Investigative Journalism. She was the sharpest and most engaged student in his section, and each almost immediately recognized the shared sensibilities in the other. Discussions in class about Seymour Hersh and Woodward and Bernstein led to more intense discourses outside of class, involving E.M. Forster and Virginia Woolf, at the student union over coffee. Eventually Rebecca spent a good portion of her free time just hanging out in John's apartment on East Walnut. There they enjoyed each other's company, studying together, talking late into the night about history and politics and books. They drank bourbon and coffee and smoked cigarettes and marijuana.

Their relationship was never complicated by sex, which was hard to explain or even imagine, since John knew Rebecca wasn't exactly saving herself for marriage. He was acutely aware that Rebecca exhibited a sexual freedom on most weekends with a procession of eager participants, none of whom stuck around very long. Once she even slept with his undergraduate acquaintance Blair Brackman, and John had pumped him for details afterwards, attempting to satisfy himself vicariously. Blair described her revelant anatomy rather clinically, which was a disappointment. And it was obvious that Blair, more a romantic than cocksman, had been quite intimidated. John, oddly enough, felt almost a paternal pride in knowing this. Rebecca was a tough cookie and could handle herself, in or out of bed.

Rebecca never expected John to ask or make a move. She felt at ease enough with him that she never consciously sent him signals of any kind. John thought about her sexually every now and again, fantasizing, but always decided against going there. Truthfully, neither one wanted to risk spoiling a good thing.

"You're the smartest girl at this place," he once said to her, "how and why you got into that fucking sorority house is beyond me."

"You keep me sane, John," she had replied, not really answering his question.

John was a big, pessimistic teddy bear, and Rebecca cherished him. She couldn't let him sink; she had to save him. And sometimes, when she let herself think about it, she wondered if he could save her.

"Maybe Deirdre will be skiing. Tis the season," Rebecca offered optimistically. "Really. You need to come. You don't get out at all. It's not healthy. It will be a fun party."

John blew out his breath, closed his eyes, and let his chin sink on his chest.

"I'll think about it," he said, weariness in his voice. "But don't count on it."

∞

Blair Brackman went much further back with Melissa Manning than did John Palopolus, certainly, and even Rebecca Harvey. None of their mutual friends shared as lengthy a scholastic provenance as he and Melissa, going all the way back to kindergarden at Prairie Elementary. A continuously shared educational experience, excluding Melissa's stint at Barstow for eighth and ninth grades at Meg's insistence, ostensibly for reasons of academic rigor, but actually to spare Meg the embarrassment of having a child in the public school system. Ultimately, after protracted arguments and tears, Meg relented, accepting that the experiment in single-sex education had failed and concluding that her eldest daughter was boy-crazy.

Melissa had been Blair's first crush in second grade, beginning with the sight of her as the Virgin Mary in the Christmas pageant. He had been staring at her from his perch as the dove in the rafter high, when something drastically changed with the wiring in his brain, a reshuffling of neuronal synapses. And though crushes generally have an expiration date, Blair's seemed completely nonperishable, persisting in more mature manifestations as his hormones changed. All of Blair's developed notions of romance, love, and sex were inextricably linked and had evolved from the existence of Melissa Manning; a fixation so ingrained that he was unable to conceive of a world in which Melissa Manning was not *the* woman in his life. When he took his first psychology course in college, he conjectured that the persistance of these pathways depended on the salient fact that his feelings had always been unrequited. With any sort of consummation, he reasoned, his emotional attachment might change or even fracture, but he had been unable to test this theory in any rigorous scientific fashion.

Of course, he had managed. Through college and the years after, he had been involved in several reasonably serious relationships of varying duration, but ultimately all had ended, typically with him being accused of having "commitment issues." In high school, he had been content with merely crossing academic paths with Melissa in most of the honors classes, including Spanish, American History, and English. They were lab partners once in Honors Biology during their junior year with Mr. Fredericks. They double-dated on a couple of occasions when she was briefly going out with Brian Russell, Blair's best friend at the time. Blair, at a high point, even accompanied Melissa to Junior Prom, but only because Mitch Harrington had come down with strep throat, and Blair had been considered a suitable last minute stand-in, trusted as subservient to clearly established boundaries. Through it all, Blair had remained philosophical as Melissa went through successions of boyfriends in high school. It was too early for them to get together; he knew that high school relationships seldom lasted. His time would come in college, and as Melissa, unrelenting, went through a succession of boyfriends at Mizzou, Blair rationalized that his time would come even later, because it just had to.

Ultimately, Mitch Harrington had been the primary obstacle during high school, and eventually would re-emerge victorious after the college years in a remarkable come-back, given that he was the anomaly who never attended. Mitch was a year older, a high school jock who played halfback on the varsity football team, forward on the varsity basketball team, and ran track, specializing in the hurdles. He was diligent but not a great student, and given all the time he spent at practices, he wasn't in any honor classes. His father, an imposing hulk of a man never seen in shirt and tie, was a tradesman and given the unfair rap of not placing much value on higher education. He simply taught Mitch what he knew; thus, his son was best schooled in the practical and the mechanical, more facile turning screws than flipping pages of books.

A vicious and successful competitor on the field, Mitch was even-tempered and congenial off it. He was non-aggressive for a jock, inducing no anxiety in pimply freshman males when they passed him in the halls of Shawnee Mission East, or more treacherously, in the showers and locker room during gym. He was good-looking too, in an outdoorsy midwestern way, with curly brown hair and freckles, green eyes and a fullish, almost pouty mouth. In summary, there was nothing much to hate about Mitch Harrington, and much to inspire jealousy in those not purely academically inclined. Even Blair had admired him in high school before Mitch's first date with Melissa. And, as luck and timing would have it, Blair had been present from the very start, even instrumental in getting them off on the right foot.

One spring weekend in May of junior year, Blair was left by himself at the house while his father attended a medical meeting in St. Louis and his mother tagged along to visit relatives. Opportunities such as these were rare, and Blair intended to take full advantage of being home alone. No raucous party—he didn't wish to spread his good fortune widely—rather, an intimate romantic dinner that catered to each and every one of his juvenile notions of romance: a small table for two, candle lit, with a fire blazing nearby—not too blazing given it was May—soft lighting, mood music, and additional touches to be determined, if attainable, such as any manner of alcoholic beverage served in a wineglass (even grain alcohol could be colored with food dye to look like Rosé). Plus, of course, a worthy partner sitting across from said organizer. From the outset, Blair had planned everything for Melissa Manning.

In his obtuse way, when he encountered her after Spanish class the Monday before, Blair asked her if she were available "to attend a dinner party" at his house on Saturday evening. Had he not been rushed and discombobulated by nerves, he might have avoided ambiguity by asking, more directly, "Will you have dinner with me on Saturday night?" As such, it wouldn't have made any difference, since Melissa already had a date with Mitch Harrington. Luckily for Melissa, she didn't think they had any firm plans, and she was confident in speaking for Mitch—known to be agreeable—that it would be a pleasure for the two of them to attend. As it happens, it was their very first date, and Blair Brackman had the unique opportunity of cooking them dinner to commemorate the auspicious occasion.

Overcoming his disappointment, Blair had to scramble—and what other choice did he have? Party of two became a party of four, and he needed a date, pronto. His go-to option was Rebecca Harvey. Rebecca was probably the most fun of any of the other girls in the honors classes, with something of a wild reputation for a smart girl. She was much sexier than Melissa and seemed significantly older and world-wise, or world-weary, which Blair found more than slightly disquieting. And for a hippie, she wore a lot of make-up and shaved her armpits, which Blair found perplexing. She wore her hair permed at the time, in the manner of the frizzies of the era, and fussed with it a lot, which he found annoying. But she was presentable enough, a friend of Melissa's, and Blair didn't think he could do any better on such short notice.

Even if Melissa wasn't his actual date, Blair could still take the opportunity to strut his stuff, impress her with his sophistication and domesticity. He marinated boneless and skinless chicken thighs from Kroger's in soy sauce and pineapple juice for two days, probably excessive, but he was taking no chances. The rest of the menu included green salad with tomato wedges and Wishbone dressing, asparagus, baked potatoes, and a Sara Lee chocolate cake with vanilla ice cream for dessert. He was able to scrounge a six pack of Coors from his cousin Marcus, but couldn't score anything more substantial or classy, although there was a certain caché to a beer that you had to drive across Kansas and into Colorado to buy. Rebecca, unsolicited, brought weed as a back-up.

The evening went swimmingly, after the initial hiccough of Blair neglecting to open the flue before lighting the fire in the den. In a very short amount of time, the entire house filled up with smoke. Had Mitch not been around to diagnose the problem and known what a flue was and how to open it, the fire department might have interrupted the proceedings. As it transpired, the small fire in the hearth was not without some practicality on that chilly May evening, given that all the windows in the house had to be open for much of the night to clear out the smoke, with all the doors propped open as well until the foursome had finished their salads.

But the additional touches bear mentioning. Candlelight from a single white candle in a Mateus bottle, just like at the Villa Capri and other more upscale pizza joints in town. Since Blair could only get an unused Mateus bottle, with none of the layered, multi-colored candle-wax drippings, he had to make his own. Thus, he began burning multi-colored candles to decorate the bottle at about the same time he began marinating the chicken. Fortunately, when the subject had come up in Social Studies, Craig Levine, who was Jewish, had suggested he use Hannukah candles for the purpose—they were skinny and melted fast. Craig was generous enough to bring in a full extra box from his parent's pantry, since finding them in grocery stores in Prairie Village in May was pretty much an impossibility. Craig Levine had been a life-saver, and Blair owed him big time.

Since Blair had set up the dining table in the den, he was obliged to bring his portable hi-fi down from his bedroom. He spread the speakers as far apart as the wires would allow, bracketing the fireplace, and selected three specific albums: "From Sergio, With Love," by Sergio Franchi, "Johnny's Greatest Hits," by Johnny Mathis, and "Mantovani's Golden Hits." He also brought the extension phone from his father's office and set it on a side table next to the divan, the wire conspicuously trailing across the wall-to-wall carpeting. At the pre-agreed upon time of seven-thirty, during the breezy salad course, classmate C.W. Dexter had been instructed to dial the house number and let the call ring seven times. When the phone first rang, Blair feigned disgust, and began silently counting to himself. While it continued to ring, he circumspectly patted his mouth with his napkin, got up from his seat, and reached down to the middle of the length of phone cord. He held the cord in his upturned fist. Six rings, seven rings.

"No one's going to bother us tonight," he said, and dramatically yanked the cord from the wall. The ringing ceased. It was a nice touch.

C.W. was again called into service at the end of the meal. At precisely nine o'clock, while the four were sipping the last of the Coors from the wine glasses, he rang the front doorbell. When Blair answered the door, the skinny bespectacled sophomore, known for his prowess in thespian circles at high school—and the first classmate to come out as openly gay a few years hence—was standing on the porch carrying a sturdy black guitar case. Inside was his prized Gibson Dove. Blair held the door open and C.W. entered without a word. Blair arranged the three dining guests and himself on the divan, the only illumination coming from the second candle of the night in its Mateus holder and a crack of light from the powder room around the corner, the pocket door purposely opened with a two inch gap. Through trial and error the night before, that specific distance had been shown to be the minimum necessary to emit enough light to forestall tripping or bumping shins on the coffee table.

While they sat quietly, expectantly, C.W. pulled out his guitar—which, as instructed, he had tuned before arriving—placed the strap over his shoulder, and began serenading them with some pre-selected ballads of C.W.'s suggestion. C.W. was of sophisticated musical taste, much of his folk education picked up from fairly regular excursions to the Vanguard Coffee House on Main Street. The evening's repertory consistent of "Changes" by Phil Ochs, "How Can You Hang on To a Dream" by Ian Tyson, and "Sweet Sir Galahad" by Joan Baez. When finished, again without saying a word, C.W. lifted the guitar strap over his head, replaced the Gibson in its case, and left the house.

Next on the agenda was free make-out time, which Blair was not as excited about with Rebecca. And the thought of Mitch and Melissa going at it in his parent's house—*his* house—was becoming increasingly upsetting the nearer the designated time approached. But the agenda was inviolable. As if prompted, Blair turned to Rebecca and uttered the words he had rehearsed for Melissa's ears only. "Did I tell you about my Peter Max poster of Hendrix? It's a black light poster, and I have a black light in my room." He got the words right, but the voice lacked conviction.

"Blow me over with a feather," responded Rebecca, with an irreverence that Blair found disturbing. "Lead the way, Tarzan."

They walked upstairs in near total darkness, save for the limited mood lighting filtering from the den and a small amount of light that infiltrated through an unshaded upstairs window from a street lamp. Blair led Rebecca into his bedroom by the hand, set her down on the bed, and found the cord switch for the black light.

And *voila*! there it was. The poster, in all its psychedelic, iridescent glory. Blair sat beside Rebecca, leaning back on his palms to admire it himself. Of necessity there would be a period of awkwardness, a transition. Rebecca decided to fill the time and began rolling a joint. He was looking down in her lap, admiring her rolling technique.

And then she looked up at him, grinning, seeking approval. He could not believe the horror his eyes encountered, straight out of Grimm's fairy tales: Rebecca Harvey's face under a black light. Later, he would reconstruct the individual elements. She obviously spot treated some of her zits with Clearasil, and they were scattered all over her face underneath the covering power. The light reflected off those dabs quite differently from the rest of her face, as did the parts that had powder. And then her contact lenses showed up as opaque, giving her eyes a zombie look. And her teeth—maybe it was fluoride treatment or maybe the front ones had partial caps; but in any case, they were a different color from the rest. As was her lipstick, that had been glossy before, but was now literally vibrating. The individual elements shone, radiated in ghastly juxtaposition.

Blair looked at her, eyes wide open, horrified.

"Wanna make out now, Blair?" said the monster, with an even larger devilish grin. She was a spotted demon. Her opaque eyes beckoned him to hell.

Rebecca was puzzled by his open-eyed, and now open-mouthed stare. Clearly, whatever the problem was, he needed some encouragement.

"Blair," she said, leaning in closer, "in case you hadn't noticed, I'm not wearing a bra."

"We need to check on Melissa and Mitch," he said urgently.

Blair ran from the room, stumbling down the stairs. At the bottom of the stairwell, he hit the main switch for all the canned ceiling lights in the den. Once awash in blinding light, the room revealed the dish-strewn small oval table, the glasses and beer cans. He could hear the soft strains, the dulcet strings of the Mantovani orchestra. Otherwise, the room was empty.

Blair was still standing, surveying the contents of the room but registering nothing, when Rebecca leisurely loped down from upstairs.

"What's the problem?" she asked, fingering the unlit joint in her hand.

"They're gone! Where are they?"

Blair was not faking the true panic in his voice.

"Where *are* they!"

Thursday, August 17, 1978

Blair was still renting his old office on the second floor, in late summer of 1978, when Melissa first became his client.

"Not sure if you'd heard or not—you know what a fucking small town Kansas City is—but Mitch and I have been having some problems, lately."

"No, I hadn't," Blair Brackman lied. Was that any way to start off their professional relationship, with a lie? "But go ahead and take a seat."

"I really appreciate you agreeing to take me on," she said.

When she had approached him with a phone call, Blair had given her a list of three other competent practitioners in K.C. that she could contact, using him as a referral, but she insisted on him. She needed his help making the break from a four-year marriage, and a relationship that had, off and on, stretched back years before that.

Blair was more than flattered that she trusted him enough to see him. Maybe she reasoned that since he knew her, her family, and most of her friends, he already had substantial insight, and the process would be quicker and easier. She could save a lot of time and money not needing to tell him things in session that he already knew, which was hard to argue with. In addition, most certainly—though she was not cognizant of the fact—Blair had her best interests at heart; they would not be working at cross purposes. Melissa wanted Mitch Harrington out of her life. And Blair really wanted that as well.

Blair prided himself upon never once violating Melissa's confidentiality—not that he was bragging, since he was a professional, and confidentiality was a professional obligation. Which isn't to say that folks around town didn't know about their professional relationship. John knew, of course, as did Rebecca, and most certainly Val. And maybe Deirdre—if John blabbed to her while intoxicated and desperately trying to ingratiate himself. God only knows who Deirdre might have told, since that one had a mouth on her, but then Rebecca wasn't exactly the soul of discretion. Actually, now that he thought of it, Rebecca was the one who told John after hearing first-hand from Melissa. Of course, Melissa had to know that anything she told Rebecca would instantly make its way to John, so it was not much different than her just telling John herself, only Rebecca saved her the trouble. Probably the only person in the dark about Melissa's counseling with Blair was her mother, Margaret Manning.

None of this was Blair's doing, because Melissa decided to reveal the arrangement to others, something he had absolutely no control over. He even mentioned that fact to her once, in a session, but she didn't seem to care who knew about the relationship. She even expressed that part of the therapy was being able to admit certain things to herself and others, and she was not ashamed of seeking help for her problems. From this perspective, her indiscretion was actually part of the process.

In Blair's view, the indiscretion was symbolic of her rejecting her past, Kansas City in particular, and demonstrating how much she didn't care about what her friends and family thought about her. But he didn't want to waste time exploring the psychological roots of that interpretation until she settled the more pressing issues with Mitch.

There were few notes from the first session, because Blair hadn't been paying too much attention to the specifics. It was the usual litany of not being understood, of not having the same interests, of growing in different directions, of the frequency of sex going south. Added to this were the stock phrases, such as "I don't know what I saw in him to begin with," "I think I may have just been trying to get back at my mother," "I was really too young to get married." Blair watched her carefully, though, her body language, her facial expressions, but not because they were necessarily revealing or clinically helpful. Melissa Manning just looked pretty terrific, and he had her all to himself for the next fifty minutes. He was being paid to look at her, to have her close by. And listen to some degree, of course, which he could always finesse with well-practiced body language and facial expressions.

Blair painstakingly worked Melissa through her issues with Mitch Harrington over a period of several months. Since the couple hadn't purchased a house together, or had any kids, the logistics of the split were fairly straightforward. The couple ultimately went through arbitration, and Blair counseled Melissa on the approach to the process, giving advice more often as a friend than a therapist.

Melissa had moved up the retail ladder, and as a buyer, was spending some time in Los Angeles and New York, but mainly did road trips to clothing outlets in Kansas, Iowa, and Arkansas. She was in no hurry to start dating again; both she and Blair admitted that she needed time off from relationships, an emotional breather. But Melissa also opted for stopping her sessions, which Blair thought unwise. He employed the analogy of a deep sea diver rising to the surface too quickly, concerned Melissa might suffer emotional "bends," regress back to old habits and behaviors that had resulted in trouble for her in the past. She had picked the wrong man to marry, for starters. Why was she inclined to be attracted to men that were not good for her? Not to mention, but unsaid, he would miss seeing her every week. How could he go on?

But she was adamant that her problems were solved, and she didn't need any more therapy. From then on, Blair occasionally ran into her around town. She was never accompanied by men, unless it was part of the old gang, like John Palopolus or C.W. Dexter. All innocent enough, especially in C.W.'s case, since he was gay. Blair was tongue-tied with her, wanting to say something—curious to see how she was doing, perhaps even have coffee with her—but unable to bring himself to make the move. He had also run into Melissa's sister Val, though, and become fairly friendly with her over time. Through their occasional meetings he was able to keep general tabs on older sister. But he could never bring himself to ask Melissa out, reasoning that it was still too early for her to get involved with the right man. Blair knew all about timing, and the timing wasn't right. But when it was, he was damned sure going to be there.

$$\infty$$

Thursday, May 15, 1980

Blair had learned from Val over a casual lunch at the House of Toy that Melissa had finally started dating again. She was doing a lot of traveling for work and making social contacts out of town. Melissa's marriage with Mitch had been over for little more than a year, roughly when her sessions with Blair had ended. Blair reasoned she was emotionally ready to embark on her one true and meaningful life-long relationship. He had waited patiently as she healed from the trauma with Mitch Harrington, and before that, as she had worked out school-girl relationship issues with any number of high school and college males, all learning experiences, in retrospect.

He was determined to immediately phone her and ask her out for dinner. The Plaza III, perhaps Jasper's. Finally, it would happen. Their life together would begin, just as he had always hoped and knew it would. With shaking hands he made the call, but she was out of town on business. He hung up on her answering machine without leaving a message, not wanting his call to be misinterpreted—or rather, interpreted correctly—without speaking to her directly. In three days, he promised himself—he couldn't bear to wait any longer—he would

try again. Nearly incapacitated at work, unable to concentrate, he paced in his apartment, zombie-like, until
bedtime, when he was unable to sleep.

But two days after his initial hang-up call, Melissa
was the one to contact him, leaving a message to make
an appointment through his business answering service.
Blair would always remember that the following appointment was on May 15, the day after the Royals were
shellacked by the Yankees sixteen to three. The associ-
ation between the game and the emotional wallopping
he was to experience for himself had acquired spiritual
significance, the game had become a metaphor.

"I'd like you to help me work through something,"
Melissa had said first thing, sitting down in the familiar
chair in front of his desk, but in his new office, "so I don't
screw things up again."

Blair nodded and was as alert as a small mammal
sensing the presence of a predator. All of his senses were
heightened in complete stillness. He sensed his nostrils
widening and assumed his pupils were dilating. For certain, his heart rate had risen dramatically. The therapist
was not day-dreaming or reminiscing. For once, a client
actually had his undivided attention.

"I'm *really* listening," he said, ignoring the unintended honesty that went unnoticed.

"I've met someone," Melissa Manning said.

Things went downhill from there. Blair played his
part gamely, ignoring a constellation of bodily symp-
toms that represented instant somatization, multi-organ
hysteria. A crampiness in his gut, as if his bowels were
in revolt, a flushed, feverish sensation in his face, achi-
ness in his joints, and worse, a creeping tightness in his
chest. Despite this he somehow managed to fight his way

through the session, even peppering her with questions with little detectable quavering in his voice.

"Interesting," was his initial response. He waited, trying to remember where his asthma inhaler was, and if there were anything left in it. He hadn't needed it for quite some time, and then only when pollen counts were unusually high. As he mentally went through the drawers in his dresser, the jackets of his pockets, the shelves of his medicine cabinet, Melissa proceeded.

"His name's Rod Schoenlieber. I met him in Des Moines after I started making trips there. Through a friend at one of the boutiques. It's gotten pretty serious, I think."

"Are you ready for this?" Blair asked.

"That's what I'm here to find out," she said. "You know me better than anyone."

"Well, I can't tell you what to do. I can only, you know . . . listen."

"I understand that."

"So . . . let me get oriented here." Blair took a very deep breath and let it out slowly. "How serious is serious? Are you . . . is there sex involved . . . for example?" Blair wasn't mindful of any other examples, but he didn't want to sound overly interested, or even perverted in some vicarious psychological way.

Melissa appeared thoughtful, almost as if it were a trick question. Blair interpreted this contemplation on her part as a struggle of defining terms. Where did deep kissing come into play? What about a hand job? He hadn't phrased it "Are you having sex with him?" but the more ambiguous, even obtuse "Is sex involved?" The syntax hadn't been intentional; he was simply accustomed to more open ended, ambiguous ways of expressing things.

The answer wasn't necessarily straightforward, either, didn't need to be straightforward. How she interpreted "is sex involved" by itself could be illuminating, provide psychological insight. Melissa Manning seemed to be struggling, but that impression, as it turns out, was Blair overly reading into things.

"All the time," she finally said.

"That would be a 'yes?'" Blair asked, objectively and only for clarification.

"A definite 'yes,'" Melissa clarified, definitively.

They both reflected on the answer in their own individual ways, resulting in a long silence. Blair was exploring depths of thought, his mind reeling. Questions—actual sentences he could see in psychedelic fashion—floated, even danced around him in a blurring swirl in his mind's eye. Melissa, conversely, was wondering if a more accurate response would have been "a lot," rather than "all the time," but concluded it didn't really make all that much difference.

"Can . . . can you *handle* it?" Blair finally asked, stammering and tripping on his words.

"Honestly, I wasn't sure . . ." Melissa began.

Blair shook his head up and down, rather vigorously.

"That's good, not being sure . . . yes . . . yes," he said.

"It's been quite a while . . ." Melissa continued.

"Yes . . . yes," reiterated Blair, finding a smooth track that he could glide over without concern for a verbal face-plant. "It's not something that you can take lightly . . . that you can just hop right into because—"

Melissa wasn't really listening to what Blair was saying, merely going on with her own line of thought. "—because, you know, he's so . . . *big*." She grimaced slightly, as if penises were bad enough when they were small, but really a trial when they peeked ostentatiously beyond the margins of an average-sized fig leaf, plus or minus two standard deviations.

"Oh." Blair deflated like a punctured balloon.

"I've gotten used to it, though," Melissa went on, with encouragement in her tone. "It's really remarkable how you just can kinda . . . stretch after a while. Of course, certain positions are better than others . . . ."

"Right. That's true."

"When I say I've gotten used to it, I don't mean to make that sound in a negative way. I mean I really like it. It was touch and go the first few times, but I don't have any issues with it anymore . . . and it's great. The sex is, I mean. Which is why we do it all the time. Or, anyway, we do it a lot."

"Well," said Blair, desperately wanting to move on if not teleported to another planet, "Sex is an important component of a healthy, mature relationship. But not the only thing, of course . . ."

"And he's not circumcised."

"That's . . . uh . . . an unexpected and interesting tidbit, I suppose."

"I'd never even seen a man uncircumcised before . . . it's kinda weird, like a turtleneck."

"Right."

"So that part, along with the fact that, well, it's just so *big*, like one of those guys in a porn film . . ."

"Right."

"You understand that I can't talk about this kind of stuff with anybody else . . ."

"That's what I'm here for," said Blair nobly. "But, I assume there's more to this guy Rod than his . . . penis."

"Of course there is," said Melissa, a shade on the defensive. "I just needed to get that part out of the way first, like Rod and I had to. I wanted to let you know that we've already had to work through some things. So I'd guess you'd call that being serious. Which is how this conversation all started, if I am remembering correctly."

Blair nodded. He was afraid to take a breath for fear that he would be unable to do so. He would go directly to Bruce Smith Drugs the minute she left and buy an over-the-counter inhaler. Hopefully that would be enough. He was tight—unfortunate word choice—but able to get air. His devastation, for the time being, was at least being oxygenated. He would make it through this session, and there would be many others, weekly. He would figure things out. There would be time. But was there hope?

"Actually," Blair said quietly, "studies have shown that most women actually prefer a circumcised . . . penis." He was overreaching. Was this the best he could do to diminish Rod?

To tell you the truth," Melissa confessed, "I can't really tell the difference when he's . . . you know . . . up and at 'em."

"Well," said Blair, "thank God for small favors."

Before this appointment, Blair had been on the brink of making his first moves on Melissa Manning, to embark on the one true meaningful relationship of his life. This news was more than a setback. Blair now realized he was up against a towering serpent with a turtleneck. He had been gobsmacked by a really big dick belonging to a guy named Rod. And there he was, Blair Brackman, with only inferior weaponry at his disposal. As her therapist, he was all ears.

Saturday, February 21, 1981

"John!"

John Palopolus turned to see Valerie Manning running toward him. Literally running, and she had no trouble doing this, since she was wearing running shoes. Unlike her sister Melissa, Val was inclined to wear sensible shoes. Above the white socks, however, she wore a presentable casual outfit consisting of khaki slacks and a turquoise scooped neck cotton blouse, topped off by a hot pink quilted jacket. As a junior high school teacher, Val tended to wear colorful clothes.

It was nearly 2 P.M., and they were both on the sidewalk along Nichols Parkway on the Country Club Plaza. Palopolus looked every bit the Princeton man—misplaced, though, as if transported to the Midwest by an evil witch—wearing a light crew neck sweater and his leather bomber jacket, also matched with khaki slacks. The jacket, cracked and weathered like his recliner, gave him a comforting feeling that made venturing outside the apartment more bearable. Clothes not entirely making the man, he appeared otherwise unkempt: hair uncombed, unshaven, and with purplish bags under his eyes, a street person with a clothes budget impersonating a Princeton man. In common with the latter, Palopolus had not bothered with socks. He wore cordovan penny loafers with tassles, scuffed and needing a shine.

Val caught up with him, not in the least out of breath. She was smiling, perky, happy to see him.

"It's been ages, John!" she said cheerfully.

"You're looking really good, Val."

"Thanks, John. And you look like ten pounds of manure in a five pound bag."

"Buttering me up like that, Valerie Manning, you must want something."

"Not at all, John. I just want to talk to you about . . . something. Coffee somewhere?"

John looked at his watch. After meeting Rebecca earlier in Westport, he had been wandering the Plaza, an escapee from his nearby apartment complex. Despite his depression, he could recognize a beautiful unseasonably warm winter day when he saw one, and his place was a pigsty. He had nothing to do, nowhere to go, and any invitation was a welcome one.

"Look at the time, Val. A little late in the day for coffee. Approaching cocktail hour."

"Maybe an Irish coffee?"

"If you're buying, I'll give you whatever you want. Blow in my ear and I'll follow you anywhere."

Val had completed her solitary errand, returning a blouse that her mother had bought at Hall's and then thought better of. This was something her mother tended to do a lot. The store credit coupon was safely tucked in her Italian leather purse along with several others she had neglected to pass along. Like her mother, Val tended to be absent-minded, but only because she was generally busy with a lot on her plate, the least of which was keeping her mother on a reasonably short leash. Other activities were mainly sports-related, as she participated in a volleyball league, a tennis league, a softball league—season dependent—and was a season ticket holder for the Royals and the Chiefs. Of course, she also coached the girls' basketball and field hockey teams at

Meadowbrook Junior High. Plus she was a member of the Friends of Art at the Nelson and did charity work for the Elks and Toys for Tots.

The closest bar being Houlihan's, they headed in that direction without discussion or logistical coordination. Conversation was terse along the way, as Palopolus needed to vent his obsession and Valerie did not want to indulge him.

"Did you know that Deirdre dumped me?"

"Of course I know. It was ages ago."

"It took a while to sink in."

"You realize she isn't the nicest person in the world."

"Niceness is over-rated. She had other redeeming qualities."

"She picked on me when I was in junior high," said Val, trying to avoid legitimate discussion. She knew John was still a wreck. "She came over for one of Mel's slumber parties and short-sheeted my bed."

"I feel better now. You win. All she did was cheat on me and then take everything."

"Well, I never liked her, if that helps, and I'm a great judge of character."

"You really don't want to talk to me about this, do you . . ." They were at the restaurant, and John was holding the door open for her.

"No, I don't," Valerie said walking past him. "That short-sheeting was extremely traumatic."

Sitting across from her at a corner table, John appraised the younger Manning daughter. Better-looking than her sister, but she didn't let it show. No make-up. Always wore her hair short, like a little Dutch boy. Fit and sinewy, but still curvy. Smarter than her sister, too. And she had a lot of spunk. She wasn't going to let him wallow about Deirdre. She had warned him about broaching the subject, her signals clear, he had shown the obligatory resistance—a hint of his inherent rebelliousness and contrariness—and now he would drop it. Or try as best he could. He could understand that no one wanted to talk about it anymore—enough was enough—and it felt like he was going through the motions anyway. He knew he had to get on with his life. He knew it had been a big mistake to marry that bitch in the first place. But she had been like a drug to him. And he was still undergoing withdrawal. Hopefully he would come out of it, and he was gaining some confidence that he might. He just couldn't see that far ahead.

The waitress was all over them for the order as soon as they sat down, taking them for drinkers and not late lunchers. She had surmised correctly.

"So, how's the field hickey team?" John joked, leaning over the table for a pretend look at Val's neck."

"Hah-hah."

"Are you still seeing Jarvis?"

Jarvis worked on the City desk at the *Star*, and John had run into them together at a few social functions connected with the newspaper. Without that mutual connection, Palopolus wouldn't have felt as connected with Val, since she was four years younger than Melissa and most of the other members of the gang from Mizzou.

"Occasionally. We're not exactly on the same page."

"Old newspaper joke," said John.

"Rather, the same place. Our timetables are different." Jarvis, Palopolus recalled, was a couple years older than he was.

"Well," said Palopolus, "if he were right for you, the timetables wouldn't matter that much."

"Maybe I'm hesitant because so many people I know are divorced."

"Well, I am, and Mel is—that's an entire two by my count, or four if you count us as individuals. And then there is your Mom, of course. But that hasn't kept your sis from going at another try, has it? What's the guy's name? Rod? St. Louis boy?"

"Rod Schoenlieber. Des Moines."

"St. Louis. Des Moines. Fucking Midwest. All the same. Sorry I asked."

The waitress set down their coffees, John's packing the additional punch. Val added cream and sugar and stirred excessively before taking a sip. She grimaced and added more cream.

"You're not really much of a coffee drinker, are you, Val? Maybe they have hot Bosco here."

She wasn't a coffee drinker, that much was obvious. But she had invited him for coffee, so she felt obligated to do her best.

Val smiled, found out. "Well, John, I invited you for coffee, so I couldn't very well—"

"—order tea? Too close to 'Tea and Sympathy?'"

She smiled, looked down at the cup and cleared her throat. John in the meantime, took a large slurp of his coffee.

"Did you know that 'Palopolus' is an Irish name?" He said after swallowing. He smiled back at her and waited. He had an inkling of what this was all about.

"Yes," he continued, without being asked, "I *did* receive an invitation to your mother's party. I know I shouldn't be telling you this, of course, because it's a . . ." He leaned low over the table, "a surprise!"

"A *real* surprise."

"Who else is coming?"

"I'm not sure."

"Wait . . . don't tell me. This really *is* your mother's party? She's not just hosting it? You're not behind it?"

Val nodded.

"I don't know who she invited," Val confessed, "except for you and . . . Deirdre." Her expression appeared part anxious, part helpless.

Palopolus took a deep breath and another sip of his beverage, smaller this time.

"I've been a shut-in lately, Val, you know that. This was going to be my coming out party." He sipped again. "You've just short-sheeted my coming out party. And I thought you were my friend."

Val shrugged. "Maybe she won't come, if she knows *you're* coming."

"No, no, no," John waggled his finger. "It doesn't work that way. She'll come all right, just to dig her stiletto heels into my gut. She takes great joy in it. And she'll bring someone, just to rub his dick into my face."

"It's your call, John. Maybe she won't come."

Palopolus shrugged, resigned. He'd consider it.

"And . . . Blair Brackman is invited as well, that's all I know."

"Blair, okay. He almost needs to get out more than I do. Can't have a party without a fly on the wall. Well, I can partially solve more of the mystery. Rebecca was invited. We were just discussing it the other day. It might even be a party if Deirdre doesn't show."

"I hope so," said Val, sounding relieved. "Maybe I've been foolish to worry about it. But Mom's handling everything. She's insisting. It really isn't about Melissa and Rod at all, it's all about her."

"It's never about the couple, Val, always about the parents and the family. If the world were a fair place, newlyweds would get an all-expense paid trip to Hawaii, with a step-by-step guide on how to become members of the Mile High Club. That would be it. Save everyone a lot of trouble. But in this case, at least I can look forward to some of Ora Lee's spectacular cooking."

Val looked down at her coffee cup and shook her head solemnly. "Ora Lee's not cooking, John. She might help with getting things in the oven and serving, but otherwise, like I said, Mom's doing everything."

John performed his ritualistic gestures of pulling out his pack of Chesterfields, tapping it against the palm of his hand, drawing the long straw, pulling his engraved silver lighter from his jacket pocket, and lighting the cigarette. He snapped the lighter shut authoritatively before replacing it in his pocket. He put elbow to table, and chin in hand, a thoughtful pose.

"I didn't realize your mother even cooked."

"She doesn't."

Palopolus took a deep drag and blew the smoke groundward and towards the wall.

"Interesting," he said.

There was a lull, then Val continued.

"While I have you here, I thought I might ask you about Blair," she began.

"What about him?"

"Is he . . . you know . . . seeing anyone?"

"You're sweet on Blair," Palopolus said flatly, a statement of fact.

"I'm . . . a bit interested, maybe. We've had coffee . . . well, not really coffee . . . well, *he* had coffee . . ."

"It doesn't matter if he had Geritol, Val. Spit it out."

"No real evening dates. Nothing like that. Always very casual, a few lunches here and there. I asked him to talk to my ninth graders on career day, about being a psychologist."

"I'm hurt." John blew out more smoke. "You didn't invite me to talk about being a burnt-out journalist."

"There's another career day coming up . . ."

"Forget it, I'm joking." said John quickly. "So you expect him to make some moves on you in front of your ninth grade class, is that it?"

Val pushed her coffee away. "He's hard for me to figure. We go way back, sort of. I remember when I first met him. I was still in junior high myself, and he came over to the house to pick up Mel for a date. Junior Prom." She thought silently for a moment. "Actually, we didn't meet that time. I was shy. I remember I was wearing my gym clothes, God only knows why. Anyway, I just I peeked around the hall doorway. Mel didn't want her little sister around, anyway. I was an embarrassment."

"Says something, considering your mother," John muttered.

She ignored the dig, as John expected her too.

"I think I had a crush on him. Well, I did. He was a high school boy, going out with my big sister, and cute. Quiet. Not aggressive or show-offey."

"He had a thing for your sister back then, you know. Even in college."

Val looked surprised. "They really didn't go out all that much."

"Doesn't matter. How did you end up seeing him again?"

"An opening at the Nelson," she said, a bit distracted by John's throw-away comment and wishing to back-track. "He was there with someone, but apparently it wasn't serious, or he wouldn't have called me after that."

"He hasn't been serious with anyone. In a tailspin, in my estimation. Some sort of existential crisis. And it takes one to know one. We used to play racquetball together, even golf occasionally. He used to jog all the time. Doesn't seem to get out much anymore. Very introspective, won't open up. And he was introspective to begin with. You need more of a natural athlete, Val, someone who can keep up with you on the basketball court. A bosom buddy in the weight room, someone to keep track of all those sets of bench presses. Someone physical, and fit. Like me." He chuckled and snuffed out his cigarette. "But don't get me wrong, I love the guy. He could count himself pretty damn lucky to end up with someone as fantastic as you."

"Thanks, John."

"You didn't ask me for coffee to tell me about the party, did you? You wanted to pump me about Mr. Brackman."

"Yeah. Sorry."

"Don't be."

"Well, I agree with you about the introspective bit, but more than that. He really seems sad. Maybe depressed."

"Damn," said John. "I must have let him drink from my glass."

Val allowed herself a crack of a smile.

"Maybe the problem is we don't have all that much in common besides Melissa. I think I'm still the little sister to him, all skinny legs and knobby knees and training bra."

"Now you're just fishing for compliments, Val. He might be depressed, but he's not comatose. Maybe he needs a bit of a push. Perhaps you've been acting like the little sister. Maybe it's time to burn that training bra of yours and show him what you're packing."

Vale smiled and seemed encouraged.

Palopolus finished off his coffee. He had made someone feel better, he had been able to step out of his self-absorption long enough to do that. It was a start.

"There's a big party coming up, Val," he went on. "My advice to you is wear your sexiest dress, put on your most provocative scent, get a few drinks in our friend Mr. Brackman, and make your move. A big time, big league move. Like our Royals last season. After all, what's the point of keeping how you feel about someone a secret?"

❧

Monday, February 23, 1981

Nigel Davies loosened his tie and unbuttoned his top collar button before riffling through the day's mail. The opulent heaviness of the envelope from America stood out from the stack like a Texas tourist at the Victoria and Albert. Not to mention, the block of four "Love" stamps. Seemed a bit excessive. Nigel began to calculate the face value by multiplication, finally resorting to the note-pad on the counter and the Monte Blanc from his shirt pocket. Looking down at the figures, he shifted his lower jaw back and forth—a habit he had acquired while pursuing his sums in primary school. The excess was at least twice as much as required. Wasteful Yanks.

He thought back on his last letter from America from Candy Decker, or rather, the former Candy Decker. That had been a Christmas card, lighter than this communique, surely. He recalled the writing on the card: overwrought, emotional scribblings covering all available blank space, which at the time had annoyed him, but not without a tinge of guilt. He couldn't blame the girl, though, since he was irresistible. He hadn't bothered to reply, as even a business-like, courteous response would have only prolonged the agony. And Nigel was anything if not humane where relationships with the fairer sex were involved.

Nigel flipped the envelope over, slid his finger under the flap, and pulled out the embossed card. Melissa Manning was giving matrimony another go, evidently. A bloke named Rod, with a funny last name. Good for her. Surprise party before the event, and please no gifts, according to the script in the lower right hand corner. No one would object to that. But the large typeface and all those exclamation marks was a bit over-emphatic, Nigel thought, the ad man in him coming out. Finally, in the lower left hand corner, once again in italics and a more appropriate font size, the invitation specified "Regrets Only." Thinking of his times with Melissa, Nigel had none. All had ended amicably, without emotional scribblings on holiday cards or scenes of any sort. Things just ran their course and in due time ended, and college life went on, no one the worse for it.

The address was an apartment on the Country Club Plaza. Nigel only remembered the previous family house in Old Mission Hills, driving there and back from Columbia for the day, or an occasional weekend visit with Melissa. An elegant, older home, all brick, with a rolling lawn and a meticulously landscaped garden. It had been, in fact, the fanciest home that the young Brit, a product of north London, had ever seen. He particularly recalled Melissa's overdone bedroom, all fluff and fringe and pastels, as well as what Americans called a recreation room on the lower level. Nigel had never heard of a recreation room, but the nomenclature was quite fitting, since he and Melissa had recreated there on a number of occasions. He had preferred the soft mattress in the bedroom, though, gaudiness aside, and his preferences had been accommodated more than once, but only when the senior Mannings were away from town on golfing jaunts and little sister was staying with nearby relatives. The recreational sex in the recreation room had always had a more furtive quality, since potential family interruptions always lurked on the horizon. But furtive or not, the sex was all good. If anything, the threat of discovery gave him more staying power.

Nigel tossed the invitation on the counter and gave his tie a further loosening. No sense in denying himself the memory of those times, his coming of age in America. He closed his eyes and thought of the Kappa House at the University of Missouri. Mel Manning—they met in a marketing class—had been his entré, and a fortuitous one. From her he had branched out among the sorority sisters. Deirdre Rehnquist had been next, her determination to bed him likely a competitiveness with Melissa, who by that juncture had neither anything to prove nor any reason to fight over a bygone lover. He himself had pleaded no contest and let himself be taken for several intense weeks. And Rebecca, of course, she came after him at every opportunity.

Unsatiable, that one, perhaps overly eager. Without question the sexiest of the bunch and a risk taker, Rebecca not surprisingly ended up pregnant—thankfully not by him but from some Delta Chi dopehead as rumor had it, and had dropped out her senior year, right before graduation. A shame, since Rebecca Harvey was sharp as a tack, an honors student getting her undergraduate degree in journalism. She had ended up a single mother, struggling to raise her daughter, and still was, last he had seen of her.

Surprisingly, the Kappa sorority sisters at Mizzou had never begrudged him his voluptuary nature. Recrimination free, he maintained his cross gender friendships with ease, and hardly ever needed male bonding. Sorority parties, football games, study dates, he was always the gracious companion. He was a Brit, after all, and only there for the junior year abroad. The co-eds at Mizzou, in their delightful naiveté, were invariably charmed by any English accent. In particular, they were ignorant of his lower crust intonations, of what it meant and how it defined him among his countrymen. In the heart of midwest America, his speech did not betray his working class upbringing in Tottenham.

Given the scholarship opportunity for the year abroad—the blessed outcome of receiving a prize in journalism and becoming a favorite of a professor at the University of West London—Nigel was able to reinvent himself, and it was liberating. No one in America knew how he had struggled, working crap jobs, laboring jobs, to save for the study year. But he had his priorities straight: he splurged for a razor cut at a well-known salon in the city right before leaving. And, naturally, he had already purchased an aubergine velour suit and a matching Liberty of London patterned shirt to go with it, from a male boutique on the King's Road. Crossing the Atlantic, then going by bus from New York to Columbia, Missouri, he could have been prepped at Eton or Harrow, for all they knew. Besides which, they had never even heard of Eton or Harrow.

No one—save one exception—was deluded enough to ever take him seriously as marriage material; still, whether platonically or sexually, he was irresistible. Not that he had lost his powers. But these days his female companions were mostly secretaries, and not of the background, culture, or wealth of the American girls with whom he had fraternized back in the day.

Nigel examined the envelope again. Candy Decker's Christmas card had borne "Love" stamps also. An intentional gesture, she had specifically eschewed the customary holiday stamps with her last, final communication. That was a typical Candy touch. Overly sentimental, ascribing the profound to the trivial. She dotted her "i's" with a small circle, and sometimes drew in a smiley face. Her Southern drawl was what every un-traveled foreigner imagined an American sounded like, and what non-Americans with poor mimicry skills would imitate if asked to talk American.

She had grown up in Tyler, Texas, and represented the classic American stereotype to the young Brit who was as naïve about Americans as they were about him. She was a tall, statuesque blonde with large round blue eyes, full red lips, and porcelain skin, all presented to their best advantage by an abundance of cosmetics. Her figure was voluptuous, but restrained by a somewhat modest taste in fashion; that is, until the swimsuit competition. She had been a beauty queen in high school, knew her way around horses, was comfortable with firearms. Predictably she was overly churchy and conservative politically, but didn't concern herself much with current events—or else knew better to initiate those sorts of conversations among her more liberal collegiate peers in the Show-Me-State.

She had waited patiently for Nigel, all the while witnessing his indulgences with Melissa, Rebecca, and Deirdre, among some others from the Kappa house, without judgment or discouragement. She was one to trust her heart, and knew in her big Southern heart of hearts that Nigel Davies was her man.

And thus, the devil-may-care Nigel Davies had unknowingly deflowered the Southern belle Candy Decker. From that moment on, until boarding his international flight to Heathrow less than a month later, she had given herself to him at every available chance with a sexual abandon that caught even Nigel off-guard. As if to compensate for twenty years of sexual repression, Candy had been at turns accommodating, then demanding in bed, but always tireless, libidinous, and uninhibited. And to his shame, Nigel had jilted her not once, but twice. On a return to the States on a business trip two or three years earlier, shortly before the Christmas message, he had not been tempted to renew his collegiate sexual adventures with any of the now mature Kappa House sisters except for Candy Decker.

Candy was an old married lady now, evidently. Married into some money, apparently. Good for her.

But it would be nice to see them all, given the excuse of Melissa Manning getting married again. Even if he had to fight off Rebecca Harvey. Or not.

He looked around at his Kensington apartment. It cost a pretty penny: spacious and modern in a fashionable neighborhood. By any standard, he considered himself a success. Still, a guest appearance in Kansas City would give his ego a boost. A triumphal return of the conquering hero would bring back old times, which were the best of times. He was due a trip stateside for the Agency anyway, and he could easily take a few extra days to trek to K.C. for a visit with old friends and lovers. Just a shift of his schedule.

Nigel stared at the invitation and wondered who else was on the guest list. Unconsciously, he shifted his lower jaw back and forth, working out the sums.

Monday, February 16, 1981, 11 A.M.

Blair placed the party invitation in the top drawer of his office desk for safekeeping a few minutes before Dickie Rawlings rang the office buzzer. Blair would ruminate more on it later. In the meantime, he felt the dread of another session with Dickie Rawlings. But as a professional he always tried, offered the best counseling services of which he was capable. And because he was financially rewarded for his efforts, the sessions with Dickie were not a complete loss.

"I'm getting paid to sit here," he constantly reminded himself during the sessions. "Paid to listen. And paid well. There are worse jobs." And then, to finish the thought, he would change things around by pondering the abundant variety of worse jobs, and select one for comparison. For the subsequent fifty minutes, he would multi-task—listening, nodding, sometimes offering a suggestion or commentary—all the while mentally digging ditches, cleaning out cesspools, unclogging the sink drains in a Japanese beauty saloon.

"So . . ." Blair began, looking across his desk at the fit, tanned thirty-something in a Ralph Lauren polo shirt and Nantucket red slacks. Dickie wore his characteristic self-satisfied smirk. He folded one of his long legs over the other, revealing a bit of ankle, beige anklets, and the white textured bottom of a Topsider.

Blair rubbed his chin and looked past his client into the middle distance—in an ironic homage to Freud of which he was fully cognizant—and reflected. Dickie, on a 24/7 regimen of narcissism, assumed that Blair was trying to remember where they had left off from the week before.

I could be the guy in the parade who walks behind the horses with a shovel and bucket, Blair thought to himself.

Generally, Blair was empathetic with his clients, shared the joy of their progress, their acquisition of insights and skills necessary to overcome personal obstacles, to become better adjusted, and possibly, dare it be said, achieve some semblance of happiness. Most of the time, Blair personally had a stake in helping them realize their potential. But then there was Dickie Rawlings.

"So . . ." Dickie flicked his overly-long in front hair back like a teenager, a habit of his. "Do you remember where we ended last week?"

Quite a cheeky, presumptuous remark from anyone else. But Blair was accustomed to Dickie's complete self-obsession, assuming his life events were of such importance that his therapist would naturally remember, having nothing better to think about. After all, the world revolved around Dickie Rawlings, the cosmos consisted of himself and the hired planets.

Blair moved his stroking hand from his chin to his forehead in slow motion, as if he were practicing Tai Chi. After a few forehead rubs, Blair ran his fingers through his hair and then placed both hands flat on the desk in front of him, a cadet waiting for the orders to begin eating.

"Let me think for a moment," Blair said. He strained to think, but all he remembered from the week before was that he had been cleaning out the primate cages.

"Weren't you . . . weren't we talking about . . . that woman you're interested in? The one at the club?"

"Right!" Dickie almost shouted, such was his gratification. "But not the woman at the Carriage Club . . . the one at Mission Hills."

"Right, I remember," said Blair, gratified himself, though not at all surprised on hitting paydirt with his educated guess. Dickie normally spent most his time relating sexual exploits with different women from different clubs. "Not the Carriage Club one . . . the Mission Hills one. Exactly. So . . . how's that going?"

Dickie interlocked his hands over his uppermost knee and pulled himself forward, his head penetrating the invisible vertical plane of Blair's desk. The body language reflected the transition from confidential, which was a given, to *extremely* confidential.

"We fucked," he said, in a voice barely above a whisper. And then he smiled, a grin barely below a guffaw.

"Well," said Blair, leaning all the way back in his chair, his head thrust back like a turkey, as if Dickie had drawn a knife. "That . . . that's progress . . . as far as establishing a relationship goes."

"And, I think we'll fuck again," said Dickie, reassuming his more relaxed position in the chair. "So . . . what do you think? Pretty good, huh?"

"Well . . ." Blair demurred, trying to visualize Dickie in some way coupling with another human, but only seeing the tail of the horse in the parade in front of his mind's eye. The tail was arching. He thought he heard a hiss, the passage of gas. He gripped the armrest of his chair, readying the shovel.

"If you think it's a good thing, Dickie . . ."

"I think it's a fucking *great* thing!"

"And what's this woman like? Do you have anything in common? Is there a possible relationship here? A future?"

"Stupid question, Blair. I'm a fucking married man. She's damn hot, though."

"Okay, then. Well, that's something." Blair was struggling to engage. Bringing up extraneous details generally worked, although rarely generating insights. But a response, in any event, and any response counted as participation, strictly speaking: *You were in a car wreck? What color was the car?*

"So, where did this . . . you know . . . take place? Obviously not your house, unless your wife's out of town . . ."

"No, no . . . she has a house of her own. She's divorced."

"Well," Blair responded, nodding almost encouragingly. "That makes things somewhat less complicated on her end. But what do you think she's after? Have you considered her own needs, her motives?"

"She was after my dick, Blair."

Blair nodded absently. Dumb question. Dickie Rawlings not only had zero personal insight, he was also a literalist.

"Yes, in the most elemental sense . . . I get that. But maybe things are more complicated for her. She's divorced, maybe she's looking for something longer term. And—you know this yourself—you're quite a good catch. You're . . . good-looking . . . in good shape . . . uh . . . you certainly dress well . . . you have a lot of money . . ."

"Shit, Blair . . . don't be so naïve. It's not about money. She's rich herself. I told you. I met her at the club, not at the Y."

"Right."

"And you know what a small town Kansas City is. Everybody with money knows everyone else with money. My folks know her folks. In fact, my dad and her dad did banking and investment business together. The families go way back. All the families do. And we're all in the same clubs. So, I actually knew her ages ago, before she left for college and married some douchebag. She was at Barstow when I was at Pem-Day. A couple years behind me, though."

Blair resisted the urge to look at this watch. He needed a wall clock, right behind Dickie's head. He reminded himself to buy one. "So you have a lot in common, a basis for a relationship . . . if it should go that way . . . if you *want* it to go that way . . ."

"You want to know her name?"

"I don't really need—"

"Deirdre. Great name, isn't it? Classy name, Deirdre. Really classy."

Blair experienced a sense of forboding. Deirdre was a great name, but not all that common. Of Irish derivation, meaning melancholy. In Celtic legend, Deirdre died of a broken heart.

"Means 'melancholy.'"

"Really! How do you know all that stuff, Blair? You're one smart guy!"

Blair shrugged. "One picks up these things . . . here and there." This particular tid-bit, Blair recalled, he had picked up from a client named Deirdre. Oh, no . . . fuck, please . . . nooooo . . .

"You want to know her *last* name?"

"That's not really necess—"

"Rehnquist. Deirdre Rehnquist!" Dickie's smirk widened to the biggest grin Blair had ever seen on that despicable face.

Dickie was laughing full out now, while Blair tried to look impassive. But there was no point, he had been set up.

"Check your appointment book, Blair, she actually has an appointment with you tomorrow afternoon. Somehow your name came up . . . what a hoot! Small fucking world! I just *love* Kansas City!"

Blair cleared his throat and attempted to compose himself. He was surprised and dismayed that his voice almost sounded professorial. And scripted.

"You realize, Dickie," he began his disclaimer, "everything that is said in this office is under the strictest confidentialy. If either you or . . . your new friend . . . feels in the least bit uncomfortable with this arrangement, I would be happy to refer either one of you, or both of you, to someone else. I would completely understand."

Blair had long understood that Dickie Rawlings didn't really want therapy, he just wanted to pay someone to brag to, to confide in, someone to have a chat with, who would not unfairly judge him. Validation, whatever the form. Plain and simple, Dickie Rawlings wanted a friend, and could afford to buy one.

"Won't be a problem at all, for either one of us," Dickie reassured him.

But Blair was staring off into the middle distance again, stroking his chin.

Dickie looked at his watch. "Gotta run. Racquetball match with Deirdre. Sorry to cut this short . . ."

Blair was watching the load drop, in three or four separate packets, in slow motion. The pile was steaming. Well packed, though, not runny at all, the lowermost portions somewhat flattened by the force and weight of the waste that followed immediately after. From the top, a thin strand of manure pointed heavenward, unruly, like Alfalfa's cowlick. There was an earthy smell to everything. Not really bad at all, rather wholesome and natural.

Dickie Rawlings untangled his long legs from the chair, made a man adjustment to his crotch, smoothed the wrinkles over his thighs with a couple downward swipes of his hands, and headed to the door. Typically, he had to have a parting shot, the last word, and Blair was not disappointed.

"So tomorrow Deirdre will tell you all about what a great fuck I am, and then you can tell me all about what she says next week!"

The door shut firmly behind him, but his laughter could still be heard fading down the corridor.

Blair gave the shovel a firm push, scraping the asphalt, and scooped up the load without difficulty. He put the bucket on the ground, and the manure, equally obligingly, slid off the shovel into the bucket.

This isn't so bad, after all, he thought, picking up the bucket by the handle and having to jog for a bit to catch up. He resumed his former safe distance behind the undulating chestnut-colored rump. Now all he had to do was walk until the next time. Easy peasy.

He looked over at the closed door.

"I look forward to it, Dickie," he answered. "I really do."

Thursday, February 26, 1981, 4 P.M.

Blair found the sessions with Melissa increasingly difficult after Rod had entered the picture. One reason, Blair surmised—but not the only one—was their shared past. Thinking that he knew her so well, he was deluded into thinking he had insight into the way she thought; that he might even know more about what she thought and felt than *she* did. Or at least, than she could recognize and admit. In which case, the purpose of her therapy was precisely the attainment of that recognition and admission. So he continually waited for his suppositions to be validated, but they seldom were. That the topic of Rod Schoenlieber began to monopolize their sessions might also have had something to do with it.

Melissa would say things that surprised him. He realized that he needed to reconsider his therapeutic approach, but wasn't sure how. Until then, he would just maintain the usual, the status quo. Mainly listen and nod, while the mind raced. Given all the talk about Rod, Blair was surprised that he hadn't become more acclimated to his invisible ghost-like presence in the room.

Frankly, he knew more about the man than he cared to, but accepted it as all part of the job. Still, he wished she would just stop talking about the guy. What a putz.

It was more awkward now that he had received the invitation to Meg Manning's surprise reception. He had decided not to mention it the previous week, procrastinating, since his thinking about Melissa and the current situation had progressed well beyond the decent bounds of obsessiveness. He had resolved to bring up the topic today, but decided to wait until the session was over. Typically, though, no appointments were scheduled after Melissa's, so he could be generous with his time, if need be. He didn't mind at all if she stuck around longer.

"I don't quite know how to bring this up . . ." he began. It was obvious to both of them that there were many possibilities. Melissa set her Burberry trenchcoat over the empty chair next to hers and eased back down into her own.

She looked at him expectantly and a bit quizzically. Her eyes, the irises a very definite blue, had that soft, watery look, like old movies filmed through gauze. But most notably, he appreciated, they bulged out at bit. Not in a way to suggest a thyroid disorder, but more like the subtle buggy-eyedness of Susan Sarandon or Lesley Ann Warren. He had always found those eyes rather appealing and sexy. But not up to the point of a thyroid condition, that was pathology, he was very clear on that. Anyway, he had to stop looking at Melissa's eyes at some point, and say what needed to be said.

"I received the invitation," he continued, looking deeper into her eyes, and unable to control a slight twitch in one of his own.

"What invitation?" she asked, genuinely surprised. It didn't take a master's degree in psychiatric social work to ascertain that she was clueless. Completely clueless. And now he had to go on.

"I guess I thought you knew . . ."

He felt like an idiot. It was a surprise party, how should she know? And worse, he was the one who had blown the surprise, against the explicit instructions in the invitation. In boldface and an overly large typeface, no less. There was no small irony in a therapist running off at the mouth about a surprise party for one of his clients. But Blair had thought things out beforehand. He never shot half-cocked, he knew that, it was not how he was trained. Not to mention, as a naturally obsessive thinker and all training aside, he considered all possibilities and their ramifications beforehand. Bringing up the invitation was definitely the proper thing to do, in his professional opinion.

First off, he firmly believed, people rarely gave anyone a surprise party that the guest of honor didn't already know about, other than in movies or television commercials. He himself had been given three such parties, although, admittedly, only one in semi-adulthood. According to the old medical joke, one case entitled the practitioner to say "In my experience," and two cases allowed him to claim "In my series." Blair had three cases, which allowed him to conclude "Time and time and time again . . ." Who could keep a secret these days? People faked being surprised at surprise parties more than women faked orgasms. In Blair's experience.

Secondly, there was the issue of one's therapist unexpectedly showing up at a social gathering. It could cause Melissa embarrassment, even discomfort, possibly even negatively impact the progress made in her therapy. The scenario would be awkward even if no one else were aware of the professional relationship. But in this instance, Val knew, and Rebecca, and of course John, and God knows who else, some or all of whom might be at the party. Of course, he could ignore the invitation althogether. But if he didn't have the courtesy to show up, Melissa's feelings might be hurt. "Why didn't you say anything?" she would lament at their next session. "I knew all about the surprise! And I was *so* hurt that you didn't come!"

That, of course, would not happen, because Blair had every intention of going, with a very specific and important reason to be there. Besides, the second rationale was complete bullshit, he figured, because he knew Melissa well enough to be certain that she would be completely comfortable with him there, would even *want* him to be there, because he'd been her friend for all these years and no one deserved to be at her surprise party more than he did. He might go so far as to say, with all due humility, that the get-together wouldn't be the same without him.

Thirdly, he needed to bring up the invitation specifically because of Melissa's relationship with her mother, which could be labeled, understatedly, as "fraught." That was common knowledge. Everyone knew about the problematic relationship. With her first marriage to Mitch Harrington—an ill-advised, inexplicable mismatch—the common assumption was that Melissa had chosen the ill-suited mate just to get back at her mother. What could punish Meg, society matron, more than a blue collar son-in-law, a tradesman?

Blair's internal point being, Melissa didn't want her mother throwing her a party of *any* kind, which was why she and Rod were having a small ceremony in the first place. If there were going to be a party against her wishes, Melissa needed to prepare herself; it *couldn't* be a surprise. There was psychological work to be done before the event, and every minute counted. If need be, Blair could coach Melissa on how to act surprised. But, without question, in his professional opinion, she needed to know. And he was going to tell her.

"Actually, I *do* know," she said, before he had the chance.

"Then . . . then . . ." Blair had been leaning over his desk, and now he plopped back into his chair, emotionally spent.

He eventually managed to sit a bit more upright and start over. "Then . . . why did you say you didn't? Why did you lie?"

"I didn't exactly lie . . . I played dumb."

"And why did you do that?"

"Not sure," said Melissa, with an unconcerned shrug of her shoulders. "I think I just did it instinctively. I always used to respond to Mom like that. Playing dumb. Just a habit, maybe."

Blair couldn't think of anything to say. If only his mind would stop racing and start processing. The fact did not escape him that she had known about the surprise party and had not even mentioned it in an earlier session. Perhaps she had a lot less anxiety about it than he thought.

Melissa, like her mother, didn't like long silences.

"Do you have the invitation? Here, I mean?"

He nodded dumbly.

"Can I see it?" she prompted.

As he opened the top drawer of the desk, he eyed her suspiciously.

"You mean you haven't seen it?"

"Nope."

"Really? You're not just playing dumb?"

"Nope. Honest injun. Val found out about the party a couple of weeks ago, by accident, but didn't get an invitation."

"Val's not invited?"

"Don't be ridiculous, Blair. Of *course* she's invited. But Mom didn't want to waste an invitation on her. So I haven't seen it. Neither of us have. Gimme." She reached out her arm and he handed over the envelope.

"Nice paper. Mom spares no expense," she quipped, as she worked the card out of its snug fit in the envelope. "Embossed. And check out the gold lining."

Blair grimaced. Melissa frequently resorted to sarcasm in matters relative to Meg, but he was uncomfortable with the tenor of this after-session session. Had this been a dramatic production, the fourth wall was collapsing.

"Jesus, Mom . . ." She had finished reading, closed her eyes, and was shaking her head. "Really corny . . . but typical Mom. Why am I not surprised ?"

Blair resumed full therapist mode.

"So what do you think about all this?"

"I'll manage. It's just . . . it's just that she's such a fucking pain in the ass."

"No anxieties, then?"

"It's a party. What can go wrong at a party? It would be nice, though, if I knew who was coming."

"You mean you don't know who's coming? Besides me, I mean?"

"It's a surprise, Blair. Shush." She put her finger in front of her mouth, but quickly saw that he was not seeing any humor in her flipness. Blair was back at the ranch, trying to do serious business.

"How can you not know who's coming? Wouldn't your Mom tell you, or doesn't *she* know that *you* know?"

"She's in the dark. Surprise! Meg in the dark. And she wants it so badly to be a surprise, what's the point in ruining it for her? Val tried to pry out the information, but Mom actually doesn't remember most of the list. Can you believe it? She can't remember . . . although, you should feel complimented, since she remembers inviting you! A.K.A. 'Sylvia and Harry's son.'"

Blair shook his head. "She's always had a problem with names. I remember as a kid, she used to call me 'Blair Blackman.'"

"I remember."

"In spite of knowing my parents for years."

Melissa started to laugh. "Half the time she even referred to *them* as the Blackmans!"

Blair shook his head again, and couldn't help but laugh with her. "Blair Blackman. More alliterative, I suppose."

When he stopped laughing, he once again realized why sessions with Melissa could be difficult.

"So you really don't know who was invited?"

"Besides you, so far only Rebecca and John, the usual suspects. And, unfortunately, Deirdre, since Mom assumed she and John were still married."

By then, of course, Blair already also knew that Deirdre had been invited. She had told him in session. But he couldn't let Melissa know that he knew. Nor could he tell Deirdre that he had been invited also, and was planning on attending.

"Of course," Melissa continued, "if John thinks that Deirdre is coming, no way in hell will he show up . . . and that would be a real shame."

Another confidentiality quandry. He also knew that Deirdre would be skiing in Aspen during that time frame, and probably wouldn't be able to make it back for the little gathering withough changing her flight reservations. And very likely her tickets were non-refundable.

How confidential were Deirdre's ski trips? She went every year. But if he happened to mention that he knew Deirdre would be skiing, Melissa might think he had a social relationship with Deirdre, or heaven forbid, might even be dating her. And if she were to ask how he knew, he would be revealing that Deirdre was a client. A clear breach of confidentiality.

Melissa also didn't know that Dickie Rawlings and his wife were on the list of guests. Blair couldn't reveal that to Melissa any more than he could have told Dickie Rawlings that he himself was invited, not only with every intention of attending, but on a mission. Blair took a moment to consider Dickie at a social gathering with a few Glenlivets down his gullet, and shuddered. Given the circumstances, perhaps he needed to rethink the whole party thing himself. He had been doing a lot of thinking, and to be honest, was a lot more anxious about the party than Melissa, evidently.

"Well," Blair said, off-handedly, "Deirdre goes skiing all the time, especially this time of year. Maybe she won't be in town."

"That would be lucky," said Melissa.

"Although . . . how would I know?" Blair shrugged innocently.

"I rather hope that bitch doesn't show up . . . John and Rebecca are the only people I care to see, really . . . except for you, of course, but I can pay to see you any time I want."

At that Blair blinked a couple of times, involuntarily, tic-like. To cover, he rubbed his eyes as if something irritating had just flown into them. Oh, nothing, just a small fleck of remorse . . .

PART TWO

The Party

March 13, 1981, 6:45 P.M.
The apartment of Margaret Manning

Meg Manning had forgotten something. She had actually forgotten several things, but of immediate concern was the ice cube tray, which she had neglected to fill with water. Both daughters always nagged her about leaving the empty ice trays in the freezer, but if that were the worst of a mother's flaws, so be it. Besides, she would have had to fill the trays multiple times, since the punch bowl was so large. Fortunately, she reached Val in time and asked her to stop at Safeway to get a bag—make that two—of ice cubes. And, on the way over, she had just remembered, Val needed to stop off at the twelfth floor and pick up the punch ladle from Mrs. Gottlieb.

Her own ladle was somewhere, but she couldn't for the life of her remember where she had left it for safekeeping. The punch bowl on the other hand—bubble-wrapped and boxed—had been easier to locate on the floor of her closet, where she continually bumped into it with her foot when she was choosing a blouse to wear every morning. Next to it was a similarly sized box containing sixteen matching cups, each individually wrapped and taped for protection against accidental droppage or natural disaster.

I need to give this damned punch set to charity, she would think to herself on those occasions when she stubbed her foot exceptionally fiercely on either of the boxes, since neither daughter wanted it. Meg had asked many times, and the answer was always negative, sometimes a simple polite "no," and other times prefaced by "I've already told you" or "Stop hounding me about the damned punch bowl," depending on their moods. Both girls had their moods, which meant that they could change their minds. Circumstances changed, Meg knew, which was why she never had gotten rid of the set. Some day Mel or Val might really want the damned punch bowl.

It occurred to Meg that she hadn't started referring to the punch bowl as "damned" until hearing that expression from Val. Mel, the more foul-mouthed daughter, was more likely to refer to the "fucking" punch bowl. But it was crystal, after all, and Waterford at that, which had cost Charlie a pretty penny when he bought it for a long lost anniversary. Fifth? Tenth? Both girls needed to be more grateful and not take things for granted. Poor people in Africa likely had to serve their punch out of something plastic, she'd remind them next time.

Well, now I'm sure glad I didn't get rid of that damned punch bowl, Meg thought immediately after deciding to host the reception for Mel and Rod. She planned to serve punch.

Meg was concerned that Ora Lee wouldn't be present for a helping hand and moral support. She wrung her hands and paced in the kitchen, looking at the culinary line-up on all the kitchen surfaces. There were two prepared trays from Wolferman's on the counter—delivered promptly at 6 P.M. as requested—wrapped tightly in layers of Saran wrap. One contained sliced meats—three varieties of ham and three varieties of salami—artfully rolled; the other, slices of hard cheeses as well as a selection of black and green olives, cherry tomatoes, baby gherkins, and pepperoncinis. Meg had set out her own special cheese plate with Brie and Camembert, the circumference of the dish haphazardly outlined by water crackers. Crackers as a decorative border, Meg realized, did not lay out as nicely as playing cards, but they would get messed up as soon as people started eating them anyway. A small sterling silver bread basket, lined with a turquoise linen napkin, contained the cracker surplus, completely unordered—just simply poured from the box—and thus looking more professionally arranged.

The major points of worry were her own creations from recipes clipped from magazines. She had chanced upon a small file box crammed with clippings—all ragged-edged and hurriedly torn out two decades earlier—in her living room bureau at the same time she stumbled across Mel's old address book. Two clippings caught her attention as she riffled throught them: the mini eggplant pasties with zucchini and red pepper, and the non-alcoholic punch made with fresh rhubarb. Both were currently in preliminary stages of preparation and producing no small amount of unease.

The large mixing bowl of puréed rhubarb mixed with sugar and water was on the top shelf of the refrigerator, covered in plastic wrap. The color of the mixture had seemed a bit pale, so Meg had improvised and added the juice from a jar of maraschino cherries she found in the back corner of her refrigerator. Finding the results still a bit subdued, Meg added more than a teaspoon of red food dye. The food coloring bottle had been difficult to open due to the congealed material under the small lid, but Meg had managed by running the top of the bottle under hot water, tapping the edges with the blunt end of a dinner knife, and finally employing a vice grip. The cap did not survive the latter maneuver, which is why Meg had used so much of the food coloring rather than wasting it. The effort had been worth it, though, as the viscous, fibrous punch base was now a brilliant, almost incandescent, crimson.

Large plastic containers of 7 Up and soda water needed to complete the beverage were on the breakfast table. Most of the table top, however, was covered by large sheets of wax paper, which bore the efforts of several hours of exhausting crafting. Earlier, Meg had rolled out pastry dough into free form sheets, cropped into roughly five to six inch squares. They only approximated squares, of course, given that most of the edges were irregular, more amoeba-like in contour. When folded and crimped along the edges with a fork, few pieces resembled one another, even remotely. Within each dough pocket, Meg had placed a heaping tablespoon of the eggplant, zucchini, and red pepper mixture. There were scores of these unbaked eggplant-zucchini-pepper appetizers just waiting to be placed in the oven on cookie sheets at three hundred fifty degrees for twenty minutes or so. Meg had determined to put in the first batch after the initial guests arrived, something she needed to remember. Normally, Ora Lee would be responsible for details such as these.

Meg slowly stepped backwards toward the kitchen entrance, as if she had set an explosive device, all the while surveying her domain, mental check list repeating internally like a mantra. She leaned back against the louvered saloon doors. They emitted an eerie creaking in protest, announcing potential energy waiting to be unleashed. They quieted, held in suspense as she stood motionless except for her eyes, roaming all corners of the room and in-between like two globes in a random orbit.

There was a dusting of flour on all the counters, the table, and on the floor, as if unexpected snow flurries had passed through. With no time to clean up, Meg would need to keep everyone out of the kitchen, even if they insisted on helping. Of course, she had to be careful where she stepped so as not to track white footprints onto the plush carpet—which wouldn't be a tragedy, since the carpet was white—but more importantly, take precautions not to powder herself or her cobalt blue cocktail dress. For the moment she was protected by a peppermint-striped kitchen apron, so the pricey dress from Saks was safe. Meg examined the palms of her hands for traces of white and found none. Encouraged, but knowing that one couldn't be too safe, she headed to her bathroom to double check. The saloon doors frolicked noisily.

She had only made it as far as the bedroom door when the doorbell rang. Meg checked her watch: a few minutes before seven, and Val wasn't even back yet with the ice and Mrs. Gottlieb's ladle. Lines of worry sprung upon her face, but she would soldier through on her own. She made her way across the generous open space in front of the sofa and coffee table to the front door of the apartment and took a deep breath before opening it.

He was a good-looking young man, not handsome in a rugged way but more the banker type, with delicate and smooth features—the type that used skin cleansers and shaving balms—and likely a non-smoker with unstained teeth. She hadn't seen his teeth yet, but was extrapolating. He was of medium height, had nicely-trimmed hair, and wore a London Fog style raincoat. His scent was a cologne that Meg couldn't place, but it was pleasant enough, kind of citrusy.

"Hello, Mrs. Manning," he said, a strained smile just revealing itself at both ends of his mouth.

Meg smiled broadly and focused on his hazel eyes. He certainly looked familiar, but she couldn't place him right off. What little of his teeth she could see through that tight smile looked white enough and straight as well. Anyway, she knew she knew him. And certainly he knew her, so she would just go with it.

"My, how long it's been," she began, certain that she was correct about that. However long it had been—and she had no idea—it had been long enough for her to forget who he was. And when she was nervous or feeling somewhat insecure, Meg Manning had a tendency to chatter, silence grating on her nerves.

"So good to see you again, dear, how are you? You're first here, you know, and Valerie is out getting ice and Mrs. Gottlieb's ladle, and I think I'll keep the coats in the bedroom since this front closet isn't big enough for a mouse—actually it is, since we had a small rodent problem a while back and I found a nest in—but that was all taken care of . . ."

Her first guest entered the apartment and began to remove his overcoat, hindered by the hands-on assistance offered by Meg, who had begun to maneuver the opposite sleeve from the one he was attempting to slip off. For a moment it seemed she was a police officer attempting to apply handcuffs, until he surrendered, and let his arms go limp. Meg folded the liberated wrap over her arm and led him into the bedroom, chatting all the way.

"You see, the guests of honor aren't here yet but it's good to see you anyway and I'm so excited about this whole thing that I'm just at sixes and sevens . . . maybe even eights and nines." Meg giggled at the exaggeration.

"Absolutely everything has been so hectic . . . so much to keep track of. I haven't gone through anything like this since my own wedding—and don't you dare ask how long ago that was!" She considered making the calculation in her head, frowning slightly as she did so, then abandoned the attempt. "Anyway, I don't remember it being this complicated—Melissa's father and I eloped as I recall. Maybe it would be easier if Melissa and Rod just forgot the whole thing and lived in sin!"

She paused again to consider what she had said, and realized she needed to correct the record. "Of course you know I'm not serious. I really enjoy the whole hullabaloo—it sort of breaks up the monotony of my Friends of Art meetings and exercise classes, if you get my meaning—but it's put me in such a tizzy. People ask me—"

"Congratulations on the upcoming nuptials," Blair Brackman interrupted.

During her yammering, Blair took the opportunity to surreptitiously appraise the room. He had never been in the apartment before; he thought he recognized the ornately carved mahogany bedroom set from the previous family home in Old Mission Hills. The bed was king-sized and covered with a powder blue satiny coverlet and several color-coordinated pillows and bolsters. The room was large, and didn't seem cramped even with the presence of a chaise lounge in a floral material—more for show than actual sitting—and an antique writing desk. Built-in wall shelves exhibited framed photographs and a variety of tchotchkes rather than books. Separate doors led to the bathroom suite—he could make out the wall tile through the partly opened door—and presumably a closet.

"Why thank you . . . good heavens, I still can't for the life of me remember your name," she admitted with a slight blush, accepting that his name would not come to her unaided, at least not that particular evening. She had planned to finesse things until Val returned and she could inquire discretely, but where was that girl, anyway?

"Brackman. Blair Brackman."

"Blair! Blair! Of course, Blair Blackman!" Meg was excited with relief. "It's been so long since you've come around! You aren't by any chance related to Sidney Blackman? Did I ask you that?"

"I spell my name with an 'R,' not an 'L,'" he explained. On prior occasions, he had just let it pass, allow her to call him Blair Blackman, which was easier to enunciate anyway. But this night was different. She needed to get his name correctly. It was important that she knew exactly who he was.

"No relation to Sidney Blackman then," she said.

"No." Blair was taking no chances. "You know my parents, actually," he added. "Harry and Sylvia Brackman." He over-enunciated the "BRAC" part, then repeated it for clarity. "BuhRACKman."

"Oh, Heavens!" Meg exclaimed. "Of course! You're Harry and Sylvia's son! How could I have forgotten that?"

Blair shook his head. Accepting it as a rhetorical question would make the conversation easier for the both of them. He shook his head again, as if he didn't have a clue. The simple answer—had the question not been rhetorical—was that Meg Manning was a complete ditz.

"And how are the folks?"

"They're doing great. In Sedona at the moment." He smiled, relieved the conversation was moving along and hopefully coming to its termination. "They send their regards," he lied. They probably would have, had they known he would be seeing her, but they didn't.

"And I send my regards right back!" said Meg.

There was a lull. Meg could have excused herself and gone into the bathroom to check herself, but Val still wasn't back, and how could she leave the only guest in the bedroom by himself? She was the hostess, after all. So they should chat, make small talk.

"Names are funny things, aren't they?" she began, feeling herself warming up to the subject. "So many different spellings, pronunciations, and then the way people change them! Why, I once knew these three Greenberg brothers. One of them changed his name to Greenstreet—it was Richard who did that, he was the oldest—and the middle one, Martin—who I went to Garfield High with—chopped it down to Greene with an 'e,' and the youngest brother changed it all the way to Chartreuse. Herbie Chartreuse. Herbie was always a little flighty. Haven't seen any of the Green—any of them in years. I can't imagine why I'm telling you this, except, oh yes, your last name.

"With an 'R.'"

"Of course," Meg went on without paying attention to what he said, "I've heard all these stories about how names were accidentally changed when immigrants got off the boat at Elvis Island. You know, the immigration men sometimes got things wrong, especially if they didn't speak foreign languages and didn't know what on earth to do with those curly-cue things over the 'n's' and that two-dotted business." Meg clarified with appropriate hand and finger gestures. "I for one certainly wouldn't know what to do with them." She considered, this was something she had never thought about before. What on earth *would* she do with them? she asked herself.

"Just leave them off, I imagine," she answered herself vaguely.

"Oh?" Blair felt his eyelids getting heavy.

"Well, anyway, you could do a lot worse than being related to the Blackmans. Wonderful people. Filthy rich."

"Similar names, but no relation," reiterated Blair, wondering what was taking Val so long with the ice. He needed rescuing.

"Too bad," Meg went on. "Well, what's in a name?"

Blair shrugged dumbly.

"Just letters, I suppose," said Meg, exhaling, signaling another potential lull that had to be avoided.

She quickly recovered. "Blair Brackman . . . Blair Brackman . . . Harry and Sylvia's son . . . ah, you're the lawyer!"

"Psychologist."

"Psychologist. I knew that. It's just that sometimes the right things don't come out. My tongue gets all tied up in knots."

Blair, exasperated, was trying his best to be empathetic, to relate to the woman.

"Like my stomach," he cautiously confided.

"Exactly. And you can't talk?"

"Can't eat."

"Oh, I see." Meg's face fell into a blank expression. "No, I don't, actually" she said.

"I'm sorry," Blair apologized. "That's something else entirely. I just jumped tracks on you."

"Well, now . . . you'd better not do that! Not today, anyway. Unless you want to give my migraine a migraine!"

Blair felt the chest tightness coming on, but tried to ignore it. Still, even Meg Manning's chattering couldn't distract him. He was beginning to panic, to feel the heat rising from his neck. He could excuse himself and ask to go to the bathroom, but what the hell? It was unfair to hide his asthma from this woman. It was no big deal and besides, he needed to nip his bronchospasms in the bud or else he'd never get through the evening, never see his plans through. If Meg wanted to talk asthma, he'd talk asthma. If she wanted to discuss her own health issues, that would be fine, and no worse than talking about immigration officers on Elvis Island.

He calmly reached into his jacket pocket and removed the inhaler. With forced casualness, he brought the inhaler to his mouth and took two healthy whiffs, then replaced the inhaler in his pocket. He avoided making eye contact with Meg during the process.

Meg looked at him in a sympathetic way, with some concern in her eyes. Blair smiled wanly, prepared to explain about his childhood asthma, which had taken a recent turn for the worse, in no small part related to her daughter. The latter detail, for the time being, he would omit.

"Onions for dinner?" she asked.

Blair gave his answer some thought. He could feel his chest loosening, a coolness coming back to his face. He took a deep breath without any difficulty.

"Yes," he replied.

"Well," Meg said, "here I'm going on like this and I haven't even hung up your coat."

"That's quite alright."

"Anywhere will be fine," she said, flinging it onto the king-sized bed. "You're the first one here, did I tell you?"

"I believe you mentioned it."

"Val had to—"

"—pick up some ice and get the ladle from Mrs. Gottlieb."

"Exactly."

"Nice of Mrs. Gottlieb to lend you her ladle."

"She's delightful, full of beans—I don't mean in a gassy way, of course," Meg said, "but her varicose veins are unbelievable. Anyway, before we spend too much time on Mrs. Gottlieb's veins, I hope you don't mind if I . . . I'm a little bit behind and I still have some loose ends to tidy up before the others . . . I think there was something I needed to do in the kitchen."

"Please, go right ahead." Blair made a solicitous gesture with his arm, a seventeenth century gesture, as if he were Sir Walter Raleigh and had just laid down a cape.

"You see what happened . . ." Meg began. Blair let his arm drop. "What happened was . . . my help couldn't make it. She came down with the hog flu or something like that and left me completely stranded. Val left school early to help out though, last minute things while I rolled the eggplant pasties. Terrible thing, that flu, especially now, before the party. Ora Lee's very reliable otherwise, you know, been with me for years."

"Nasty thing to catch," said Blair, who remembered Ora Lee quite clearly as a saint.

"Anyway, so you'll forgive me if I can't chat right now. You can make yourself at home in the living room until Val and the other guests arrive. Shouldn't be long."

"Thank you. I will." Blair wasn't ready to go into the living room, not ready to see anyone. He needed to prepare, especially given that little episode of shortness of breath. Meg Manning anticipated a move toward the living room on Blair's part, but he didn't make one. He seemed glued in place, both feet planted on the bedroom carpet.

"You know the living room," she said. "We just came through it."

"Yes," said Blair. "I thought I might use the bathroom first. It's right over there, isn't it?" he asked, pointing at the tiled room.

"Yes. Right through that door there. Well, I'll see you again soon."

"Yes."

Meg had made it halfway out when she turned, an afterthought, but an important one.

"And, Blair . . ."

"Yes?"

"Be sure to shake it real good when you're done. Give it a good shake. So it won't drip."

"Excuse me?"

"You know . . . shake it. *Shake it!*" She made a shaking gesture with her hand, as if she held an invisible maraca and the beat was quite up-tempo.

Blair's eyes were transfixed on her jiggling hand. He blinked and could only think that he was wearing dark colored pants, so it was not a problem. But, unconsciously, he looked down at his pants, to confirm they were dark. His expression must have been blank, if not confused.

"That toilet will sing all evening if you don't give the handle a good . . . oh my goodness . . . you didn't think . . . I didn't mean . . ."

A mortified Meg Manning fled her own bedroom. Had she remembered to go into the bathroom herself for a final once-over, she would have removed her peppermint-striped apron, which concealed most of the expensive blue cocktail dress from Saks. Missing her chance, she would be wearing the apron all evening.

❧

Val Manning walked down the hall from the elevator, a plastic bag of ice hanging from each arm and a silver-plated ladle tucked precariously under her chin. She felt beads of sweat on her forehead and dampness in her armpits, and regretted not having removed the fleece liner from her knee-length jacket that morning. She set down the bags on the floor outside the threshold—on either side of the sisal mat expressing a cheerful but in-discriminate "Welcome to the Manning's"—to unlock the door to her mother's apartment.

The living room was empty, so Val assumed her mother was in the bedroom applying finishing touches to her clothes and make-up—she surely needed to with all the flour floating around the place. Front door open and with the ladle under her chin, Val retrieved both ice bags and carried them into the kitchen, thrusting her chest at the saloon doors as she passed through. The double-louvered doors rattled angrily as they continued to swing back and forth with diminishing conviction until stopping entirely. Val set down the ladle and placed both ice bags in the smaller side of the double sink, a tight fit. She tore open the top of one of the bags with her fingers, then tore it some more before lifting the bag back out from the sink and tromping across the living room, cradling it low and in front of her with both arms like a third trimester pregnancy.

Meg had positioned her dining room table against the far wall of the contiguous dining area. Covered with a white tablecloth, it was empty for the time being except for the Waterford punch bowl, a showy crystal centerpiece surrounded by matching crystal cups. Val dumped about half the bag of cubes, stepped back to assess whether it was an appropriate amount, and determining that it didn't much matter and probably wouldn't satisfy her mother no matter how much she deposited, transported the half-emptied bag back through the louvers to its designated resting spot in the kitchen sink. Then she returned to the living room and collapsed on the sofa, her legs splayed out straight in front of her.

Val gazed down at her black pumps and distractedly moved her feet on their heel pivots as if they were windshield wipers. Slouching, her butt barely maintained contact with the front edge of the sofa cushion. She wriggled out of her jacket and leaned back against it; a button jabbed into her shoulder but she didn't bother to change her position. Instead, she concentrated on the wiper-like movement of her feet, alternating with them going the same direction, pointing together, then moving in counterpoint, pointing first towards one other and then away. She imagined each foot having a different gender; it was a pedal relationship, sometimes synchronous, sometimes rocky and discordant. Relationships could be like playing footsies.

Just for a moment, she promised herself, she would rest and stare at her feet. Val Manning was known for being infatiguable, but that usually referred to energy expended in the physical realm. Emotional energy was much more taxing, and spending more than two or three consecutive hours with her mother took a metabolic toll comparable to running a marathon in the heat. Whether she could completely revive, given the possible social ordeal to come, was in doubt.

The day had been exhausting. She had come straight to the apartment from a tough Friday at school—the kids were particularly antsy for some unknown reason, perhaps related to gravitational effects from the moon impacting their ever susceptible hormones. At the apartment she found her mother exceptionally on edge, for very known reasons but also possibly exacerbated by gravitational effects, clearly needing help but reluctant to accept any. Meg's appearance was also a mess; she was perspiring heavily, with a large stiff lock of hair flopping into one eye, unmoored from the earlier spraying. Since Meg didn't want to touch her face or hair with flour-covered hands, she had been continually tucking out her lower lip and blowing upwards to blow the hair away, with only limited and intermittent success. She was blowing so incessantly at times, that Val thought she might pass out from hyperventilation.

Val had watched her mother fold the eggplant and zucchini mini-pies for over an hour, at first coaching and then watching with incredulity, but could only convince her mother to let her fold a few herself.

"If you do more than a few, Val, dear," she had complained, "too many of them will look alike. That's not the style I'm going for."

Such was her mother's rationalization for the inability to perform any fine motor action consistently. The mini-pies showed an incredible spectrum of diversity for being composed of identical material, rivaling the variety within species of birds or even insects. Val had finally given up, since she needed to shower and change clothes, and went back to her own apartment. She had just entered the shower and was dripping wet when the phone began ringing; it was Meg, of course, asking her to stop off at Safeway for ice and then to pick up the ladle from Mrs. Gottlieb on the way up to the apartment. Now, sprawled on the sofa, Val was hesitant to take anything out from the kitchen, not even the innocuous cheese and meat plates from Wolferman's, or heaven forbid, get involved with concocting the punch, until she had her mother's explicit permission and instructions. She had been brazen enough already, just with the ice. But at least she could put the ladle with the punch bowl and glasses. She forced herself to her feet.

When she emerged from the kitchen, ladle gripped in her fist, John Palopolus had entered the apartment through the open door, his leather bombardier jacket draped over his arm.

He emitted three disparaging "tsks" as soon as he saw her. "Strange men have been known to enter open doors in this neighborhood."

"Some day my prince will come," replied Val, "and it would be a shame if he couldn't get in."

Palopolus, never one to concede a repartee, continued, "Then again, if I had known that you were prepared to ward off attackers with a giant spoon, I might have reconsidered and—"

"This is Mrs. Gottlieb's ladle—"

"—chosen instead to assault Mrs. Gottlieb, who is obviously defenseless. How about a little kiss, sweetheart?"

"Good to see you, John." Val presented a cheek for him to kiss, then, indicating the ladle, walked to the table to set it down beside the punch bowl.

"Want anything else as long as I'm warmed up?" John said in a louder voice to Val's back.

"You're sure in a good mood," she said, returning. "Let me take your jacket." She took the neatly folded garment, and sheepishly admitted that she wasn't sure where her mother wanted the coats to go. She set it down on the sofa next to her own jacket; transport to the front closet or the bedroom could be arranged later.

"Rebecca told me a couple days ago that Deirdre is still in Aspen and won't be coming, so I'm here to have a good time. It's someone else's funeral this time—I've already had mine." John looked over at the near empty serving table. "And I'm the first? Too early?"

Val shook her head. "Mom's just a bit behind and I'm afraid to take charge. You know how she can get. I think she's in the bedroom making last minute dress changes, debating her lipstick color, and having a nervous breakdown."

"Your mother? Calm, controlled Margaret Manning? Come, come now, you're joking. By the way, Val, you're looking good, if I have to say so myself." He gave her the once over in exaggerated fashion, then repeated the up and down visual tour. She wore a scooped-neck dress with a floral pattern, cut well above the knees. The scoop neck explored lower depths than Val's usual more conservative fare, and John's eyes had paused noticeably, with raised eyebrows, when they momentarily lingered at her cleavage. "Nice to see a bit of breast. Been brushing up on your pop psychology so you'll have something to discuss with that certain someone?" He winked at her.

Val blushed, uncertain whether it was from John's pointed attention to her décolletage or the reference to Blair Brackman, both of which she found embarrassing.

John looked back to the door. "Wonder what's keeping Rebecca? I saw her parking as I was coming up. Wait!" John crouched down slightly, jutted his head forward, and spread his arms apart, palms down, in a pose of attentiveness. "I think I smell that cheap French perfume . . . hear those heavy stiletto-heeled footsteps, those overworked thighs . . ."

As Rebecca strode in, Palopolus straightened dramatically and extended a sweeping, introductory arm. "And here she is now . . . the Virgin Queen!"

"Screw you, John, I've had a helluva day, and you know I can't deal with you when I'm sober . . ."

"We'll take care of that," replied John. "The usual? Lighter fluid?" He looked around. "I'm afraid all we have at the moment is a punchbowl full of ice cubes. Val, show us some mercy."

"Mom has a special punch planned, but this appears to be an emergency." Val walked to the serving table, which sat just beneath the built-in bar. Reaching over it, she pulled open the double doors to reveal a well-stocked liquor cabinet, with duplicate unopened bottles of both clear and amber spirits, along with a selection of glassware covering the entire wine, champagne, and cocktail spectrum. Val busied herself making up two generous tumblers of Scotch, pilfering ice cubes from the punch bowl, while Rebecca delved into the details of her day. None for herself; she needed a clear head.

"Listen, you won't believe this day—how are you, anyway, Val? The old man Higgenbotham pinches my ass again this morning—not only that, but Braverman's secretary calls in sick—that flu is going around—and I get stuck with twice the work. I pick up the kid after school—she gripes at me the whole way home for being late—then gets down to the real problem: all of her friend's mothers wear bras. Eight years old. Serves me right for slaving to send her to private school."

She took the tumbler from Val and held the glass up for an attempted toast with John, but he already had the glass up to his lips and was drinking, looking at her over the top of the rim. He made an upward motion with his elbow as an acknowledgement, and Rebecca steamed on.

"Thanks, Val. Anyway, we drive all the way to Winstead's for a burger and the kid spills her half-melted frosty into my lap. So I go back home to change, schlep to Leawood to drop her at her slumber party, and now I've spent the last fifteen minutes trying to parallel park because some jerk-off in a Lincoln who thinks he owns the world takes up a space and a half."

"I guess I shouldn't complain," said Val.

"So where is everybody?" Rebecca asked.

Val shrugged.

"Maybe it's a very exclusive guest list . . . just us," said Rebecca.

"That would be nice. And the eminent Herr Brackman," added John, looking over at Val.

Val took a deep breath and shrugged again.

"Maybe we should just assume no one else is coming and start partying ourselves. Where's the food, Val? Let's get a move on. I've been on a liquid diet all day, saving myself for this feast."

Val gave John a helpless look and yet another shrug.

After only a short moment of ennui-laden silence that felt considerably longer, a flustered Meg Manning emerged from the bedroom, wearing her kitchen apron over her blue cocktail dress. Muttering to herself, she was looking downward, shaking her head—and, oddly, her right hand. She jumped, startled, acutely aware that the party had started, that she was in the presence of company for whom she was the hostess.

"Oh, dear," she said "how utterly awful what I said . . . and you startled me so."

"Mom, what the—" Val began.

"Nothing but a Freudian skip, dear. Oh . . . hello everyone!"

The introductions commenced, predictably of a more complex and extended nature had Meg Manning not been a participant.

"You already know . . ." began Val, indicating John.

"Hello, Mrs. Manning, good to see you, as always," said John, taking his cue, smiling amiably and behaving for the time being.

"Of *course* I do," confirmed Meg. "This is . . . uh . . . uh . . ."

"John," said John.

"John," said Meg.

"Palopolus," said John.

"Palopolus," repeated Meg, remembering he had a funny name for an Italian. "And you're Becky, isn't that right?"

"Rebecca Harvey, Mrs. Manning. Pleased to see you again."

"But they call you 'Becky,' right?"

"No," said Rebecca.

"They call her many things," Palopolus interjected, signaling an end to a restraint on bad behavior, "but 'Becky' isn't one of them."

"I could have sworn—" said Meg, noting the open front door, "Val, dear, don't you know that strange men have been known to enter open doors in this neighborhood?" John and Val couldn't contain small smiles at the trademark remark. Meg closed the door securely and flipped the latch for good measure.

"Mom," Val had a plaintive tone in her voice. "The punch isn't ready and none of the food is out. Can I help you bring things in from the kitch—"

"Absolutely not, dear, I'm taking care of everything. Now, you all just sit down and make yourselves comfortable, and I'll have the punch fixed up and all the food out on the table before you can say 'Swiss Family Robinson.'"

The three sat on the sofa, lined up like actors at an audition call. Rebecca slipped off her coat and held it in her lap. Val leaned back on her own—the button from her jacket jabbed her in the shoulder again—and John, not bothering to lift his folded leather jacket from the seat, ued it as an additional cushion. They watched together, spellbound, as Meg Manning made repeated trips back and forth from the kitchen, punctuated each time by the swinging and racket of the louvered saloon doors.

The spectacle was hypnotic. Meg first brought out the slushy rhubarb mixture and emptied it into the punch bowl with a large serving spoon. She returned with a two-liter bottle of 7 Up, which she meticulously poured on top of the ice. She then proceeded to fetch another two-liter bottle, this one of soda water, which she also poured, with great care, into the bowl. And so on, until she had placed both the meat and cheese plates from Wolferman's, a small container of toothpicks to spear the olives and gherkins, cloth napkins, and scavenged portions from her silver service, each item requiring a dedicated trip.

While Meg was in the living room tending to her transports the sofa occupiers were silent, but as soon as she disappeared through the doors and was out of earshot, terse conversation resumed.

"John and I are curious about the groom, Val."

"The infamous Rod," said John.

"I haven't spent all that much time with him, actually." Val looked at the two contemplatively sipping their Scotch, not without envy. "He's alright. He grows on you. I imagine he won't exactly be on your wavelength, but if he makes Mel happy . . ."

"How romantic!" Rebecca rolled her eyes. "What's he do again?"

"A salesman."

"Sounds deadly."

All quieted while Meg brought in the cheese plate with the semi-softs and spent an inordinate amount of time rearranging crackers along its edge. Some had fallen on the floor en route. Meg picked these up and absently slipped them into her apron pocket, and was gathering reinforcements from the cavalry of crackers she had set out the trip before.

When she finally exited the room again, Val said, "I think I may have a drink myself."

"Punch looks tempting," mocked John. "Makes my eyes hurt just looking at it. Doesn't appear to contain any alcohol, from what I've seen."

"Doesn't. Mom insisted. A new recipe. Exotic. Experimental. Made from rhubarb."

"Interesting," mused John, pausing as he customarily did before one of his zingers. "High fiber."

"I'll start with the Scotch," said Val, pushing herself up from the couch. She poured her drink into the tumbler and was replacing the bottle in the cabinet when she heard Palopolus exclaim "Shit!"

"What's going on?" she asked, returning to her seat.

"Shit shit shit!" said John, now slumped back and holding the drink in his lap.

"What?" Val persisted.

"Deirdre is coming," said Rebecca. "She was in Aspen but found an earlier flight and cut her trip short. She left a message on my answering machine earlier today."

"And Rebecca didn't even let me know," John fumed. "She told me day before yesterday that Deirdre wouldn't be coming. You could have called me and you didn't. Some fucking friend you are . . ."

"You need to get out, John, and I knew you wouldn't come if I told you. And see how much fun we're having already?" Rebecca swirled her drink around in her glass before taking another swig.

Palopolus did a bad job of appearing to accept the new reality.

"It doesn't fucking matter," he said. "No reason we can't be together socially. Small town, Kansas City, right? Impossible to avoid each other forever."

"It's been a year and a half since the divorce, for Christ's sake!" Rebecca's exasperation came at the cost of an increase in conversational volume. The echoing sound was squelched by the banging of the saloon doors as Meg entered. She hurried to the center of the room and stopped. Her hands were empty. She appeared confused, an impression amplified by the fact that she was muttering to herself. She abruptly turned around and hurried back into the kitchen.

John resumed when the doors had come to rest.

"We're both adult about the whole thing."

"Don't make me puke," said Rebecca, keeping her volume down with effort. "Val, this fool calls me up every other night for a shoulder to cry on. Same old crap. The fact remains, Palopolus—and you know I love you or I wouldn't say it—you're the biggest damn weenie in the entire world and that bitch wouldn't piss on you if you were on fire."

"Not every other night," said John.

"He's letting that woman totally destroy him. He's lost his job and all he does is sit around, smoke, drink, and pop pills."

"Aw, come on," said John, reaching into his pocket for his pack of cigarettes, then thinking better of it. Meg would go ape-shit, and there were no ashtrays in sight. But it was worth a try. "Val, do you think we might be able to borrow an ashtray from Mrs. Gottlieb?"

Val shook her head and glared at him in the same way she castigated Damon Beiriger, the worst trouble maker in her eighth grade class. Palopolus, like Damon Beiriger, relented after bestowing a token dirty look.

Meg noisily entered, again empty-handed. She looked around the room, as if trying to find something, but not sure what. If she saw it, though, it would come to her. In the meantime, she realized that only Val and two others, Becky and the Italian, were in the room.

"Our other guest . . ." she began hesitantly, "he's still in the bathroom?"

"Someone's here already? Who?" Val was completely surprised. How had anyone slipped by her?

"Blair something or other with an 'R.'"

"My shrink's here! I'm saved!" John exclaimed.

"That's Blair Brackman with a 'B.'" corrected Val.

"I know that, dear, but he's no relation to Sidney because I already asked."

"Their names aren't the—"

"And you can't just leave the coats all over the place, Val. Take them into the bedroom and put them on the bed. You know how small the closet is."

"Sure Mom, I will. In a minute—"

"And I'm forgetting something," said Meg, her face clouding as if blinds were closing over it, "something else I just know I was about to do . . ." Her sudden smile evidenced the shades being pulled open. "The hors d'oeuvres! Val! Did you turn on the oven?"

"You didn't want me to—no, not yet," she said, resigned to being blamed for something that was not her fault.

"I'll take care of it," Meg said. "You take care of the coats." She quick-stepped back into the kitchen. The three of them jumped slightly this time when the doors clattered; either Meg had pushed more forcefully in her eagerness, or they were becoming sensitized, the relentless slamming and shuddering working as a mild form of torture.

Val stood up and picked up her own jacket and took Rebecca's, while an accommodating John lifted his buttocks slightly off the cushion so Val could slip his folded bomber jacket out from under him, yanking out the tablecloth from under a heavy place setting of dishes.

"You lost your job?" she asked him before heading to the bedroom. "The break from the column wasn't temporary?"

"I'm doing freelance. Just a transition period. Jarvis is handling the column."

"If he writes anything at all, he's writing porn," Rebecca said.

"It's only the occasional piece! And its *soft* porn!" John protested. "And it pays the rent, dammit!"

"If only the Princeton Glee Club could see you now . . ." Rebecca tilted her glass for the last watered down drops. She let one of the smaller ice cubes slip between her molars and crunched it ostentatiously to emphasize her point.

ᴄᴏ∞ᴏ

It was just the two of them, Rebecca and John, sitting beside one another on the living room sofa in complete silence. Until the doorbell rang.

John's body convulsed.

"Who's that?"

"How should I know?" Rebecca answered snippily, "I'll find out though . . ."

She started to get up but Palopolus grabbed her arm, a drowning man reaching for rope.

"Wait! I mean—"

Meg peeked her head out over the top of the louvers like a nosy neighbor peering over a fence.

"Did I hear the doorbell?"

John hesitated before answering. "Yes, you did."

"Anybody there?" Meg softly pushed open the doors, clasping each one from the top. She stood in place, arms fully stretched, like the sheriff of Dodge City about to enter the Long Branch Saloon.

"There's no way of telling with the door closed, for God's sake," said Rebecca, tugging away from John. He would not let go.

"But the doorbell rang," Meg confirmed in a non-confirmatory tone. "I believe so. Yes, it did!" Meg took a couple tentative steps into the room, prompting an intense rejoinder from the doors when she set them free. "Oh, I see. Then you haven't answered it yet!"

"That was the next step," said John, still restraining a wriggling Rebecca.

The doorbell rang again. And again in quick succession.

"Well, that was *definitely* the doorbell that time," said Meg.

"No question about it," said John.

Meg gave the two an odd look, but one still within the realm of politeness.

"Don't bother, I'll get it," she said.

As Meg walked toward the door, John abruptly released Rebecca's arm and rushed to the far corner of the room, where he proceeded to pull a pill container from his pocket, shakily open it, drop a tablet into his hand, and gulp it down with the remaining diluted whiskey in his glass.

Meg watched him, frozen in her tracks midway to the door.

"Breath mint," said John, in response to her inquiring eyes.

"Onions for dinner," Meg affirmed.

John nodded.

"So, then," said Meg. "We all agree that the doorbell rang and I'm about to answer it." She appeared to have lost confidence. "Well, here goes . . ."

∽

"If you had waited any longer—whoever you are—I would be standing in a puddle."

"Oh, Dickie . . ." Candy Rawlings chastised her husband, as she often found herself doing when he had been drinking.

The couple were pushing the spring season, but could have stepped out from the pages of a fashion magazine. Dickie aspired to the Tom Wolfe look, with a cream colored three-piece suit, a starched white shirt with thin pale blue stripes, and an apricot-hued tie. He wore brown and peach saddle oxfords with thinly ribbed peach socks barely visible. Candy had more of the country music awards ceremony look to her, wearing a tight white cocktail dress with an assortment of silver sequins in a pattern that suggested an aboriginal dream painting. The dress had a plunging neckline and tightly conformed to her curvaceous body, with her breasts bursting straight outwards like two guard dogs pulling on their chains at the sight of an intruder. She was a blue-eyed blonde with a heavy-handed application of make-up and perfectly coiffed sprayed hair. Outfit aside, Candy Rawlings exuded a wholesome innocence, accompanied by an intellectually dense, vapid aura—she was not very bright, and if she were, she hid it beautifully—a physical and mental hybrid of Daisy May and Little Annie Fannie. She was holding a yellow daffodil.

Momentarily deterred by his wife's admonitions, Dickie stuck out his hand and introduced himself.

"Pleased to meet you, Mrs. . . ."

"Meg. Just Meg."

Dickie wore his hair reasonably short along the back and sides, but long on top—like a California surfer boy—hanging down and curving to the right. Dickie flicked his head to get the locks away from his right eye, as was his habit. On occasion, he would scoop the front locks back with his left hand, and secure the offending strands behind his right ear. His hair was long enough to stay there, looped over and behind that ear for a reasonable amount of time, provided he remained relatively still.

"Just Meg, I'm Dickie Rawlings and this is my Southern Belle of a wife Candy, and we've just returned from a marvelous though overpriced dinner at Plaza III, where I literally drank myself to the gills."

"Oh, Dickie!"

"And in all seriousness if I don't find a toilet immediately—*immédiatement*—I shall be forced to actually *douse* my hostess . . ."

"Oh, *Dickie!*"

". . . and I, not to mention my wife, would be frightfully embarrassed as we will all be reading about it in the society pages of the *Kansas City Star*, such as they are."

Meg, a bit shell-shocked, managed to lift her arm and point to the door leading to the bedroom. Dickie brushed by her with an "Ah-hah! Hello, everyone!"

"When you're done you have to shake . . . never mind," said Meg, catching herself as Dickie disappeared through the bedroom door. She turned her hostess-with-the-mostess attention to Candy, posed like a statue, holding the flower in both hands, her upper body undulating in what might have been a provocative manner had it not been more identifiable as self-conscious squirming.

"So pleased to meet you! Candy, is it?" effused Meg. "I'm Melissa's mother. What a beautiful flower!"

"Why, thank you!" drawled Candy.

Rebecca had made her way over to John, now both within close range of the liquor cabinet.

"Brother!" Rebecca said in a hoarse whisper. "If it isn't the tight-ass from Tin Mountain, Tennessee. And it looks like you took that breath mint for nothing, Palopolus."

Candy was in a comfortable conversation zone with Meg.

"The man at the restaurant gave it to me," she said coyly. "Why, some of the drinks had little flowers floating around in them, just like a lil' ole lily pond. I'm really sorry Dickie had so much to drink, but they were so pretty and they had these big long straws, and well . . . even I had a teensy weensy taste of one, and I don't usually drink 'cause it makes me throw up."

"Well, that's wonderful, dear," said Meg. "I don't mean about the throwing up part."

"'Course not." Candy wore one of her pageant smiles.

"I mean about drinking. I'm not much of a drinker myself. My husband had a drinking problem. I don't even like to keep alcohol in the house, but I do it for the kids. Mother's sacrifice, you know."

"Is he dead? Your husband?" Candy looked devastated, like the time she had been asked the question about the Vietnam War in the semi-finals.

"My husband? Charlie? Dear me, no. We're divorced. For years and years—don't you *dare* ask how many years . . ." She chuckled, to indicate she was joking, just banter, and not being rude.

"Oh, no, I wouldn't think of it." Candy said, shaking her head, serious business, not appreciating the nature of the banter.

"But it's a great comfort to me to *pretend* he's dead. Until the first of every month when he comes miraculously to life—long enough to sign and mail my alimony check. Or else I call my lawyer. But why am I going on about my dear departed when—but you must simply try the punch. It's absolutely delicious and it doesn't have a drop of alcohol in it!"

"How wonderful! You know it's been so long since I've been to a party that didn't have a spike in the bowl!"

By this time, John had generously freshened up his own tumbler, as well as Rebecca's, retrieving additional ice cubes from the punch bowl with Mrs. Gottlieb's ladle. He gallantly picked up an overturned punch glass and poured in a couple dips of punch.

"Allow me, Candy," he said, walking it over to her. "When the others get here, you'll have to fight your way to the bowl."

"Oh, John," a pleased Meg feigned protesting, "it's not *that* good!"

"Mrs. Manning, in all honesty, I don't think I've seen a punch like this since Bonnie Baumgardner's sixth birthday in 1954."

"Really?"

"Of course I can't drink it myself, unfortunately, since I've developed an allergy to all non-alcoholic punches."

"What a shame!"

"It makes him throw up," piped up Rebecca from the table, as she breached the intact round of Camembert and placed a slice of it on a cracker.

"How awful!" lamented Meg.

Rebecca wasn't sure what had gotten into her, but she was feeling some guilt about her attitude toward Candy; she could at least try to be civil, and perhaps was even capable of it. She had seen little of Candy since their college days—back then she had been Candy Decker—and not surprisingly they hadn't been friends. Rebecca could now admit that it had been mostly her own fault—she had been antagonistic and often downright mean to the conservative, old-fashioned Southern girl. Candy never held it against her, always pretending as if nothing untoward were between them, like an eager puppy holding no grudge against its owner after getting smacked for crapping on the carpet.

Candy had been well liked at Mizzou, appreciated for being authentic despite many classmates doubting that her vein of authenticity could actually exist in twentieth century America. A sweet and kind person at heart, Candy had represented a "type" Rebecca simply couldn't stomach. A war was going on, how could anyone just ignore it, not be really pissed off at the Establishment? The two were opposite extremes at the Kappa house: Candy the epitome of the stereotypical sorority doll, and Rebecca the rebellious hippie girl. In truth, Rebecca had been more of the anomaly in that crowd. She never really understood what she was doing in a sorority house, anyway, nor did others. And it was still a mystery how she got in to begin with, but she suspected Melissa had put in a good word for her. They had shared a bedroom, either because Mel preferred it that way, or had stepped up when none of the other Kappa sisters wanted to share personal space with a hippie slut.

"Tell me, Candy," said Rebecca, sidling up to Candy, "do you ever hear from Nigel?"

"Pardon me?"

"You know . . . Nigel Davies."

"That name sounds awfully familiar . . ."

"English chap. Friend of Melissa's from junior year. The exchange student from London."

"I . . . I've never been to England," Candy squirmed, "but I hear it's nice."

Meg was following along. "It seems I've heard that name lately . . ." she said, wrinkling her nose as she struggled to remember.

Rebecca had tried to be civil, but Candy was being completely disingenuous and it irritated the hell out of her. So much for keeping the gloves on.

"No, dear," she said to Candy with as much condescension as she could impregnate into two words, "you must be confused. He's in advertising and he works for J. Walter Thompson in London. He's been back to the States a few times since college. I'm sure you remember the last time he was in the city . . . shortly before your wedding."

". . . but I can't seem to remember where." Meg was no longer tracking, preoccupied with her own lost thoughts, grasping into the recesses of her brain as if trying to remember a dream.

John now joined the fray.

"Ladies man," he contributed. "Seducing young virgins sort of a hobby of his."

Dickie emerged from the bedroom, a look of consternation on his face. Candy leapt at the legitimate opportunity to disengage and direct the conversation her own way.

"I wore *white* for my wedding, if you understand what I'm trying to say. Didn't I Dickie?"

"Of course she wore white," her husband responded, joining the group in the center of the room. "Snow White. In fact, at Bedford Forest High, Candy was voted 'Most Likely To Retain Her Hymen.'"

Candy blushed through her amply applied blush. "You know how embarrassed I get when you brag, Dickie—"

"She came marching down the aisle with a crown of flowers on her head and seven little midgets carrying her gown along. There was this cute dopey-looking one who kept farting all the time."

"Oh, Dickie!"

"Darling, please don't 'Oh, Dickie' me. You know how it makes my skin crawl." He flicked the hair out of his eyes petulantly.

"I'm sorry, sugar plum."

"I think I could use a drink," said Dickie.

"Try the punch," said Meg.

"It's delicious, Dickie," said Candy.

"Then let me get you a refill and I'll try some myself," he offered, his mood ever malleable.

"You just help yourself, honey pie, I think I'll go powder my nose," said Candy. She walked stiffly toward the bedroom door. Certain that no one could see her front side, she let the veneer drop. The bottom half of her face slacked, her eyes stared ahead and went glassy.

She looked like she had been eliminated from the pageant in an early round and was valiantly holding back the tears. She tried to think happy thoughts, though, like her mother had taught her to do in such circumstances.

Dickie scooped the punch into a fresh cup and set the ladle down on the table. There were deep red stains in the spots where the tablecloth had become wet. Instantly he had produced another stain, which continued to grow as he watched it with fascination. The ladle left a trail wherever it was set down, and the serving table was beginning to look like a crime scene.

"What's in this?" he asked, holding the brilliantly crimson liquid close to his face and looking through its surprising opacity.

"Rhubarb," Meg boasted.

"You don't say. Outstanding. If it's any good I'll have to get the recipe to the steward at the club," Dickie said. "Cheers, good people," he added, raising his glass.

∞

Before the arrival of C.W. Dexter, John and Dickie—two men of differing disposition and values who did not especially like one another—agreed that the punch needed some fixing.

"Weirdest Kool-Aid I've ever tasted," Dickie said. "Needs a little something, doesn't it?"

"Definitely," John concurred. "A lotta little something." With Meg checking on the progress of the hors d'oeuvres in the kitchen, John opened the liquor cabinet and pulled out two unopened bottles of Smirnoffs. He handed one to Dickie, and in unison—great minds thinking alike—they twisted off the caps and poured the entire contents of both bottles into the mixture.

"Do you think two's enough?" Dickie asked.

"Depends," John answered. "I'm winging this without a recipe. Is there room in the bowl?"

"It's a rather large punch bowl. Waterford."

"In that case . . ." John perused the liquor cabinet for possibilities and located a full bottle of Bacardi. "Try this." He handed it over to Dickie, who opened and poured.

"Ahhhhh . . ." he said, admiring the gurgles and splashing sounds.

John replaced the two empty Smirnoff bottles in the cabinet, adding the empty bottle of Bacardi after Dickie had completed his task.

Palopolus closed the double doors of the liquor cabinet. There would be no further need to open it again that evening. He picked up the ladle and stirred the mixture thoroughly. Then he placed the ladle down to produce yet another expanding stain.

He filled Dickie's glass, then his own. They raised them together.

"A toast to Bonnie Baumgardner," said John.

Dickie conveyed a look of non-comprehension.

"Nevermind that," said John. "How about: 'What hath Meg Manning wrought?'"

While knowing that his time alone—the time he needed to gather himself—would be limited perhaps to minutes, if not seconds, Blair savored the solitude in Meg

Manning's bedroom. The plush and foreign personal space was relaxing. And there were poignant tethers to his own circumstances, like Melissa's high school graduation photograph. And yet another on the bureau of her with Val, taken at the duck pond at Loose Park, when Melissa was likely in her senior year at Shawnee Mission East.

How ironic, he thought, that after all this time and consideration, his long awaited opportunity had finally come and there he was, emotionally readied but without having formulated an actual plan. Not all the details scripted out, anyway, but perhaps it was better that way. Tied to something too specific he might have trouble improvising, adapting to whatever reactions he encountered. But knowing the interested parties so well, he was confident that he could successfully anticipate any and all responses. Humans were so damned predictable.

He started for the bathroom, realized he really didn't need to go, and paced for a few seconds at the foot of the bed. Passing the full-length mirror on the closet door, he encountered a presentable image and admired it. He realized he could stand a bit straighter, which he did, then shuffled his feet a few inches on the carpet to center himself in the frame. Seeing himself as he would be seen, he cleared his throat. A throat clearing—brusque and confident and conveying gravitas by its timbre—would get their attention, like tapping on a glass with a spoon in the manner of a Best Man preparing the wedding guests for a toast. The Best Man tapping the glass image was more than a little ironic, and Blair found himself cracking a smile. Perhaps he could find a spoon and tap his own glass, which went to why one shouldn't be tied down by specific plans.

Blair noted that the man in the mirror was smiling slightly and immediately remedied the lack of decorum by transforming the man's expression to solemn with the rapidity of a mime. He cleared his throat again before speaking.

"I suppose you're all wondering why I have taken this opportunity." He paused for dramatic effect. "Most of you are my friends, many of you I have seen in a professional capacity . . ."

Blair, self-editing on the fly, stopped himself and shook his head. "No good, too pretentious," he chastised himself, sotto voce. He began again.

"I have something very important to say to you all, and now . . . now that I have to piece things together . . . piece things together . . ."

Stuck, Blair let his shoulders sag. Perhaps having written something up and memorized it might not have been a bad idea, he mused, feeling a slight tightness in his chest and pulling out his inhaler. He took a hit before proceeding.

"I've been listening too long. Period. And now I may not be speaking as articulately as I would like precisely because . . . I've been listening too long. Period. But now . . . tonight . . . I can no longer let my profession get in the way of my life. Does that surprise you? Does it?"

The increase in volume, but even more the strain he saw in the man's face, stunned him. It was a Dorian Gray moment and Blair realized that he had to maintain better control. He certainly had a few pent up feelings—it wasn't as if he didn't have insight into the situation. After all, he was a fucking psychologist and did this for a living. Certainly he didn't want to start off alienating everybody.

Starting again, roughly from where he left off, if he could remember . . .

". . . been listening so long . . . blah blah blah . . . does that surprise you? Perhaps it hadn't *occurred* to you—as you poured out your collective hearts—that I have feelings too."

Blair was back on track, but it only took him a sentence or two more to realize he was on the wrong train. Nonetheless he went on, planning to disembark at the next stop. Better that he express some of his repressed feelings in rehearsal, purge them. Thus released, they would not get in the way when he needed to exhibit complete control. Never did it cross his mind that his self-therapeutic strategy—often taking years to accomplish for his clients—was not a reasonable expectation.

"Imagine, will you," he continued, now pacing before the mirror, "a client comes to me with asthma. Asthma. He comes to me so I can help his breathing. So I listen and nod, all the while thinking, 'I can't go another forty minutes without my inhaler!' But he keeps babbling on with the lung power of Pavarotti and I turn blue!"

Blair turned to the mirror and looked deeply into himself, practically touching the reflecting surface with his nose. Had he been staring at a pool like Narcissus, he would have plunged headlong into water, the mythological hunter captured in a blooper reel.

"Shrink!" he blurted, "Shrink thyself!"

The unanticipated response, "You do that with mirrors?" nearly jolted him off his feet. Fortunately, it was Val who had entered the bedroom carrying several outer garments. If he had to be found in an embarrassing position—not to mention seen convulsing as if an electric current has passed though his body—he could think of a no more understanding person to witness it than Val.

"Just talking to myself," said Blair, flipping around and composing himself the best he could with all the routine mannerisms: adjusting his tie, hunching his shoulders a couple times in succession to get the hang of his sports coat just right, brushing back his hair with a casual hand, slapping both thigh fronts as if cigarette ashes or crumbs had fallen on them or he were shooing away house flies working in tandem. As he displayed his repertoire of preening gestures— heavy-handed stage business in such combination—Val gently laid three coats on the bedspread, arranging them neatly side-by-side.

"Sounded more like a knock-down drag-out," she said, walking around the bed to stand nearer to him.

"One of me is very volatile," Blair responded.

Val looked at him appraisingly.

"The party has officially started. John and Rebecca—"

"Good. Good." An impatient, non-responsive response. He had spoken over her, in a rush, obviously anxious to bypass the pleasantries and cut to the chase. "Are they here? I mean . . . you know . . . Mel . . ."

"Not yet."

"Good. I mean—"

"You have a thing for her, don't you?" It was Val's turn to speak over him, and it was intoned as a statement, not a question. Things were beginning to make sense, and in a flash they all fell into place.

"What are you . . . a *thing*? I don't know what you're talk—"

She stepped on his words again, she couldn't help it.

"You're in love with her." She said it again, drawing the words out more. Val felt like she was about to cry, but for the moment the sweep and intensity of her feelings—the conflicting emotions of dread and curiosity—temporarily lent her enough detachment to hold tears at bay. She was the supporting actress in a movie, the girl next door who doesn't get the guy, watching herself and feeling sad, thinking that she would have written the film another way. It would have worked better the other way.

"I heard you the first time," said Blair.

"I'm sorry," Val said. Sorry that she had repeated herself unnecessarily, sorry that he was losing the woman he loved to another man, sorry for herself. "I remember when you came to the house to pick her up for Junior Prom."

"You were just a kid."

"Eighth grade. The same age as the kids I teach now. I was hiding and peeking from the other room when you brought her home. I saw you kiss her at the door. I was so jealous. I thought you were the neatest boy in the world."

"Not really much of a kiss," Blair recalled.

"Well, I remember it," said Val. "It was the first time ever I caught my sister kissing a boy."

"Time marches on. Things change," said Blair.

"Some things don't change, apparently," said Val.

"You're right, Val." He sat on the edge of the bed, suddenly spent. "She's still the only woman in my life."

"Come on . . ."

"All the others . . . games to pass the time, like gin rummy or checkers. More like solitaire, I guess."

"I don't want to hear this," Val said, betraying her words by not moving. She was transfixed, she was paralyzed. Which game was she? Old Maid?

"You see, dammit! I've been listening to people so long that I don't know how to talk any more. I woke up this morning and . . . you can't imagine what it's been like. Listening to her every week, and then getting her check for eight-five bucks. I feel like a prostitute. And I can't ever say 'Keep your damn money, don't you understand I love you?'"

"No, you can't, I imagine, if that's how you really feel." Val could no longer make eye contact. "But it's not as if there aren't others who care about you. Maybe you're not really listening . . ."

He wasn't listening, apparently, at least at that moment, since he continued without acknowledging that she had said anything.

"That first love . . . before sex, before heartbreak, before cynicism. Every morning since I heard about the engagement—she told me in my office, long before even you or your mother knew—I look in the mirror and say 'Blair Brackman, you are thirty years old. Can you ever love like that again?' And, you know, I'm scared . . . really scared."

"Blair—"

"Don't say anything." Blair pulled out his inhaler, contemplated it for a moment, then gave in, rationalizing that another small puff couldn't hurt.

"I thought you outgrew your asthma."

"This? Breath freshener. Ask your Mom. Onions for dinner." He took a hit from the inhaler, then a long, deep breath. "All sorts of revelations, huh? I'm a desperate man, Val, and I could do a desperate thing."

"You're frightening me, Blair. You almost sound suicidal."

"Homicidal. I'd like to kill Rod Schoenlieber."

"You haven't even met him!"

"I know him well enough," Blair attempted to make a disparaging scoffing sound but ended up snorting, which was disparaging enough. "His shoe size. Boxers, not briefs. The weird way he takes a child's toothbrush and uses it vertically. Believe me, I know more about him than I want to—"

Dickie Rawlings, a *crème de la crème* vision in *crème*, barged through the bedroom door. He was in a hurry, hunched over, knees inwardly together, his right hand clenching his privates.

"Excusez moi, où est la pissoir?"

Dickie figured it out before either of them had a chance to respond and trotted directly into the bathroom, slamming the door shut.

Val went over to the open bedroom door and closed it, then walked back to Blair.

He went on as if she had never left him, unfazed by the unwelcome momentary vision of Dickie Rawlings.

"For the past ten months he's all I've heard about. 'Does he love me? Am I playing too hard to get? Should I have slept with him so soon?'"

"Melissa asked you that?"

"Yep. You betcha."

"Jeez, Louise, what did you tell her?"

"I told her that what was past was past, she had acted on impulse to have sex with him, she was involved with the wrong person—someone who was bad for her—and she should sleep with me instead."

"You didn't. That's unethical! I don't believe you!"

"What do ethics have to do with it? You're right, I didn't. I gave her the standard rigmarole. You know, she had to make her own decisions, do what she felt was best for her . . ."

"And that whole time . . ." Val was shaking her head, for the moment no longer feeling sorry for herself as much as feeling sorry for Blair, poor guy. "You must have died."

Blair closed his eyes, thinking back and rubbing his hands together like the lady in the Scottish play when he finally spoke again.

"Prometheus had a picnic compared to me," he said.

Val paused, overcome with curiosity. She was considering how she could put her question in an inoffensive manner, while still asking what was clearly an offensive question.

"So, she's slept with him. I'd be stunned if she hadn't. But, he doesn't exactly strike me as . . . as a master of . . . of swordplay, so to speak. It must be . . . you know, decent for her . . ."

"Decent. You must mean indecent."

"Are they . . . are they doing it a lot?"

"These are treacherous sexual times, Val, not like the good old days when 'safe sex' meant pushing the bed away from the wall so you wouldn't concuss yourself."

"Don't change the subject."

"I'm a professional, for Christ's sake, Val, and this is a violation of—"

"She's my sister. I've got a pretty good idea, anyway. Spill the beans."

"You don't expect me to remember everything, do you?" He got up from the bed, but with Val in front of him he couldn't easily pace, so he just stood in place, pacing internally.

"They rut like fucking animals! Welcome to the fucking monkey house! Are you happy now?" He plopped back down onto the bed.

Val was chastised and embarrassed, although without question glad she had asked. But now she felt remorse, sorry that she had upset Blair by asking the question that she was going to ask no matter what. And where the hell had she come up with 'swordplay'?'

"I'm sorry I asked," she apologized unconvincingly.

"It's worse than that," Blair said, now the picture of despair and resignation.

"What?"

"He's . . . he's exceptionally well-hung."

"Oh. I see." Val tried extremely hard to remain expressionless and had no inkling if she were succeeding or not.

"And I can only assume in a deformed 'take me into the circus tent to see the freak' kind of way."

"Oh, I see," Val said again, tongue-tied. "Well." She tried to adopt a philosophical tone. "They say that most women would rather be tickled—"

"—than be *rammed* by a humongous *Rod*?" Blair sniggered. "That entire 'size doesn't matter' thing is a complete myth, perpetrated by a long line of academics with particularly small penises!"

Val wasn't sure how to respond. She didn't want to delve into the realm of personal sexual experiences with Blair Brackman at the moment, or express any reassurances about his own manifestations of manhood, which could come across as patronizing or emasculating or both.

"You'll get over her," she settled on saying, looking down, then realizing that he might be thinking she was checking out the size of his shoes. She quickly moved her eyes back up to his.

"It's not over yet," Blair said, with menace.

⁓∞⁓

The bathroom door clicked open.

"'The pleasures of the piss it's said, far exceed those of the bed.' Heard that one?"

"At your wedding, Dickie. Still feel the same way?" Blair answered, lifting himself off the edge of the bed to stand up next to Val.

Dickie Rawlings first checked his fly, then took off his overcoat and carelessly tossed it on the bed. He swept a hand over the right side of his forehead, fingers scraping across skin like an earthmover, transporting hair to its designated location behind the ear lobe.

"Dear boy, eighteen months of marriage to Candy has only reaffirmed my initial philosophy."

"That's a horrible thing to say." Val, like most people, was not a particular fan of Dickie Rawlings.

"Horrible, but true. Fortunately for me, I admire fidelity in a spouse as much as a pig admires the opera."

He paused and gave Val the once over. He misread her look of disgust for one of surprise, a manifestation of his lack of self-awareness.

"You look shocked. Well don't be. I defy any man to live with that woman and tolerate her Scarlett O'Hara complex, or whatever the hell it is. And every time I manage to break through that Frigidaire of flesh she giggles herself straight away into the hiccoughs! She still undresses in the closet, for God's sake. With the light out even. Thrashing about in the dark. Do you have any idea how much time I spend picking up my ties from the closet floor? Have you ever seen such a desperate man?"

"Get in line," said Blair.

"Break my heart," said Val. "Can't you pay someone to pick up your ties?"

"Worry not . . . I'll make do," he said. The conversation was going nowhere, so Dickie made for the door without further ceremony. He had been a bit rude coming into the party in such a rush, but he felt considerably better now. He needed to make amends and charm everyone's socks off.

"Asshole," said Val, once the door closed.

"Maybe misunderstood," said Blair.

"Hardly. But I suppose one could feel sorry for him."

Blair bristled. "I feel sorry for *me*! The one thing about Dickie Rawlings . . . he may be an asshole, but he's a doer—"

"—who sells two houses a year and lives off Daddy's dividends. He's a spoiled preppie." Val interrupted.

"That has nothing to do with it. When Dickie Rawlings wants something, he gets it. Simple as that. No one will ever crumple him underfoot. He has the courage to make a positive effort to make his own destiny, to change it if he wants, albeit, uh . . ."

"Misdirected," said Val.

"Misdirected," Blair demurred. "But still, I could learn from him. Actions don't have to be misdirected.

Just this one time I should learn . . . what might be my very last opportunity . . ."

"I don't understand what you're talking about, Blair. He's an asshole." And then it occurred to her that Dickie, the asshole, was not the one who had hurt her so deeply. Perhaps all sorts of people, maybe everyone, were misunderstood. She would contemplate that notion sometime later, when she allowed herself a good cry and a pint of Häagen Dazs rum raisin straight from the carton.

⌘

When Candy came into the bedroom, Blair realized that any further chance for solitude and contemplation had gone by the wayside.

Unlike her husband, she didn't barge in. In quite the contrast, she slowly opened the door and peeked her beautiful blonde head around it. She was never at a loss for an appropriate opening.

"Peek-a-boo! Am I interrupting an important conversation?"

"Of course not, Candy," said Val. "Please come in. We were just talking about your husband. How are you?"

"Just fine and dandy." Purse hooked over her arm, she was holding a nearly empty glass of punch with a flower stem pressed beside it and her coat, fur-like, if not real fur. In either case, that she looked stunning in the coat was never in doubt. She placed it inside out on the growing pile on the bed, with only small portions of animal hair provocatively exposed. Blair then remembered it was real. Dickie had told him in session, complaining about how much it had cost.

"What a lovely flower!" Val said, affirming to Blair that she was proficient at small talk.

"Isn't it now?" effused Candy. "I need to put it in some water so it will keep. Is there a little container somewhere?"

"Why don't you put it in a punch glass?" said Blair, trying to sound helpful, and would have sounded so, had he been able to prevent his eyes from rolling.

"Now that's a very good idea!" said Candy, who knew when not to notice an eye roll. She had a life-long experience with eye rolls, but remained charitable, almost Christ-like, as far as they were concerned. *Forgive them, Lord, for they knoweth not how their eyes doeth roll.*

"Let me take that for you, and I'll put some water in it." Val extended her hand for the glass. Candy held up a finger indicating Val should wait, flashed a big white toothy smile, and tilted her head back to swallow the few drops of punch remaining.

Blair watched her attentively. The head back, arm up gesture produced a strange and wonderful, but difficult to describe, non-synchronous movement of her breasts, which was the counter-balance to eye rolling in response to Candy. The eyes could roll—roam about, searching for something better to look at—but they would always settle back on her. Candy Rawlings, grits and corn pone and all, was extremely hard to look away from.

"Isn't this just the most lovely apartment? And such a lovely party?" Candy asked Blair, as Val was in the bathroom filling the punch glass with water.

"Very nice," said Blair. "Very nice. Have the bride-to-be and groom-to-be showed up?

"Not yet! Maybe they're chickening out, poor things! Wouldn't that be just awful, now?"

"Tragic," said Blair.

"What's tragic?" asked Val, emerging from the bathroom, punch glass in hand. Candy appreciatively took the glass and set her flower in it.

"Long story," said Blair.

"Listen," said Candy, "y'all wouldn't mind . . . would you excuse me if I powder my nose a spot?" She had already opened the clasp of her purse with one hand, and had proceeded to hand Blair the punch glass *avec* flower to hold.

"I don't mind at all," said Blair.

"You can't help but look beautiful, no matter what you do, Candy."

"You're so kind, Val, but of course you can't mean it."

"She means it," said Blair.

"Oh, you sweet things . . ."

Blair and Val watched as Candy expertly performed an unnecessary touch up from the cosmetics counter she had managed to fit into a relatively small purse.

"Really," she said, looking into the mirror of her compact, "I just don't know what to say!" She proceeded to chat as she re-applied eye shadow, eyeliner, mascara, lipstick, and face powder with impressive speed and dexterity. She spoke with animation, her facial expressions in constant flux, a moving canvas. Remarkably, her artistic master strokes compensated with pinpoint precision. The display was a bravura performance, showing off highly developed fine motor coordination and extraordinary powers of concentration. In her sphere, Candy displayed great talent, perhaps true genius.

"Why, if I weren't an old married lady I'd give you a great big kiss! It's my upbringing, you know? My momma had me putting on lipstick before I could walk! And in high school I carried around an electric hair curler in my pocketbook! 'Course now I have to keep up for my sweet thing of a husband . . . I wouldn't want to go looking like some old bag and lose that man of mine."

Even the preoccupied Blair couldn't fail to appreciate the poignancy of her chatter, particularly knowing how Dickie slept around on her. But he was in no mental state to focus on others for very long; he had his own problems. Still, he wondered if Candy Rawlings could apply make-up while being shot from a cannon.

Candy's chatter then segued into a seemingly more purposeful direction. Blair became alert—it was his training after all, he couldn't help himself, any more than a pointer could keep its tail tucked between its legs with someone waving a rabbit in its face.

"Uh . . . Val," she began, treading lightly, "I was talking with someone the other day—I can't for the life of me remember who—and somebody's name came up, just in the course of some silly conversation. I can't remember what about . . ."

"Who?" asked Val.

Blair's ears were up.

"Some man . . . from England," Candy continued. "From England, I think it was. London's in England, right?"

Blair rolled his eyes without allowing his ears to move.

Confirmation that London was, in fact, in England was not forthcoming, so all parties concerned accepted Candy's geographical question as a rhetorical one.

"His name was funny . . ." Candy continued.

"Nigel?" Val ventured.

"Nigel. Let me see . . . Nigel, Nigel, Nigel . . . why yes, that might have been it."

"Nigel Davies," said Blair.

"I can't remember why his name came up or anything, but I do recall meeting him a long time ago, way back when. He's . . . he's sort of . . ."

"Charming. Cultivated. Sexy," Val offered.

"Not you too, Val," said Blair, pursing his lips. "It's just the accent."

"He doesn't have to say a word," countered Val. "He's in England, though. Too bad. I haven't seen him in months. Nobody has."

"Oh, well," said Candy, disguising her relief. Rebecca had just been trying to get under her skin, so typical of Rebecca, nothing had really changed from college. "I was just sort of wondering. No particular reason." She snapped her compact closed with the finality of a falling guillotine and replaced it in her purse.

"Aren't you two coming in? There's some lovely punch!"

"I really should help Mom," Val said to Blair as Candy made to leave. "You coming?"

"Momentarily," he said.

"Maybe you need to think things through," she said, "so as not to hurt anybody . . ."

"Anybody else," she finished to herself.

John tensed when he heard the knock on the door. Reflexively, he set down his newly fortified glass of punch in case he had to make a run for it. Then he recognized the cadence of the six taps, metered to the first two measures of "Some Enchanted Evening." It was C.W. Dexter's particular knock. By this time, Rebecca, heading toward the door, was responding in full voice, *"You may see a stranger . . ."*

She opened the door dramatically, and they both continued as a duet, completing the musical phrase before exchanging hugs and kisses, making big smoochy sounds as if a case of champagne corks were being rapid-fired in sequence from their bottles.

"He's arrived!" intoned a suddenly cheerful John from the food and drinks table, picking up his punch glass and holding it up in a remote toast to the newcomer.

"The perfect guest!" C.W. Dexter shouted back, disentangling himself from Rebecca. He pushed the bridge of his large round tortoise-shell eyeglasses snugly against the middle of his forehead, a practiced theatrical gesture. "Hide the women and children," he said, ". . . and the men, of course!"

C.W. wore a floppy khaki parka over a plaid sport coat and a thin cashmere crew neck sweater. His light brown hair was curly and bushy, never combed, just fluffed up with his hands after showering. He was tall, masculinely handsome and fit, and at first glance would seem more appropriately decked out in an expensive three-piece suit from Jack Henry's as a floor model. But C.W. Dexter was a performer, once on the stage, and now in real life. And his plaid sports coat, despite looking cheap and designed for the aesthetics of a car salesman, was imported and had been quite expensive. Not just any man could wear it with such aplomb.

Rebecca escorted him the few steps to Meg.

"Mrs. Manning," she said, "you must remember C.W. Dexter. C.W., as we all know, is just the finest decorator in the world."

"Oh, darling . . . how you flatter me! Don't stop . . . I love it! I love it!"

"Of course I remember," Meg said confidently, adding "I think."

"I don't believe we've ever had the pleasure," said C.W.

"Now I remember . . . we haven't met at all! But I *have* heard so much about you! Let me take your coat—"

"Here, I'll get it," said a solicitous Rebecca, running interference and assisting in the garment removal.

C.W. had been a junior and senior high school accomplice, but had left most of the pack and headed to California for college at U.C. Santa Cruz. A track star in high school, he hung out in thespian circles, participating in all the plays and musicals that didn't conflict with track practice. Much of his free time in those days was spent studying and playing guitar and writing melancholy songs. An only child, he had recognized early on that his sexuality was at odds with what seemed to be the entire world. He compensated by being the loneliest and most gregarious student in the school district. Everyone loved C.W. Dexter, always an entertaining companion. Of the group that night, only Rebecca, John, and Blair knew about his suicide attempt junior year, which they had not discovered until much later.

At Santa Cruz, C.W. ran track and majored in Theater and Drama. There he met the love of his life, and he and Brandon, also an actor, became inseparable. After graduation, they moved to Los Angeles and embarked on stage careers. It was the predictable slog, with the two of them spending most of their valuable audition time in a succession of jobs, waiting tables, tutoring high school students, driving taxi cabs. Brandon had ambitions to go to New York, but C.W. was more easily disillusioned and was wearing out. For these reasons and others, mainly in the form of another young actor who had designs on Brandon as much as Brandon had on Broadway, the relationship went sour. Complicating matters was the failing health of both of C.W.'s parents. Clarence Werner Dexter, Sr. had worsening diabetes and heart disease and his mother suffered from a collagen vascular disease. C.W. Dexter had returned to Kansas City two years earlier, perkier than ever. Again, only Rebecca, John, and Blair saw through it.

C.W.'s flamboyant and over the top pose seemed to work well with the rich Kansas City matrons who employed him—and overpaid him—for home decorating. Other than set design, he had no training in the field, but was a quick study. Much of his success involved establishing a personal rapport with his clients, whom he amused and delighted. Business was booming. He would occasionally grace the stages of the Missouri Repertory Theatre in a comedic role; he could certainly do tragedy—he lived it after all—but considered it bad for business. His well-heeled society female clients loved seeing him playing himself on stage. He had not been in another relationship, meaningful or otherwise, since Brandon.

"Why in the world don't you leave?" Rebecca would perennially ask him. Occasionally they would meet for drinks, and after a few, C.W. would lapse into his actual self—thoughtful, soft-spoken, and depressed. But not for very long.

"I'm a homosexual man living in Kansas City, where rich people have absolutely no taste. What could be better than that?"

In fact, he could easily leave, relieve himself of the burden of being the dutiful son, visiting his parents at least four times a week, running errands, going shopping, taking them to doctor's appointments, whatever it took to make their lives easier. All he had to do was tell them he was gay. They were devout Christians, after all, good God-fearing Kansas folk. Problem solved. No question, they would disown him and immediately expel him from their lives. As a plus, they might suffer some heartbreak of their own, give them something in common with him, a possible basis for something more than a superficial caretaker relationship. It was a Hobson's choice, but C.W. was prepared to pull the ripcord once he had a parachute. Until then, he would surround himself with paint chips and color swatches.

"Melissa here yet?" he asked, looking around, and along the way nodding at Dickie Rawlings, whom he despised, and Candy, whom he had trouble wrapping his head around.

"Coming any minute," said Meg, nervously looking at her watch.

"I'm *so* excited. I haven't met Rod, of course, but I've heard. Very . . . uh . . . interesting place you've got here, Mrs. Manning."

"Why, thank you," said Meg. "Coming from you that's a real compliment! Let me get you some punch."

"This décor is a bit like old opened soda," confided C.W. to Rebecca, assuming Meg, who has well on her way to the punch bowl, was safely out of earshot.

"Isn't it?" said Rebecca.

"Oh, no," responded Meg, scooping her special mixture into a punch glass, "it's made with fresh rhubarb. But don't tell anyone." She paused, noting the level of the punch in the bowl. Was it her imagination? Was the color a bit faded?

"The secret will die with me," said C.W., taking the crystal cup from her. "Thank you." He took a sip, smacked his lips, and blinked.

"Mother's own recipe," said Dickie, watching his reaction.

"I've already officially switched to the punch. Never mix, never worry," said John.

C.W., recovering, was sipping the liquid cautiously, as if it were hot.

"Vodka base, is it?" he asked Meg.

"One hundred percent non-alcoholic! Isn't that amazing?"

"The things they're doing with soy beans these days!"

"Rhubarb."

"I simply *must* get that recipe!" said C.W. "And probably a taxi."

Rebecca took his free elbow. "Let's dump your coat and I can show you the rest of the apartment," she said.

"I'd love your suggestions . . ." said Meg, still beaming from the punch compliment, and excited to get any free advice from the decorator whom she remembered hearing about, arguably the best in Kansas City.

"And I love being suggestive!" said C.W. "Lead the way, Rebecca."

C.W. paused to crane his neck over the saloon doors to the kitchen as they passed by.

"Looking for Miss Kitty," he whispered into Rebecca's ear.

"Let me refill your punch glass, my dear," Dickie said to his wife.

"But Dickie, Pumpkin Pie, I have water in here . . . and my *flower!*"

"How about *them* pumpkins, banana nose," said John, abandoning any remaining verbal filters.

Dickie ignored him. "Well, we'll just have to arrange for a new glass so my little princess can have some more punch."

"Don't worry," said Meg, well into her hostess mode, omnipresent and able to float wispily into any conversation taking place in the room, "there are plenty of glasses. It's a set of sixteen."

John extended his empty glass over the bowl as Dickie approached.

"Top me off, rhubarb face," he said.

"Don't get cruel with me, John, you know how nasty I can be to the lower classes." Nonetheless, he poured a ladle-full of punch into John's glass before filling one for Candy.

"And how about you, Mrs. Manning?" asked Dickie. "Some punch?"

"If you can believe it, I haven't even tried it myself!" she exclaimed. "But I absolutely love *fruity*-tasting things!"

"You're in for a real surprise, Mrs. Manning," said John.

"You twisted my arm," giggled Meg.

Val returned from the bedroom while Dickie was graciously pouring for Meg. The younger Manning daughter looked despondent. She walked straight over to John.

"'Why the long face? the bartender said to the horse.'"

"I'm a little worried about Blair," she said in an undertone. "He's . . . he's in kind of a . . . state."

"Then remedy it," said John. "You're the one that has a crush on the man. I just pay him for his services."

"You don't get it . . . you don't *get* what's going on." Val was looking at the carpet.

"Try some punch," said John. "It will make everything better."

"That's a switch," Val mumbled, her thoughts still swirling.

"I've decided to go on the rhubarb wagon," said John.

Meg and Candy sampled the drink at approximately the same time.

"Goodness!" exclaimed Meg.

"My, oh my . . ." exclaimed Candy.

Both women emitted coughs, which they eventually were able to control.

"I think . . . it must have . . . gone down the wrong tube," Candy managed to say. Of the two, she appeared more severely affected; her cough briefly lapsed into choking.

Dickie held up his glass and peered through the liquid. "Wonderful fruit, rhubarb . . . or is it a veggie?"

"It doesn't seem quite—I mean it's good and fruity-tasting—but more of a kick than . . ." Meg was now sipping additional punch and reflecting, as if sampling soup to decide if it needed more salt.

"Peculiar thing about rhubarb," John began in a didactic manner, "it gets more tart as it sits around in the air . . . an oxidation of some sort."

"I've never heard that!" exclaimed Meg.

Dickie chimed in. "Have you ever seen a rhubarb pie left uncovered for long?"

"There's always Saran wrap or something . . ." John adeptly contributed to the improvisation.

Meg thought and took a bigger sip. "Well, now that you mention it . . . once you get used to it . . . I think I like it better this way, in fact. You know, uncovered."

"You two should be ashamed," Val said to John, shaking her head in mock disgust. "You're no better than a couple of junior high schoolers."

"I was under the impression that you *liked* junior high schoolers, Val," John quipped. "After all, you spend most of the fucking day with them."

"Punch for me, John," said Val, relenting.

"Anything you say, my dear." John made his way to the bowl.

The doorbell rang.

John stopped in his tracks midway to the punch bowl.

"Who's that?" he said in too loud a voice and an almost accusing tone.

"Why that's probably them now!" exclaimed Meg, still cradling the punch glass in both hands.

"I'll get it," said Val.

This moment, which marked the arrival of Deirdre Rehnquist and her date Milton Perkins, coincided with the sudden disappearance of John Palopolus. Fortunately, his punch glass was nearly empty; otherwise he might have spilled his drink on himself—and worse, the carpet—during his hasty escape to the bedroom.

∽∞∾

"Why, Blair Brackman, you anti-social thing!" Rebecca said, tossing C.W.'s coat onto the bed.

"Hello, Rebecca, C.W.," said Blair sullenly.

"I'm just giving C.W. the royal tour. He's never been here before," Rebecca explained.

Blair was unresponsive, and Rebecca was perceptive.

"You can't stay in here all night, Blair honey, but you might have the right idea. I'm getting bad vibes about this evening."

C.W. made a brief foray into the bathroom.

"Is this place awful or what? 'Contemporary Dentist Office.' Who did the design, anyway, Spiro Agnew?" C.W. had returned and realized that he was talking to himself. Rebecca's focus was on Blair, and the atmosphere had become intense during C.W.'s few seconds in the bathroom.

"Oh, for Christ's sake, Blair," Rebecca was saying. "You're as transparent as cellophane! I thought you outgrew her like your asthma!"

"Who's her?" C.W. ventured. "Oh, you mean Melissa. Have you met him yet?"

"Who?" stalled Blair.

"Rod! Who else? Don't play coy!"

"Not exactly," said Blair.

Rebecca eyed him attentively but dispassionately, as if watching a dog—not her own—heaving on someone else's carpet.

"Well, that makes three of us," said C.W., "and frankly, I haven't been this excited since Mac proposed to Rachel on 'Another World'—"

John Palopolus barged through the door, remarkably transformed. Only a few moments before, he had been pleasantly drinking punch; now he was sweating and appeared panic-stricken.

"Christ! Quick! Somebody hide me!" he pleaded, his eyes bulging from their sockets as he realized he had escaped to a moderately sized bedroom. His expression was that of a criminal chased unwittingly into a blind alley. He ran into the bathroom, which he quickly learned was simply another blind alley, only smaller and less plush.

"Evening, John," Blair said to the air.

"It's a fucking one-bedroom apartment, John," said Rebecca.

John emerged, blinking rapidly and out of breath, a trapped animal.

"Horrible bathroom, isn't it?" said C.W., who relished the opportunity to douse a fire with gasoline. "Constipating. I'd plug right up if I had to do my business in there."

"Christ!" John pulled his pillbox from his jacket pocket and dosed himself.

"Particularly those gold faucet handles made to look like albatross wings or something."

"You're no help! Jesus!"

John was a desperate man without an exit strategy. He had selected flight over fight, and was committed to it. But despite his agitation, he was still capable of relevant cognition. The only other door in the room was covered in a mirror: obviously the closet, and since the coats were on the bed—and, unlike the bathroom, no one would be using it—John could wait things out safely there, like he did in the basement during tornadoes when he was a kid. At the moment, given the circumstances, his rationale seemed quite reasonable. He would wait things out, like in a tornado.

Course of action determined, John exploded from where he stood—a frightened rabbit darting from the shelter of a small shrub—and sequestered himself in Meg Manning's closet, closing the door after himself definitively.

"Maybe I set him off," said C.W., feeling guilty.

"He didn't need setting off," said Rebecca, closing her eyes and shaking her head.

Blair, saying nothing and observing all, pushed a portion of a coat aside and sat on the edge of the bed.

"Obviously Deirdre's arrived," Rebecca observed unnecessarily. "Honestly, John," she said, speaking toward the mirror, "you're such a child."

"She's an absolute bitch, John," added C.W., still trying to make amends for his perceived overstep. "I don't blame you at all. Compared to her, Eva Braun was Heidi! I mean it!"

"You're no help," Rebecca chastised C.W. And, again to the mirror, "Don't be ridiculous, John. Come out!"

Not a creature was stirring behind the mirrored door. Rebecca asked one more time. "Come out, John!"

Again, with no response forthcoming, Rebecca said, "I'm done here. C.W. and I are going back to the party. Blair, you talk to him."

"Why?" Blair asked plaintively.

"This is not the way I intend to spend my evening, talking to a mirror like the fucking Queen in Snow White."

"I'll be the fucking Queen," offered C.W., a line that might have provoked a hearty laugh if presented under different circumstances.

"I've had a hellacious day," Rebecca went on without cracking a smile, "the details of which I won't bore you with right now, and I'm thirsty. You'll talk to him, won't you, Blair?"

"Do I have a choice?"

"It's what you do, isn't it?"

"I actually mainly listen," said Blair. Thus prompted back into his rehearsal mode, he went on, "In fact, I've been listening too—"

Rebecca cut him off. "—Well, do whatever the hell you do."

"I've seen enough," said C.W. "Let's leave these two alone. Mush, mush, Rebecca, darling."

"Deirdre! What a pleasant surprise! I thought you were skiing in Aspen!" Val lied, closing the door behind Deirdre Rehnquist and her escort, a stranger to Val.

"I *was*, Val darling, but I flew back a couple of days early. I wouldn't miss this for the world!"

Deirdre Rehnquist was petite, though she appeared taller from a distance because of her slimness. She wore a taupe Suzie Wong type dress, high-collared and showing a lot of leg that was worth showing, with her dark brown hair in a French twist. Her forearms displayed a collection of bangles, and the slightest of motions made her jangle like a walking set of wind chimes.

As Deirdre swept past, Val was nearly overcome with *Joy*, a fragrance she owned and generally liked, within limits.

The escort was helping Deirdre off with her coat, a stylish short fox jacket.

"Val, I'd like you to meet a new friend of mine, Milton Perkins," she said, one arm still lifted and the bracelets cascading down until impeded at the elbow. "Milton is in town giving readings. He's a poet. I just met him an hour ago at one of them and insisted that he come with me. Hope you don't mind. He's so cute."

The poet was short and slight in stature, with wispy thin brown, disobedient hair. He wore a corduroy sport jacket with elbow patches and baggy khakis that sagged at the knees. No shirt, just a V-neck sweater, presumably over a V-neck undershirt. A vision in earth tones—ocher, brown, beige—and obviously one who occupied the correct side of hygiene but felt no further obligations. Was his attire shabby chic or just shabby poor—who could tell these days?

In any case Milton was blushing, obviously wondering what he had done to deserve landing a catch like Deirdre, if only to accompany her to a party. Under other circumstances, he would assume she was affording poetry, and its makers, the respect that they deserved. But Deirdre Rehnquist didn't seem to know all that much about poetry, nor did her interest go much beyond the mere mentioning that he was a poet. Still, Milton had the entire evening to figure things out, and he assumed he would, given that he was a poet. If worse came to worse, he could write a poem expressing confusion. And if he were lucky and got laid, he might consider giving up the art form altogether.

"Good to meet you," said Milton, with the fox coat now in his arms. He was still wearing his own coat, notable mainly for its toggle buttons.

"Likewise, Milton," said Val, warmly. "Where are you in town from?" she asked.

"Oh, just Independence," he said, sheepishly. Living less than twelve miles away, he wasn't accustomed to wowing people geographically. Besides, there was no point in boasting that it was the home of the Truman Library to a bunch of Kansas City folks.

"I suppose Independence barely makes the cut for out-of-town," he admitted. But Deirdre had said that he was from out of town, not him.

"Love those Thomas Hart Benton murals in the Truman Library," Val said, recovering. She had been expecting to hear some appropriately snide remark from John—how could he possibly resist?—and was surprised at the silence. Meg approached and was waiting expectantly for introductions.

"Make yourself at home, Milton, glad to have you here. I'd like you to meet my mother Meg, Candy and Dickie Rawlings, and John—" John's absence from the room suddenly explained no rude comment about Independence.

Entropic group greetings were transmitted from across the room. Meg, naturally, was the only one determined to dwell.

"Dee-dra, isn't it?"

"Deirdre. Mel and I were in junior high and and college together, Mrs. Manning. And our families knew one another from the Club."

"Oh, yes. Indian Hills?"

"Mission Hills."

"Of course. Now let me get this straight. You're no relation to William Perkins. William and Betty?"

"No, no, no . . . my last name is Rehnquist. *This* is Milton Perkins." Deirdre jerkily pulled him forward by his arm, jangling deafeningly. She waited for the noise to settle before speaking again. "Milton is a poet."

"Of course, Rehn-quist," said Meg, a wrinkled forehead betraying her affirmations. "Our families knew each other through the club. Rehnquist. I remember now. Honestly, I don't know how I could confuse something like that! And a poet! How literary!"

"I've never seen you at Mission Hills before, Deirdre," Dickie Rawlings lied, establishing an alibi. He gave Milton the twice over. Was this the competition? Seriously? "I'll have to call you if we ever need a fourth. You do play tennis, don't you?"

"When I'm not skiing," she replied, playing along. "Do ring me up . . . if you ever need a fourth."

"I don't ever think I've met a real live poet before!" said Meg.

"Uh-huh," said Milton.

"Most poets don't come into their own until long after they're dead," said Dickie.

C.W. and Rebecca emerged from the bedroom. Rebecca and Deirdre immediately found their gazes instinctively drawn to one another, as is always the case between two people who share a mutual and intense dislike.

"Deirdre, dear! It's been ages!" said Rebecca, not intending to come within arm's length, let alone cheek-pecking distance. "I *thought* I heard you come in," she continued, thinking that Deirdre hadn't needed to ring the bell—only stand outside the door and shake.

"As you *well* know," said Deirdre, "I just got in from Aspen. I left a message on your machine that I'd be coming tonight."

"Never check that damn machine," said Rebecca. "Put on a little weight? Trying to keep that girlish figure by skiing, I suppose."

"It might do you some good to take up an outdoor sport yourself, Rebecca, dear. You know, something you do on your feet."

"Drinks, anyone?" Dickie offered. The attempt to mediate was not an unselfish gesture, although Dickie would have been pleased to pass it off as one. In truth, he didn't want Deirdre to get riled up by Rebecca, which might divert her attentions away from him.

"There's a *fabulous* punch," piped Candy.

"Scotch rocks," ordered Deirdre, ignoring Candy.

"I'll have to concur with Candy about the punch in this instance, Deirdre," said Dickie. "In fact, I must insist . . ."

"Non-alcoholic but quite tart, from sitting around uncovered, you know?" Meg explained.

"Well . . ." Deirdre was understandably hesitant.

"I made it from a special secret recipe . . . with rhu-barb!" Meg added, sure of closing the deal with the information reveal.

"It must be the best-kept secret in the world," said C.W.

"I suppose I'll try it then," relented Deirdre.

"Milton, is it?" asked Dickie, extending the offer by inference.

"Yes, make it two, please."

C.W. sidled over to the newest male arrival. He was up for some performance art, and inflicting himself on an obviously insecure heterosexual might be amusing, or at least pass the time. From what he had seen so far, the party wasn't going to be very entertaining unless he did his part. And according to C.W.'s social philosophy, a gay man was the slave of duty when it came to enlivening a party.

"I don't believe we've met," C.W. said to Milton.

Deirdre intervened. "I'm so sorry, how rude of me. Milton, this is C.W. Dexter, and Rebecca Harvey. Re-becca, C.W. . . . Milton Perkins. Milton is a—"

"—poet," interjected Dickie from the punch bowl.

"Poet," said Deirdre.

"How marvelous!" said C.W.

"A pleasure, Milton," said Rebecca. She looked at Milton with an expression suggesting she had just bitten into a bad nut.

Milton addressed Val. "And you must be the bride-to-be . . ."

"Sister, rather, the maid-of-honor-to-be," she said.

"I see," said Milton. "Well, congratulations in any case."

Val went on. "For some odd reason, the lucky couple haven't made the scene yet, but they're expected soon. And they're in for a real surprise. By the way," she addressed the assembled multitude, "start eating all that food on the table. Don't feel like you have to wait."

"Super punch," said Deirdre, imbibing her first taste, "but you're joking about it being non-alcohol—"

"Shush, dear," said Dickie, "that's the secret!"

Meg had been patiently waiting for an opportunity to speak. It seemed that the opportunity had arrived.

"Perkins," she said. "I hate to dwell on this . . ."

"Mom—please!" said Val.

"Just one little thing, dear. Bear with me. Milton, *you* don't happen to be related to William and Betty . . ."

"I'm afraid not. Perkins is my pseudonym . . . just the name I write under."

"Oh, I see. But, then, what's your real name? I mean, I won't call you that or anything—"

"Mom!" said Val, more insistently. She knew that no matter how threatening her voice, there would be no stopping her mother. She had tried anyway, half-heartedly, out of habit.

"That's quite alright," Milton assured Val. He looked back at Meg. "My real name is Morris . . . Morris Chartreuse."

Meg's mouth dropped open wide enough for a root canal.

"Chartreuse! You're kidding! Herbie Chartreuse's son!"

"Why, yes," said the poet, genuinely but not pleasantly surprised. "Herbert Chartreuse is my father."

Everyone in the room silently shared in the revelation. Dickie had given Candy a cracker smeared with Camembert, but paused momentarily before preparing one for himself. Who *was* this douchebag? he mused.

"I can't believe it!" shouted Meg. "What a coincidence! Herbie Chartreuse and I grew up together!" She brought down the volume, going from exclamation to exposition for the benefit of all. "Of course, his name wasn't Chartreuse back then . . ."

Milton was shaking his head, partly agreeing that "no, that wasn't his name," but also trying to convey "no, you don't really have to go on with this story." He was experiencing ambivalence, which would be worth a poem, perhaps, albeit one too uncomfortable to write. Honesty, even in poetry, was not without boundaries.

"You see . . ." Meg was saying, "there were these three Greenberg brothers . . ." She began fanning herself with her free hand. "Oh, well, you all wouldn't be interested in that, I suppose, but it is quite coincidental . . . and is this room hot?"

"It is a bit stuffy," said Dickie, jamming the entire cracker in his mouth. "Have some . . . more . . . punch to cool you off," he mumbled through chews.

"Why thank you," said Meg, awkwardly making her way over to hand him her glass. "Phew!"

Dickie, out of common decency, suggested that the punch would taste better with some cheese and crackers, and perhaps also some slices of meat. The effect was similar to a well-considered wine pairing, he informed her, offering to make her up a plate. She accepted, feeling a bit light-headed and leaning against the table.

In the meantime, C.W. had made his move to monopolize Milton's attentions.

"I simply *love* poetry . . . and poets as well. Especially famous ones. Are you famous?"

"Does he look dead?" Dickie asked, skewering some salami with a toothpick to add to Meg's plate.

"Well, I hate to boast," said Milton, ignoring whom he now considered the preppie asshole, "but I have just had a collection of my poems published in a book."

"Really? What's it called?" an enraptured C.W. asked.

"'Castration and Other Love Poems.'"

"I'll order a copy," said C.W.

Meg was composing herself by the table, waiting for the light-headedness to pass.

"I know what I forgot!" she exclaimed, just as Dickie held the plate out for her. "Those little thingies you stick on. Everybody needs one. I put them here somewhere . . ."

"Name tags, Mom, and I don't really think we need them," said Val.

"But I bought them especially the other day," Meg protested, taking the plate from Dickie and promptly setting it down on the table. "They were on sale . . ."

"We don't need them, Mom," said Val.

"It's so confusing with all these new names and faces. For Mel's sake, when she gets here . . ."

"They're all Melissa's friends," Val pointed out.

But Meg was already on her way to the bedroom, where she remembered she might have left them.

The group had gathered around the table and was serving themselves in earnest. Only Candy, Deirdre and

Milton availed themselves of plates; the rest grazed with fingers and toothpicks, shuffling amongst themselves as if placeholders in a line.

C.W speared a large green olive and offered it to Milton, who declined vigorously.

"Milton . . . you don't mind if I call you Milton, do you?"

"No, not at all. That's my name."

"Well, then, Milton, have you seen much of the city?"

"I just live in Independence—"

"—I'd be more than happy to squire you around. Take you clubbing. Or jazz. You must like jazz. I'll take you to Milton's Tap Room. No relation, I assume."

Milton ignored the obvious sarcasm, not wanting to get too chummy with this guy. But Deirdre was talking to the preppie.

Candy, disregarded by Rebecca, and with Deirdre and Dickie chatting away at the moment, sought some give and take with the poet.

"Do you write anything like Rod McKuen?" she asked Milton. "He's my favorite . . . favorite *heavy* poet."

"No," said Milton, trying to be polite, "I don't suppose I write that sort of poetry."

"Milton's excellent, I'm sure," piped up Deirdre.

"And probably a good poet as well," said C.W. suggestively.

Dickie found himself drawn into the literary circle as well.

"Do you write things like 'I love you in blue, I love you in red, but most of all, I love you in . . .'"

"Oh, Dickie!"

". . . 'blue'?"

"Oh, *Dickie!*"

"Afraid not," said Milton, prepared to put the jerk in his place once and for all with the power of words. He had his canned, oft-used response at the ready, which he had rehearsed enough—most recently for the earlier presentation that afternoon at "Bargain Books"—to make it sound nearly extemporaneous.

"Actually," he began, addressing the room in its entirety, "I'm more concerned with dehumanization in our industrialized society. I attempt to evoke these feelings of mechanized emotions—because that, in fact, is how the structural societal decay is influencing our everyday existential existence—through glimpses of the perversion of interpersonal relationships . . ."

He made eye contact with them as individuals in turn, as was his practice, but lost concentration when his eyes turned to Candy's cleavage. Hers was a poetical savage breast that could not be soothed, at least not when it appeared to be heaving expectantly. Candy was making a Herculean effort to understand at least some of what he was saying, which produced a nuanced mammary movement difficult to describe.

". . . paralleled by the construction of my poems: erotic stanzas . . . I mean *erratic* stanzas," he corrected, hoping no one had noticed, "with no dependence on traditional forms." He paused dramatically, in preparation for the big finish. "I feel that only in this way can I accurately depict the brutality, the self-destructive essence of the environment with which the poet is forced to cope."

"Sour grapes love poems?" Dickie asked.

"My concern," said Milton, "is if there's a place for love in mechanized society."

"Hmm," said Dickie, "why don't you ask a mechanic? Rebecca?"

Candy was overwhelmed. "Phew! Land sake's alive, I don't think you write anything like Rod McKuen!"

"I'm sure they're not so difficult when you hear them . . ." Deirdre momentarily looked up from slicing a segment of Brie, ". . . even for *you*, Candy."

"I'm referring to the conceptual framework, Candy," Milton went on to explain, "which is a bit more complicated but not entirely crucial in appreciating the poems. I believe that good art succeeds on many levels."

"I think if poets got laid more often, literature would be all the better for it." said Dickie. "I mean, there would be much less poetry. More punch, anyone?"

"What you said, I think it's fascinating, Milton, I really do." C.W. flashed him a winning smile.

Still bristling at Dickie's insulting remark, Milton wasn't able to come up with an appropriate retort, the main problem being that Milton, on the frequent occasions of being horny and depressed—often considered the merits of Dickie's assertion.

"It *is* fascinating," said Deirdre. "You'll have to come to his next reading, C.W."

"Of course. I'd be delighted. When is it?"

"This Tuesday at three, at the Lenexa Library," Milton said.

"I'll make a reservation," said C.W., turning to give Rebecca a wink.

∞

"I could use a top off, if you don't mind, Dickie," said Deirdre, holding out her empty punch glass. She looked at him provocatively, which he returned in kind.

"I thought you skied instead," said Rebecca, ruining a touching moment.

"I was referring to the drink, Rebecca, dear. Clean up your act." The tone was clearly not a friendly scold. The punch had done wonders in destroying the few inhibitions comprising the group's baseline.

"Clean up?" Rebecca responded in equal parts volume and incredulity. "I don't believe in sweeping my dirt under the rug, unlike some people I know."

Meg cheerfully re-entered the room, a spring in her step, holding up a small packet.

"Here's the—"

"Listen, you nympho . . ." Deirdre said, voice raised.

Meg stopped in her tracks, her feet exhibiting quicker reflexes than her mouth.

"—name tags," she finished softly.

"Children, children," Val used her work skills, unmodified, to defuse the situation. "Recess hasn't started yet. And everyone wants recess, right?"

C.W. did his bit to calm things down, killing two birds with one stone.

"I'd really love to hear some of your poetry now, Milton. I don't think I can wait until Tuesday. Why don't we step over to a quiet corner and you can give me an exclusive preview. Here, let me get you some more punch first."

"I think I need a double of something," said Val, looking over at her mother, who was frozen in place, processing.

"The punch, wasn't it?" said Dickie.

"You expect me to remember? Sounds good."

Meg unfroze and scurried over to Val. She spoke in a hoarse, conspiratorial whisper.

"Everything's . . . I mean . . . everyone's doing alright, aren't they? I mean . . . enjoying themselves?"

"Couldn't be better, Mom," said Val, wincing as she reminded herself that the guests of honor hadn't even shown up yet. It was going to be an extremely long evening.

Meanwhile, C.W. had procured a drink for Milton and was leading him to the unoccupied sofa.

"Here's your drink, Milton."

"Maybe I shouldn't," said the poet, looking nervously over at his escort.

"Oh, she'll be alright, won't you, Deirdre? You don't mind if I borrow your date for a little talk about the arts, do you? I mean, what are parties for if people aren't going to mingle, right? Mingle, mingle?"

"I found the name tags," Meg announced to the group.

"I'll take care of those for you," said Dickie, snatching them from her hand. "You might get confused. Here, have some more *puncho sorpreso* . . ."

"Why, thank you," said Meg. Val shot a pointed look at Dickie—which was duly noted and ignored—then reconsidered her thoughts of intervening. Best-case scenario was that Meg had one more drink and passed out on the bed for the remainder of the evening. Val found herself actually crossing her fingers.

"It's a party, for Christ's sake," said Dickie, stirring the punch before hoisting the loaded ladle. "Lord knows we're going to need it. Marriages are so depressing. Especially this one. Why, Melissa biting the dust again is the end of an era."

"It surprised *me*," said Deirdre, "after all those *other* engagements fell through."

"And it isn't too hot in here or anything?" asked Meg, using her free hand as a fan.

"Perfect temp," said Rebecca.

"Well, I know I'm forgetting something," said Meg. "Let's see . . . I got the name tags, the thermostat's fine—although I seem to be having these flashes, maybe I forgot to take my estrogen this morning—no, no, I did—but there was something else . . ."

"Do you want me to check on the hors d'oeuvres?" asked Val.

"The hors d'oeuvres! Why I almost totally forgot!"

Meg headed to the kitchen, conscious of some balance issues. Her scurry was now more of a shuffle on the carpet, with short overlapping strides like a beginning ice skater. She stopped and turned at the saloon doors.

"By the way, Val," she said to the room, "that Brackman fellow won't go five feet from that bathroom. I think he has the run-offs, if you know what I mean. Do you think we should get him some Pepto-Bismol or something?"

～∞～

For a while after Rebecca and C.W. left Blair in the bedroom with a closeted John Palopolus—probably only a minute or two but feeling much longer—Blair sat on the edge of the bed and relished the quiet. He was used to long silences in sessions. He closed his eyes and tried to meditate, unsuccessfully.

Finally he stood up, assisting with his arms, as if a heavy burden were now upon his shoulders.

"John? John? Listen to me, John," he said, standing at the mirror, distracted by the fatigued visage gazing back at him. "Some free, friendly advice. Knock if you can hear me, John."

The response was half-hearted, more like a heavy push that caused the door to rattle in its frame, but counted as a knock nonetheless.

Blair, thus prompted, continued. "You know as well as I do that the only difference between a neurotic and a non-neurotic is circumstance. John, the only reason you're in the closet as opposed to me—I'll tell you why—you got the jump on me, John. There are two types of people, the quick and the wet, and you got the damn jump on me!"

The closet door swung open.

"That's not *my* problem," said John, standing stiffly in the dark.

"Now don't you feel foolish?"

"I like it in here."

"You can't run away from Deirdre for the rest of your life."

"I'm a desperate man," said John.

"Really," said Blair.

"She shafted me, Blair, you know what that woman did to me."

"You let her do it to you."

"Only because I loved her. And can't explain or understand why. But I loved her. Can you possibly understand what that's like?"

Blair was listening, and understood, apparently, since he noticed his chest was tightening. He pulled out his inhaler and gave himself a puff.

"There will be others, other chances." He replaced the inhaler in his jacket pocket. "Plenty of opportunities. You . . . you're a great catch."

"Am I missing something here? Did 'overweight, broke, and alcoholic' come into fashion while I was in the closet?"

"Don't put yourself down."

"I should leave it to others, right? Cut the crap, Blair."

"Trust me."

"You know I had it made in the shade . . ."

"Sure." Blair rolled his eyes and went back to the edge of the bed to sit down. Perhaps getting John to reveal himself had been a mistake.

"Good job, great house in Leawood with two double electric garage doors, eight-foot hot tub with sixteen jets and a double lounger, the speedboat for the Ozarks . . ."

"The Mercedes," Blair reminded him.

"Right. Thanks. The Mercedes, the Carriage Club, the Kansas City Club. You know how much the dues have gone up over the past—"

"—I get the picture, really and truly I do," Blair interrupted.

"And do you know what I'm doing now? Can you possibly imagine what I'm doing now?"

Blair hazarded a guess. "Writing porn for nickels and dimes?"

"Writing porn for nickels and dimes," said John. "You knew."

"You mentioned it again on Wednesday."

"I can never be sure if you're really listening," said John.

"I listen," said Blair, "That's all I do. In fact, I've been listening too long. I—"

"—former columnist for the *Star*, contributor to the *Atlantic, Harper's, Mother Jones*," John interrupted him. "I could go on."

"I said I got the picture," said Blair, irritably. Again, a chance for him to rehearse had been denied him.

"Writing porn." John shook his head, as if he couldn't actually believe it himself. "Well, it pays the rent."

"There you go," said Blair. "Something positive."

"I just couldn't cut it. It's not enough to know which fork to use. The little Greek boy goes to Princeton on scholarship and thinks he can go from one world to another. I couldn't, Blair. Nobody can. She systematically destroyed me, worked me over like a piece of Kentucky Fried and threw me out like chewed over bones."

"And you still love her." Blair was biting into his lower lip.

"Who can understand why somebody loves someone? It's irrational." He waited for Blair to respond. Blair didn't, so he went on. "I'd give anything in the world to get her back. Can you relate to that?"

Blair still didn't speak. For once, he was the one initiating the long silence. During the interval he was noticing that his chest was already tightening again. He resisted the temptation to dose himself.

John broke the silence.

"And you know what happened . . ." He waited for the cue, and narrowed an eye, becoming impatient.

"Yes," Blair finally said.

"She started with the men," he began, his eye unnarrowing, as Blair closed both of his own. "We were sleeping in separate rooms by then. So I'll admit I was drinking; still, I couldn't help knowing what was going on. Who ever heard of an illicit affair where the lover sneaks in through an electric garage door? I mean, couldn't she have at least attempted the clandestine business? Two-thirty in the morning . . . rrrrrrr-Ka-Boom! Enough to wake the dead."

At the sound of the bedroom door opening, John immediately retreated back into the closet, slamming the door, leaving Blair alone on the bed, sad for John and even sadder for himself.

It was a false alarm though, since Meg, not Deirdre, made her entrance.

"Oh, hello!" she said, brightly.

"Hello."

"You're still in here, then."

"Yes. Yes, I am."

"I see." No explanation or admission forthcoming, Meg filled in the potential dead space by explaining her own presence. "I'm looking for those, you know, those name-thingies, the sticky little slips that say: 'Hello, my name is . . . blank', and then you write your name in the blank. There are so many new faces here . . . of course, I knew them all at one time, but now it's so confusing that I thought . . ." she paused. "You realize, a lot of people are here now."

"Uh-huh."

"You . . . uh . . . might even say the party's off and running."

"Good," said Blair, attempting to insert some warmth in his tone.

"And, you've got your coat hung up, or laid out, alright?"

"Yes, thank you."

"Would you care for a drink or anything?"

"I'm fine. I'll be right in . . . uh . . . as soon as I use the bathroom."

"I see." She pointed, narrowing an eye like John had done. "Well, it's right over there."

"Right. Thank you," said Blair.

Blair followed her movements impassively. It dawned on him that Meg was going to look in the closet for her 'name-thingies.'

Before he knew it, she had opened the door, screamed "Eeek! A man! There's a man in there!" and slammed the door. She now had her back against the mirror, arms at her side, palms pressed firmly against the glassy surface, in a barricade stance. She was panting heavily. Blair was grateful that she didn't continue to scream; she had experienced quite a surprise, but his own nonchalance had likely served to fend off hysterics.

"Yes, yes there is," Blair said calmly. "John Palopolus. Nothing to worry about. He isn't trying on your clothes or anything. He's . . . uh . . . meditating. Big on meditation, John is. Does it everywhere."

"He's alright, then?" She was nearly convinced, only another word or two of reassurance would seal the deal. She unpressed her hands from the mirror and put them in her apron side pockets.

"Perfectly. At peace."

Meg's look of fright became one of hostessly concern. "Can I get him anything? I hope mothballs don't put him off his mantra or anything. Maybe he'd do better in the broom closet in the kitchen . . . goodness, here the thingies are in my pocket!" Meg pulled both hands from her apron pockets at the same time to show him. She only needed to display the package of name tags in her left hand, but also inadvertently exhibited the objects in her right one: three crackers that had fallen on the carpet and been retrieved earlier. Blair found himself looking at the crackers, not knowing why.

"I put them in my pocket so as not forget! Honestly, I'm in such a state! Maybe I should jump right in that closet and meditate with John! I don't mean . . . no hanky-panky of course . . . see you soon, then?"

"Certainly. Lovely party, Mrs. Manning."

"Why, thank you." She smiled at him, and again pointed in the general direction of the toilet before leaving the room. She intended to close the bedroom door softly, but the latch was left unengaged, the door barely cracked.

John emerged from his closet haven.

"I didn't believe it possible that that woman could actually make *me* feel stupid. I need a drink," he said, his eyes adjusting to the light.

"Have one," said Blair, encouraged that John would leave and he would be left alone again. "I could use one myself."

"Settled then," said John. "Fetch them for the both of us. I recommend the punch."

"I don't feel like facing the crowd just yet. Has Melissa shown?"

"No, maybe she's backing out. That would be something, huh?"

"Something," said Blair.

"And I bet you'd be real upset, huh? Am I right? Rebecca told me a while ago that you were still carrying the torch, but I thought she was telling tales. You take your own advice? Don't tell me you of all people can't let it go . . ."

"Let's talk about *you*, John," said Blair, snapping into sudden defensiveness. "How about parochial school girls in short plaid skirts? We haven't delved into that one for a while. All we talk about is Deirdre. Deirdre, Deirdre, Deirdre."

"I don't care anymore," said John. "I'm numb and crippled with pain."

"Well, I'm not," said Blair. "I've decided, John. I'm breaking up this marriage. Now . . . tonight . . . as soon as I step out of this room."

"Go soak your head. You've lost touch." John let out a puff of air, a dismissive sound perfected by the French.

"Keep it to yourself! Understand what I'm saying?" Blair growled from the back of his throat, his jaw clenched.

"Hey, calm down . . ." John came over to the bed and sat down beside him. He put an arm over Blair's shoulder and gave him a quick squeeze before bringing his arm back. "Come on, buddy . . ."

"I don't like the person I've become, Palopolus. I listen too much. I don't do anything anymore. When I got the invitation to this little gathering I realized it was now or never. This is my last chance. And if it means risking everything . . . my career, my friendships, maybe even my love . . . well . . ."

"Well *what*?" asked John, not quite believing what he was hearing.

"So it goes," said Blair, tears welling in his eyes.

"You need to mull things over," John said. "Don't do anything rash. Maybe you should direct your attentions elsewhere, but still close to home. Let me give you some advice you once gave me—"

"The last thing I need is my own good advice—"

"The only thing to do with good advice is pass it on." Deirdre Rehnquist had quietly waltzed through the bedroom door. She tossed her coat on the bed and stood, stance wide, slinking into one hip, a hand on the other. Her body language was hardly demure; despite weighing in at barely over a hundred pounds, she was formidable, her expression intense.

Both men stood up quickly.

"Hello, Deirdre. Been awhile." John cleared his throat slightly between sentences.

Blair was observing, trying not to alter the dynamics of an uncomfortable encounter.

"So it has, hasn't it? How's every little thing?"

"Fine. Wonderful. I mean . . . haven't been better. And you?"

"Just peachy," said Deirdre.

"You remember Blair?"

"Of course. How are you, Blair?"

Blair was guarded.

"The same as John," he said.

"Well," said Deirdre, shifting her weight onto the other hip, "I'm glad things are so copacetic. I just got back from Aspen, by the way."

"Oh?" John acted surprised. "How was it?"

"Marvelous."

"Good, very good," John continued with banality. "A lot of powder, then?"

"Heaps and heaps," said Deirdre.

"Great," said John, "nothing better than heaps and heaps of powder."

"Indeed. Uh . . . I brought a friend with me tonight, John. Milton Perkins. A poet. I'm sure you'll enjoy talking about poetic things with him."

"Oh, yes, of course," said John. "Well, I think I'll get some punch."

And with that, John Palopolus made an unceremonious exit.

"Here's your name tag, dear," Dickie said, removing the sticky back and gently pressing the colorfully-bordered identifier on the oval of white sequined fabric that nestled Candy's left breast. He balled up the backing and tossed it onto the serving table, next to the rest of the package.

"Why, thank you, sugar," she said.

Rebecca cast an eye at the hapless Milton, who had been backed into a corner of the room farthest from the punch bowl by C.W. She was generally amused by C.W.'s pranks, although they sometimes had a mean-spirited edge. Seeing how the alcohol was flowing, Rebecca would intervene if need be—her maternal instincts coming out—and save the poor dwarf wordsmith. She could bestow her own false affections on Milton as easily as C.W., especially if it would irritate Deirdre.

"Be careful, Milton," she bellowed across the room. "You're not talking to your ordinary run-of-the-mill poetry lover."

"You hush up, Rebecca, you snot!" C.W. shot back. "Milton's absolutely intriguing! We're talking about geriatrics."

"Geriatrics," said Candy, drawing out each of the four syllables. "What's geriatrics, Dickie?"

"Why do you think I bought you *Webster's New World Dictionary* for your birthday, Candy? Excuse me, I'll be back pronto. Nature calls."

Nature was indeed calling, but less in the form of a full bladder than in the form of Deirdre Rehnquist. He had seen her head to the bedroom shortly before, ostensibly to dispose of her coat. Or was it something else? A signal for a dangerous liaison, perhaps? Noting that her miserable ex-hubbie John Palopolus had just come out of the room, looking predictably glum and shaken—she could certainly dispense with him in short order—Dickie quickly calculated the room's occupants and determined that Deirdre would be alone in the bedroom, if not in the bathroom, freshening up for him. Alone other than Blair, of course, who would not present a problem.

John, on the way to the punch bowl, passed Dickie on his way to the bedroom, and they bumped shoulders, each believing they had been the one to initiate contact.

"A little dry in here," said John to no one in particular. He picked up Mrs. Gottlieb's ladle and filled his glass to the brim, avoiding the ice cubes.

On the opposite side of the room, the discussion involving geriatrics had become defensive.

"Actually, I think your misconstruing my thesis somewhat," Milton said to C.W.

C.W. opened the conversation up to others. "Milton thinks," he said in the general direction of Rebecca, "that old age is something to look forward to because one doesn't have to worry about the burden of sexual performance anymore."

"What burden is that?" replied Rebecca.

"That might be hard for you to relate to, Rebecca," said C.W.

Milton, a stickler for precise language, felt obliged to correct C.W.'s partial misinterpretation. "What I meant is . . . that in our mechanized society . . ."

Meg entered the room, carrying a silver tray with an unusual, doughy-appearing collection of hors d'oeuvres. The selection was obviously of enough interest to divert the conversation away from the mechanized society. Milton gave up on the topic, deciding to cut his losses before the indignities compounded. He stopped speaking, as if he had not been speaking at all, but merely swallowing a belch.

"Uh, excuse me, everyone," Meg announced sheepishly. "The hors d'oeuvres are ready, I think. They may be a bit on the . . . rare side . . . because I don't think I had the oven on quite high enough."

"How high was it on?" Val asked reflexively.

"Yes, how high was it?" added John, manifesting his own tipsiness.

"Well," Meg answered, "it wasn't really on at all. Actually, that's not entirely true. The temperature was set at three-fifty, but the knob on the right . . ."

"You forgot to set the knob on the right to 'bake,'" said Val.

"Why, that's right, dear, how did you guess?"

"I think you're done that before, maybe the last time you tried to cook without Ora Lee," her daughter answered.

"But they're alright like this," said a confident Meg. "You see, this recipe doesn't require baking. I just thought it would be nice to warm them up a little. But the natives eat them just like this."

"Natives?" Candy saw another opportunity to get more involved in the party talk.

"I'm so glad you asked, dear. This is a special African recipe made with eggplant and zucchini."

"From the people who brought you the famous rhubarb punch." John topped off his nearly full glass of punch.

"They're delicious," Meg said, "especially if you don't like crispy things."

John was unrestrained. "The natives are known for their hors d'oeuvres," he said, with the authority of one who had just completed an assignment for *National Geographic*. "I've never yet been to a cocktail party in the bush where the appetizers weren't out of this world. Cannibals, I hear, traditionally start off with a canapé made from a vegetarian. How's the water hole situation? Val? Rebecca?"

"Sure," said Rebecca.

"Please," said Val, "More punch. I beg of you." She took Rebecca's glass and went over to the punch table.

John was more than feeling the effects of the drink—aided by his popping of the Valiums—and was staring blankly into the punch bowl as he stirred the mixture vigorously with the ladle. Momentarily, he was fixated on the resemblance to water swirling in a flushing toilet. A vision in red.

He appraised Val with unfocused eyes and said in an undertone, "What you said about Blair. I'm worried myself."

"Do you think he'll make a scene?"

"Hopefully he'll talk himself out of it. He's never shown himself to be a man of action for as long as I've known him." John focused enough to recognize the look of hurt in her eyes. Things for Val were more complicated than the relationship between Blair and Melissa. "But how do you feel about damaged goods *now*? I'm referring to Herr Brackman, of course."

"Apparently that doesn't get in the way of his feelings for Melissa, does it?" Val watched John pour punch for Rebecca and then held out her own glass. "I suspect you could call *her* damaged goods, too, although I love her and it's a mean thing to say. But I'm drunk. And it's a really mean thing to say. Anyway," she took a deep breath and sighed, "this isn't about me at the moment."

Across the room, Meg tried to peddle her appetizers, with no success.

"Eggplant does the most God-awful things to me!" said C.W, declining her offer and holding up his non-drink-holding hand like a traffic cop.

"Maybe later," Milton demurred.

"Come on now, everybody, don't be shy," said Meg, approaching Candy with the platter. "Here, Candy, be adventuresome." Meg couldn't help but notice Candy's name tag. Of all the people in the room, Candy's name was the only one she could remember with reliability.

"But . . . but I thought your name was Candy Ralston and your name tag says . . . Leftist?"

Rebecca, the closest guest, came to Meg's aid.

Craning her neck forward she read the tag, straight-faced.

"That says 'Left Tit.'"

"Goodness, is that your pseudonym?" asked Meg.

"*DICKIE!*" yelled Candy, but he was not in the room to hear her.

"I think it's a joke," said John.

Candy's blush extended from her face down her neck, nearly to the name tag, which she immediately tore off. "Mercy me! I'm going to have to talk with that husband of mine! I'm so embarrassed I don't know if I can even chew!"

"Oh, *try* dear," said Meg, holding the tray out insistently. "Come on . . . courage!"

Candy was flustered but tried to compose herself and concentrate on the task at hand—a welcome diversion. She was surveying the contents of the tray, puzzled and indecisive, when the doorbell rang.

"I'll get it . . . it's got to be them," Val said, setting her drink down on the table and managing to jog to the front door.

"I just don't know which type to pick! They all look so good!" said Candy.

"They're all exactly the same inside, dear," said Meg. "I just rolled some of them up differently. Valerie did the neat ones."

"Oh," said Candy.

Candy moved her hand over a couple of different prospects, as if considering which chess piece to move, while Val opened the door.

An impeccably manicured Englishman in an exquisitely fitted grey-plaid suit and black cashmere greatcoat was holding a bouquet of flowers and smiling broadly. Val opened her mouth to speak, but was too surprised. She beamed at the man and stepped forward, holding out her arms for a hug.

The hug was a reasonably long one, and Candy had enough time to make her selection before the couple separated. Val stood back and let Nigel Davies make his entrance, announcing himself thusly:

"Surprise! Hallo, friends and lovers!"

"OH!" gasped Candy, as she fainted.

Before crumpling to the carpet, her hands relaxed, relinquishing both her half-full glass of neon red punch and the hors d'oeuvre she had deemed the pick of the litter.

"OH!" gasped Meg, tilting the tray forward. The appetizers—in their varied shapes and sizes but all with a surface somewhat tacky to the touch—quickly succumbed to gravity, slid off the platter, and careened to the carpet. Some of them landed, and appeared to adhere to, the supine and motionless Candy Rawlings.

Deirdre Rehnquist stared at the door through which her ex-husband had just exited, or rather, fled.

"How is he doing, Blair?" she asked.

"Do you really care, or are you just making conversation?" he answered.

"A little of both," said Deirdre.

Blair was thinking of an appropriate response when Dickie Rawlings burst through the door as he had done earlier. This time he stopped in front of Deirdre instead of seeking out the toilet. His urge was not to urinate, although of comparable intensity.

"I trust I'm not intruding," he said to Blair, though looking at Deirdre.

"Not in the least," said Blair.

"Then if you'd be so kind, Blair, I haven't much time and I'd like a word with Deirdre."

"No problem."

Over the course of their affair Dickie and Deirdre had discovered that they enjoyed role-playing as an enticement to their sexual expressions. This fortuitous circumstance had gone well beyond "chance" encounters in sex shops, where, as strangers meeting for the first time, they selected devices for one another's pleasure. They had, in fact, taken their performance art to patronizing a costume rental shop in mid-town with some regularity. The rendezvous had by necessity been at her house, where Dickie had thus far turned up as a TWA pilot to her TWA stewardess, Gatsby to her Daisy, and Frederic, in a fey pirate outfit, to her Mabel. Romance at short notice was a talent they shared. Now, confronting one another in the bedroom, only costumed in cocktail party attire, they would have to improvise. Naturally they gravitated towards actors in a Noel Coward play, with Dickie playing to type, since he had never heard of Noel Coward, let alone seen one of his productions.

"I'm glad we have this moment alone," he said.

"Alone?" Deirdre inquired, arching an eyebrow. She indicated Blair with a tilt of her head, then winked at the latter.

"Oh him," said Dickie, derisively. "He doesn't count. He's a therapist. *My* therapist, in fact."

"You don't say!" said Deirdre, acting astonished. "Mine too!" She gave Blair an ironic smile, then melded it into a seductive one as she turned to face Dickie.

"There you go," said Dickie. "He has professional obligations. Confidentiality. It's as if he isn't here at all."

"Don't fucking mind me," said Blair.

"And besides," Dickie went on, "if he listens—which he's very good at, by the way—we won't have to tell him what happened tonight. So between us we can save a couple of C notes. What say I skip next week's appointment, old chap?"

"No problem," said Blair.

"Mine too?" asked Deirdre.

"Done," said Blair, feeling a wave of depression encompass him.

Blair effectively neutralized, Dickie dismissed him from his mind.

"Now where were we?" he asked Deirdre.

"Alone," she replied.

"Did I tell you how much I like your hair?"

"No."

"I do. The shade is exquisite."

"Thank you."

"You're welcome. It's exactly the color of my wife's."

"No, it isn't."

"Hers isn't natural."

"Neither is mine."

"I see. Where are we going to dinner tomorrow?"

"How about the Colony? They have a lobster tank."

"Perfect. Seven o'clock?"

"Fine," said Deirdre.

"I'll meet you," said Dickie.

"Perfect. What about your wife?" said Deirdre.

"She hates seafood, makes her break out in hives. And she throws up when she drinks as well. I think it's psychosomatic, don't you, Blair?"

"Possibly an allergy," said Blair. He had been observing their exchanges as if at a tennis match, and while loath to admit he was feeling left out, he was pleased to be cast for a cameo.

"Could be, I suppose," shrugged Dickie.

"What I meant was . . . won't she mind?" Deirdre was dabbing at the edge of her lower lip, as if she had chanced upon a new erogenous zone and was testing its preparedness.

"Oh, *that's* what you meant," said Dickie. "Well, you see, she and I have this understanding."

"Really?" said Deirdre.

"Really?" said Blair.

"Yes. Really." Dickie broke character only long enough to flash a dirty look at Blair. "She asks no questions about things she doesn't know about. Settled, then?"

"Can you afford dinner . . . and me, Mr. Rawlings?"

"Put your trust in my trust fund," said Dickie. "I'm embarrassingly wealthy."

"I know your family," said Deirdre.

"I know yours," said Dickie. "May I kiss you then?"

"Must you ask?"

Blair had thought the little performance would come to its natural end with the embrace and kiss, and was crestfallen to helplessly observe—as if watching a spreading skin rash in time-lapse—the transformation into full blown passion.

"Aw, come on guys," he finally said, like a boxing referee trying to coax apart clinching adversaries.

But they were now writhing on the bed, and Dickie's hand had definitely made the passage up Deirdre's dress.

"Guys, come on . . ." Blair said again. He was no longer a character in their drama. Dickie and Deirdre were now in a soundproof space, immune to any and all of his vocal utterances, preparing to copulate before his very eyes.

"For Christ's sake!" said Blair, doing the only thing in his power to do, which was to cover them with all the garments available on the bed. His camouflaging work complete, he stood back and watched the coats move about. They appeared to take on a life of their own, adjusting themselves—sometimes together, sometimes in sequence—to make themselves more comfortable or to scratch an itch. And they made sounds as well.

The outerwear morphed from two adjacent humps into a single larger one, now occupying—fortunately as would shortly be seen—only one side of the king bed.

Despite the darkness and the fervor, animal instinct caused the beast with six coats to abruptly fall into complete stillness upon the sudden and unexpected opening of the bedroom door.

Candy Rawlings going to ground during the party had resulted in only minor pandemonium. Meg, of course, had taken it the hardest, somehow convinced that Candy had a food hypersensitivity and been stricken by eggplant anaphylaxis. C.W. reacted as if frightened by a mouse, fingers fluttering as if he were playing a fugue by Bach, screaming "I can't look! I can't look!" in a shrill voice. Cooler heads prevailed, with Rebecca and Val focusing on the punch splash on the rug, wondering if it could possibly be removed.

Val immediately reassured her mother, unsuccessfully, that Candy had only passed out, and rushed into the kitchen for a rag with cold water to dampen down the stain. Rebecca, in the meantime, gathered the spilled hors d'oeuvres.

"Swooned, more appropriately," John Palopolus said, kneeling down to support Candy's head, which fortunately had not struck anything hard.

"Good grief, help somebody!" screamed Meg, flapping her arms like a bird and running about directionless.

"Nigel, you haven't lost your magic," said Rebecca, still gathering lopsided vegetable matter.

"Call an ambulance!" Meg yelled desperately, as Val returned with the wet cloth. "Call the fire department! She needs epinephrine!"

"She'll be alright, Mom," Val reiterated emphatically, realizing that the attempts to calm her mother and remove the crimson stain from the white carpet had equal likelihoods for success. She briefly considered applying the wet cloth to Candy's forehead, but deemed the carpet's condition to be more critical.

Milton Perkins, the relative stranger amongst them, was anxious to be of help, but none were aware of his specialized talents. "I took junior life saving," he said.

"Someone go fill up the bathtub so the poet can save her," said John.

"Thanks, Milton," said Val, trying to make the diminutive guest feel at home. "Maybe you and John could carry her into the bedroom."

Which they did, Milton ending up with Candy's legs as he waddled backwards toward the bedroom door.

∞

Blair tried to act casually as John and Milton entered, carrying the unconscious Candy into the room like a pair of stretcher-bearers without a stretcher. He forced himself not to look at the mound on the bed. Out of sight, out of mind.

Making sure they had their timing synchronized, the two men took a couple preparatory swings before slinging Candy onto the free side of the bed. When she landed the mattress reverberated from the impact, and the beast made of fur, wool, and gabardine bounced slightly.

"*Que pasa?*" asked Blair.

"Passed out like a light," said John, tugging the bottom of Candy's dress down to a less immodest position. "Unexpected visitor from England."

"Nigel's in town?"

Milton went into the bathroom, and returned with the cup Meg used to rinse her mouth after brushing her teeth, half-filled with water. Candy was coming around, moaning, and Milton put the cup to her lips and raised it a little too eagerly. The water oozed from the corners of her mouth like an overfilled sink. Milton watched in fascination as rivulets meandered down Candy's chin and neck and channeled into the recess between her breasts. Determining that she was not thirsty and that water streaming under the front of her dress seemed to have a salutary effect, Milton set the cup down on the bedside nightstand.

"She's coming around," said Blair.

"There you go, Candy," said John. "You're alright."

Candy, frightened and disoriented, looked around and blinked repeatedly without speaking.

"Will she be alright? Do you know what happened?" asked Milton, concern in his voice.

"She's fine," said Blair.

"Doing fine, Candy. Take 'er easy," said John.

Candy, as if awakened from a nightmare, propped herself up on her elbows. "Oh, Dickie? Where am I? Oh Dickie, oh Dickie . . ."

While she was proceeding thusly, the coat beast underwent a drastic transformation, a primitive mitosis in which roughly half of the creature in the form of a disheveled Deirdre Rehnquist was propelled off the opposite side of the bed onto the floor. She landed, limbs akimbo, with a loud thud, despite the plush shag carpeting. Nearly simultaneously, the top half of Dickie Rawlings popped up from beneath his mosaic of covers. He propped himself on one elbow and leaned solicitously toward his wife.

"Here I am, darling . . . right beside you, dear one . . ." His tone conveyed the good fortune of having been so close by in a time of need.

"What the hell . . ." said Milton as he watched Deirdre stumble up from the floor in a rather undignified and poorly coordinated fashion. Recovering as all the men in the room watched—except for Dickie, who was busy comforting his wife—Deirdre tended to her dress and casually primped, tossing her hair, as if nothing untoward had happened. There she was, Botticelli's Venus in full bodily form, except attired in a cocktail dress and emerging from a mattress instead of a clamshell. The illusion would have been more convincing had Deirdre not been obligated to reposition the pair of panties—scanty and lavender—that rode down on her ankles. Sneaking them up unobtrusively was complicated by the unfortunate jangling of her bangles.

"Oh, anywhere will be fine for your coat, Deirdre," deadpanned Blair.

John, receiving a mortal blow to his soul, could say nothing. He flushed and felt his heart stop. As if the thought of Deirdre with that scum bucket Dickie Rawlings wasn't horrible enough, John was the one who had bought her those lavender panties.

"What the hell . . ." Milton repeated, not for poetic effect, but reflecting a loss for words.

"Sugar plum was with you all the time, dearest," said Dickie.

"Oh, Dickie . . . oh, Dickie . . ."

"Please don't 'Oh, Dickie' me, dear," said Dickie, trying to restrain his irritation. The hand that stroked her forehead inadvertently pushed harder.

Deirdre gathered herself enough to speak, and addressed the duo of John and Milton. "I see you two have met." The irony of her being in the same room with the ghosts of sexual past, present, and perhaps future, did not occur to her.

"Not formally," John said breathlessly.

"Easily remedied," said Deirdre, matter-of-factly. "Milton Perkins, I'd like you to meet my ex-husband, John Palopolus."

"Uh . . . a pleasure, I'm sure," said Milton.

"Don't be so sure," said John, finding enough air to flow pass his vocal cords. "We have a lot in common, you twerp . . ."

"Pardon me?" asked Milton, eyebrows rising.

"Deirdre should prove quite the inspiration, Milton, is what I meant. After all, it seems that men write the best poetry for the worst women."

"Eat shit and die, John," said Deirdre.

"Uh, Deirdre . . ." Milton didn't think it out of line to make an innocent inquiry; the situation was odd to say the least, and he hadn't been given any backstory. Perhaps it wasn't the time to bring this up, in front of the ex, but the sight of the lavender panties—he made the mental note that they were the color of wild irises in a Sedalia meadow on an unseasonably warm spring day—had him rattled. "What exactly were you doing in the bed . . .?"

"I'll explain later, Milton, but I'd like a drink at the moment, if you don't mind." Deirdre brushed past him and headed out the door, assuming he would follow her obediently, which he did.

"I think I need my make-up purse, Dickie, I must look a fright," said a recovering Candy, still in a cuddling position with Dickie.

"Wriggle your way out of *this* one, asshole," said John, with renewed aggression now that Deirdre had departed.

"I own no explanations to the likes of you," said Dickie, stroking Candy's forehead even harder.

"I think my head's okay now, honey pie," said Candy. "It's starting to burn, sugar . . . but, oh, Dickie . . . creampuff . . ."

"The fuck you don't . . ." said John, red in the face.

In general, Blair was confident that he could distinguish between verbal posturing and the threat of actual violence. At the moment, however, he was experiencing a crisis of confidence. He needed to intervene: John was clearly on the verge of initiating fisticuffs with Dickie Rawlings, and there was not much more time to listen. Candy, unknowingly, was the only thing between her husband and a brawl. But if she had to leave and powder her nose . . .

Blair was paralyzed. Just as with Melissa, he found himself unable to act. Which was *his* problem, and one that he was fully capable of acting upon, given his training. He would break up the fight before it began. He wouldn't let it happen. He would assert himself, and instead of listening, take charge and say something for a change.

And Blair Brackman knew he could have done it and *would* have done it, despite a slight tightening in his chest, had Melissa Manning and her fiancé Rod Schoenlieber not decided, at that exact moment, to enter the bedroom with their coats.

❧

"That's what you get for seducing Southern Belles," Rebecca said to Nigel, without indictment.

"I can't look! Is she gone? Is she gone?" asked C.W.

"I just feel *horrid*!" exclaimed Nigel Davies. "I had *no* idea . . ."

"Help yourself to some punch, Nigel," Val said, on her knees, pressing the wet rag into the stain on the carpet. "And you can dump those hors d'oeuvres into the trash can, under the serving table," she said to Rebecca. Within seconds, the cloth in her hand looked like a bloodied surgical sponge from a trauma operating room suite. Remarkably, and in seeming violation of the laws of thermodynamics, the splotch on the carpet had undergone no appreciable change. Val nonetheless pushed down harder, palm over back of hand and arms straight, as if doing CPR.

Melissa and Rod, who had arrived one elevator trip after Nigel, had been standing in the doorway for the good portion of an extremely lengthy minute, watching the events in dispassionate silence as if standing in the back of a movie theatre, wondering if they were in the right movie. Given the theatrical preview, Melissa was hesitant to enter her own party, and Rod wasn't about to initiate a move without his fiancée's prompting. So they stood together silently in the doorway, not even exchanging glances, with no one in the room aware of their presence. But with Candy apparently safely tucked into the bedroom with her escorts, Val settled into the carpet, and Meg seemingly quiet at the moment—at least no longer running around screaming, but whimpering on the sofa—Melissa figured it was as good a time as any to make themselves known.

"Mother?" she asked tentatively, stepping into the room, leading Rod by the hand. She used a quiet, non-obtrusive voice, so as not to further shock an emotionally labile Meg, potentially precipitating a relapse of hysterics.

"Melissa!" exclaimed Meg, jumping up from the sofa and rushing over to her daughter and future son-in-law with small hurried steps and outstretched arms.

"What's going on?" Melissa innocently asked. "What a *total* surprise! We thought we were just going to have dinner with you somewhere! And just look at this!"

"Looks like a party started without us," said Rod, who, a stranger to sarcasm, meant it quite literally. "A surprise party! Well, you sure had *me*!" He wore a cotton open-necked plaid shirt—in a color and pattern that suggested it should have been flannel—and crisp, un-faded tapered jeans. In common with Milton, his overcoat had toggle buttons. Melissa wore a conservative white blouse and black slacks, topped off with a short wool jacket trimmed in black leather.

"I'm so glad you're finally here," Meg said tearfully. "Everything is so hectic and Candy just passed out and I spilled the entire tray of—"

"I see," said Melissa, stemming the tide. "Just calm down, Mom. It's okay." Knowing all the dirt about Nigel and Candy, she already had pieced things together pretty well, certainly more than Meg could.

"Oh, Rod," Meg went on, "I'm so relieved you finally—"

"Sorry we're late," he preempted her.

"That's quite alright, quite alright," said Meg, wanting to say much more but not knowing where to begin. And she was woozy.

"Rod just came off the road and we've been rushing like crazy. And Nigel! When did you get in town? What a surprise!"

"No less than forty-five minutes ago," the Englishman replied, pouring himself some punch. He had set the flower bouquet on the table, where it could stay, and wither if need be. He didn't feel like asking for a vase in light of what had just happened. "I just had time enough to drop off my bag at the Raphael."

"And already one woman has bitten the dust," said C.W. "Honestly, these English types are too much. Everyone realizes that it's just the accent, right?"

"Poor Candy," said Melissa. "Wait . . . before going any further, I want everyone to meet my fiancé, Rod Schoenlieber. That's Rebecca Harvey by the trash can, Nigel Davies by the punch bowl—an old, old friend from England—and C.W. Dexter, the authority on accents over yonder."

"We've been waiting like buzzards," said C.W. "And, by the way, the English only sound that way because of the air whizzing past those really bad teeth."

"So *you're* the Nigel from England!" said Meg. "I remember now the invitation and how I ran out of stamps."

"Never too many 'Love' stamps," said the Brit.

"But I still don't understand what you're doing here!" said Melissa.

"Well," Nigel took his first sip of punch and reacted with a startled expression and a "wow" under-toned to himself. "I received an invitation from your mother, and since I needed to plan a trip to the States at some point anyway, I managed to shift my schedule." Upon hearing the latter word pronounced as 'shed' mated with 'yule,' C.W. rolled his eyes.

Deirdre, followed by Milton, came through the bedroom door just in time for the tail end of the introductions.

"Mel, darling!" effused Deirdre. She rushed over to Melissa, leading with her cheek. There was a perfunctory embrace, accompanied by banging bangles, and a single peck apiece. Milton despondently walked over and stood at arm's length behind Deirdre, akin to a manservant suffering from chronic depression.

"Deirdre, I'd like you to meet Rod . . ."

"Delighted. And this is my friend Milton Perkins, a visiting poet."

Milton bowed like a minor character in a Chekov play.

"Is Candy doing alright?" Val interrupted.

"Fine, is she?" added Nigel.

Milton squeezed his lips together and nodded. Then, to clarify and avoid any ambiguity, he managed to speak. "She's fine. Resting."

Melissa took a deep breath, relieved to have the introductions behind her. "You know, this is all such a . . .such a surprise."

"I *knew* you would love it, dear" said Meg. "So many of your friends were able to make it! And to be honest, it's all been a bit of a surprise for me too, since I misplaced the list and couldn't remember who I invited. Or Ora Lee may have accidentally thrown it out."

"Then we won't hold you responsible," said C.W.

"Well, any friends of Melissa's are friends of mine," said Rod, prompting looks of disbelief among a group too jaded to appreciate the social utility of clichés.

"I can't wait to catch up with you all," said Melissa, "but I want to to check on Candy."

"Me too!" said Rod, earnestly.

Barely a handful of words had come out of his mouth, and already he wasn't making a good impression. It was a tough crowd.

"Candy, are you alright?"

Melissa asking about Candy's health was the first order of business when she entered the bedroom with Rod. Blair and John were also there, she immediately noticed, as was Dickie Rawlings, lying, strangely enough, next to his wife in her mother's bed. The lower half of his cream-colored suit was covered by coats. The oddity of the situation had apparently just occurred to Candy as well.

"I'm just fine, Melissa, honey" said Candy, sounding every bit her little ole self. "But Dickie, sugar, what in heaven's name are you doing in *bed* with me?"

"Now just go easy, dear," said Dickie, removing himself from his side of the bed and leaving a closet's worth of coats helter-skelter on the coverlet.

"Hello, there," said Rod, either pretending to ignore the bed scenario or devoid of curiosity.

"Not to interrupt," said Melissa, wondering what exactly she *had* interrupted, "but this is my fiancé, Rod Schoenlieber. Candy Rawlings—"

"Don't get up," said Rod chivalrously.

"—her husband Dickie Rawlings, John Palopolus, and Blair Brackman."

"I've heard so much about you," said Rod, an exemplar of sincerity.

"Likewise, I'm sure," said Blair, ominously.

"Well!" said Melissa with an enormous audible sigh, aware that a mysterious tension encompassed all of them like a foul odor wafting from the bathroom.

"We were afraid you weren't going to make it," said Blair, still focusing an ocular laser beam at Rod. He had not blinked in a long time.

"No, no, we just got a little behind," said Melissa. "Rod didn't get in from Chillicothe until after six, and by the time . . . and then we had to shower and change," Melissa concluded, catching herself.

"Couldn't wear those old road traveling clothes for my own party now, could I? Had to get into something a bit more, you know, dressy," said Rod, proudly looking down at his plaid shirt and denims.

"And comfortable," added Melissa, aware that her former crowd had a variant notion of the dress code.

"Like your Bass Weejuns and brown argyle socks," said Blair.

"Exactly! How did you guess?" Rod was impressed. He was wearing neither his Bass Weejuns nor his brown argyle socks, since the latter were in the dirty clothes hamper and the former had dried mud on them. He naturally assumed that Blair had performed a parlor trick and might next ask him to pick a number between one and ten.

"He's observant. He's a psychologist," Melissa answered quickly, revealing to Blair that Rod had no clue about their professional relationship.

"How interesting! I didn't know that," confirmed Rod.

"There are many, many things you don't know yet," said Blair, channeling both Vincent Price and Rod Serling.

"I'll say," said Rod. "Melissa has sure opened up my world."

John, frightened by Blair's demeanor, sought to redirect the conversation anywhere besides where it seemed to be heading. For the moment, he even forgot about wanting to coldcock Dickie Rawlings. "What's your line of work, Rod?"

"I sell."

"I see. But what *exactly* do you sell?"

"Oh, I wouldn't want to bore you," said Rod, who personally found his own employment fascinating, "but I work for Ma Bell. That's what she used to be called, anyway. The name's always changing but I still like to think of her as Ma Bell. My Ma Bell. I don't know why, maybe because it reminds me of . . . of—"

"Your ma?" Blair suggested stonily.

"I never thought of it that way," Rod continued, now pensive and frowning, which Blair assumed was the expression Rod generally made when required to think. "Anyway, I sell circuit boards for specialized communications networks. Maybe you've seen those neat commercials . . ."

"Circuit boards," said Dickie flatly, making his presence known. He considered that someone could be filming an episode for *Candid Camera*, and if so, he wanted to be included. Candy, riveted by the discourse, moved her head back and forth toward each speaker.

"And where would we be without circuit boards?" said Melissa.

John began speaking and stopped, intimidated by the thought of unintended self-mockery. The conversation seeming beyond sarcasm, he deflected. "I think, in consideration of everyone's sanity, we should just take that as a rhetorical question."

"I don't believe I've ever met anyone who sells circuit boards!" said Candy. "Do you carry a whole lot of little sample circuit boards in a briefcase?"

"Let's not get too technical, dear," said Dickie, who didn't want his wife to embarrass herself if there were, in fact, a hidden camera in the room. His recent leading role in a porn flick, were a camera actually present, did not occur to him.

"Rod has a very good job," said Melissa.

"I'm the only circuit board salesman in the region, and that includes Joplin, Sikeston, Springfield, and DeSoto."

"Wow," said John. "that just about covers *all* the specialized communication hubs in southern Missouri."

"Yes, it does," said Rod. "Me and another guy have the whole thing, actually. I cover south of I-70 and Phil Minkin—"

"—covers north of I-70," said Blair Brackman.

"You know Phil Minkin?" Rod asked, incredulously. "Such a small world, isn't it?"

"These things are important to know," said Blair, adopting the tone of a hypnotist. "It's important to learn things about new people. That's my job."

"You're a psychologist."

"Indeed. You see, I approach a new person as a potentially disruptive force, the way a fighter might face an opponent. Sizing up his strengths, weaknesses, all the while bobbing back and forth, assessing, formulating a course of action so that the strike will come quickly, unexpected, and to the mark. Understand?"

"Yes . . . yes . . . I think I see what you mean, kind of. I'm not much of a boxing fan, but I see the analogy, in a way."

"I don't think you do," said Blair.

"Yes, well, Blair's very perceptive," said Melissa, also confused by the analogy. "Well, I guess this whole place is the closet!" She tossed her coat onto the bed, avoiding

Candy, who was now sitting up, and Rod followed suit. "Somehow, I'm not quite in the party mood."

Blair was acting queerly, John was drunk, and God only knew what was going on with Dickie and Candy. And worse, no one seemed to be taking to Rod.

"Come on, dear," Rod said.

"Mother working so hard . . . sometimes I wish we had eloped. Mother eloped. It saves a lot of headache."

"What headache?" said Rod. "This is fun! I'm meeting all sorts of nice people!" He outstretched his arm, indicating the group in closest proximity, the especially interesting folk in the bedroom.

"Someone came up to me today," Melissa continued, "and asked me what the colors in my wedding dress were. I had no idea! It was so *embarrassing*! I can't even remember the color of my dress!"

"White," said Rod.

"Lovely!" said Candy.

"White satin, corset style, with floral netting accented with pearls on each flower, and a pleated sheer outer skirt," said Blair.

How did the guy do it? Rod wondered, ever more impressed.

"Melissa and I are very traditional, aren't we, honey?" said Rod.

"I wore white at my wedding!" Candy popped up like a jack-in-the-box. "Didn't I, Dickie?"

"For the thousandth time she wore white! Pure as the driven snow, blinding white!" said Dickie.

"I'm very traditional too, Rod," said Candy. "Some folks say I'm old-fashioned, behind the times."

"Never!" said John.

"Don't let that bother you, Candy. People used to think I was square," said Rod.

"Really!" said Blair.

"Yes!" said Rod, beaming.

Melissa was feeling more uncomfortable.

"Shall we go back in and drink up?" she said to her beau.

"All the action's in the other room," said Rod, encouraging the others to join them.

No one did.

∞

"What a sweet man," said Candy, still sitting on the bed but now deeply immersed in her make-up ritual. She had already made the exact comment several times in fairly rapid succession. Clearly, she couldn't articulate exactly *why* he was such a sweet man.

"Yes, dear. But if you're sufficiently recovered, I'd like to have another drink myself," said Dickie. He had only recently returned with her purse from the living room, as requested, and was not inclined to tarry as Candy did her face, particularly with Deirdre in the other room.

"Oh . . . uh . . . I think I'd better stay in here and rest up. I'm still a little . . . dizzy."

"Have it your way," said Dickie as he disappeared into the party room.

"Rod's a complete doofus," said Blair.

"I was just having some fun," said John, "but I've never seen you like this before."

188

"I don't understand what Melissa sees in him. I have to save her from herself!"

"Maybe he's got a big dick," said John, making a joke.

"Fuck you," said Blair.

"Goodness!" said Candy.

"I don't think that stain is going to come up, Val," Rebecca said as the guests of honor left to see Candy. "Now your mother can get that puppy you always wanted."

Val nodded and went into the kitchen for another wet rag. She wasn't expecting positive results, but perhaps more cold water would help keep the crimson from setting until professional carpet cleaners could give it a shot.

"You don't need to worry," said C.W. "The stain goes with the color scheme . . . *anything* goes with the color scheme."

Val returned with the largest piece of absorbent material she could find in the kitchen, folded over once and soaked in the sink. She held it away from her body since it was actively dripping, and plopped it down on the discoloration.

"There," she said with finality. For good measure, she stepped on the saturated towel with her foot for a three count.

Meg watched, but didn't seen to register the significance of red food dye—with rhubarb punch serving as a delivery device—on a white carpet. At the moment, she was afraid her reception was not yet an unqualified success.

"Val, do you suppose everyone is having a good time? I'm worried."

"It's a wonderful party, Mom. Just perfect. Maybe you should make some more hors d'oeuvres . . ."

"My goodness! I almost forgot again! First the hors d'oeuvres in the oven, and then I should check on poor Candy . . ." And she was gone.

"Don't forget the knob on the right this time," Val shouted impotently. She would check for herself as soon as she had another drink.

Rebecca abandoned the stained spot and sidled over to Nigel.

"Nigel, you look beautiful," she said. "You know where you can reach me of course . . ."

Nigel wouldn't have minded reaching Rebecca any-where, but was reminded that she had a daughter, which complicated matters.

"Have you no shame, Rebecca? Really?" said C.W.

"You'll have to come to the club as my guest before you leave, Nigel," said Deirdre.

"I think I'll help myself to a refill," said Nigel, forc-ing a restrained smile, self-conscious that he could be too much of a flirt, much too irresistable for his own good. Given the unfortunate situation with Candy—who had yet to return from the bedroom to show her exquisite powdered face—he needed to hold back, if that were at all possible.

"And I'd be delighted," he said to Deirdre, pushing the ladle into the punch. He noted, without surprise, that both Rebecaa and Deirdre had decided it was time to get refills as well. He felt the warmth of their bodies on either side of him just before their distinct, but equally provocative scents reached his nostrils.

"What line of work are you in, Mr. Davies?" asked Milton. Nigel managed to squeeze around from the punchbowl, breaking free of the two women like the first one out of a crowded elevator.

"Nigel. I'm in advertising actually, affiliated with J. Walter Thompson in the States."

"That's only his hobby. He's mainly a heartbreaker and homewrecker."

"Now, Rebecca, love . . ."

"Milton," said C.W., seeking to regain possession, "remind me to tell you my theory on English men . . . it goes along with what we were saying before . . ."

"You used to be a super tennis player," said Deirdre, steering the conversation back to her own agenda.

"You'll be disappointed. I'm out of practice."

"Don't believe him," said Rebecca.

"But back to the real subject. I'm so happy about Melissa . . . and sad."

"You had your chance!" said Val, the words coming out a bit louder than she had intended.

"That's one thing he's had plenty of. Look no further, Nigel," smiled Rebecca. "Unfortunately, I'm not the marrying sort, but why buy the cow when—"

"Nothing like a challenge!" said Nigel. "This is super punch, by the way. And Deirdre, I've been meaning to ask you . . . how's your ex?"

"Just fine," said Deirdre dismissively.

"He was going through a crisis of some sort the last time I was in K.C.," Nigel persisted.

"He's always going through some sort of crisis . . . it's called his life."

"We all do our bit," said Rebecca, firing a volley across Deirdre's bow.

Val instinctively intervened.

"Does anyone else feel like the world is coming to an end, or is it just me?" she said.

"It just came to me!" blurted C.W., genuinely excited. "Marvin Gottlieb! Did Marvin Gottlieb decorate this place?"

"I think he did," said Val. "In fact, his mother lives a few floors below us. How did you guess?"

"I should have known. He leaves his mark like a cockapoo on a hydrant! He did my dentist's office, and not unlike this place, to be truthful. No offense, Val, but really! I just knew it! The instant I walked in here my jaws began to ache and I had the taste of Lavoris in my mouth."

"C.W, behave!" said Rebecca.

C.W., on a roll and going downhill, would have continued had not Melissa and Rod suddenly emerged from the bedroom, having deposited their coats and checked on Candy. Instead, he loudly began humming the wedding march. The others in the room joined in.

"Enough of that," said Melissa, good naturedly, indulging them until they had finished the entire thing. Upon which, they all broke into exuberant applause.

"Better get used to it, luv," said Nigel.

"This bride needs a stiff one . . ." said Melissa, not intending a double entendre.

"I'll say, doesn't everyone?" said Deidre.

"Not as much as you do," said Rebecca.

Melissa, anxious to move the conversation into safer territory than genitalia, asked "How's the punch?"

There was universal, enthusiastic assent in the room.

Val headed to the bowl. "I'll get it. And how about some for you, Rod?"

"Love punch," said Rod.

"It's rhubarb," said Val.

"Love rhubarb," said Rod.

∞

Candy was stalling, Blair was mentally preparing himself, and John wasn't sure he wanted to leave Blair by himself. None of the trio were particularly enjoying each other's company, but neither were they inclined to join the party. They remained frozen in the same spots for a while, each silently pondering individual motivations and needs, when the somewhat tipsy hostess came in to check on them.

"I was so worried! Are you alright, Candy, dear?"

"Just fine, Mrs. Manning."

"And how about you, Baird? You know what I mean."

"I'm afraid I don't," said the newly christened Baird.

"The bathroom business . . ." said Meg, tilting her head as an indicator.

"Oh?"

"I have some Pepto-Bismol but it may be too old. Does it have an expiration, do you know? Should I check for mold?"

"I don't know what you're talking about," said Blair, trying not to sound peevish, "but I'm sure I'm fine."

"Such a touchy topic!" said Meg, deciding to drop the subject. The Blackman fellow didn't seem to be in a very good mood, which was understandable if Montezuma's revenge were involved. "Coming to the party, then? I'm so afraid people aren't having a good time. But I've put more hors d'oeuvres in the oven and I think we can play some games."

"Games?" John asked in disbelief.

"Party games," said Meg. "They're so much fun! You too, Candy, dear! There's the most charming Englishman you'd simply love to meet. You passed out the minute he came in. I've never heard of the rhubarb punch acting that way! Maybe it was sitting out in the open too long . . ."

"I have to use the powder room first," said Candy, shakily.

"If it's alright with Mr. Blackman . . . I mean, if he doesn't need it first." Meg suddenly noticed that Candy didn't look well; a certain peakedness was peeking through her rouge. "Goodness! I hope it isn't catching! We all may be coming down with that hog flu, and me with a one bathroom apartment!"

Meg fluttered out.

"I better leave before I catch anything," said John, following her lead. He had given up on influencing Blair, and he desperately needed more punch.

∞

"Not that I want to get personal or anything . . ." C.W. Dexter began.

"He wouldn't want that," said Milton, thrusting a rapier of words.

". . . but I've been meaning to ask you, Rod. Where on earth did you get the name 'Rod'? Somewhat suggestive, isn't it? You know . . . 'Rod.'"

"I never looked at it that way," said Rod benignly. "It's not that uncommon a name. There's a baseball player named 'Rod.' And someone told me once there's even a poet named Rod." Turning to Milton, he asked "Do you know him?"

"Not personally," said Milton.

"Rob McKuen! My wife's favorite poet!" blurted Dickie, recently emerged from the bedroom. "And I'm so pleased the conversation has turned to suggestive things."

"It would seem that you're interested in suggestive things." Milton glared pointedly at Dickie, and then at Deirdre, standing by the serving table, to see if his comment elicited any change in her expression. Annoyingly, she looked placidly content and was munching on some cheese like a cow chewing its cud.

"Well, the mechanized society leaves me a bit limp, if you know what I mean, Milton," said Dickie. "And don't get your undies in a knot."

Milton was set off by the dig, enraged as his mind raced for the right words. Just the mental exertion made him red in the face, a cartoon character with steam about to blow from both ears.

"That will be quite enough," said Deirdre impassively. She lazily reached over for a gherkin. The punch appeared to have calmed her.

"Oh, no . . . do go on," said Rebecca, for whom the punch was having an opposite effect.

"What are they talking about?" asked Rod, who, despite having been the main topic of the conversation, found himself suddenly lost, without a conversational compass.

"Now don't get all riled up, Milton," said C.W., hoping to rile him up.

"There's plenty of punch, isn't there?" asked Meg, nervously uncertain about the discussion at the moment. She had discovered, though, that just mentioning the punch seemed to make everyone happier. Rhubarb seemed to be the only thing this collection of very different people had in common. Besides Melissa, of course.

"Shall I add a little more club soda?" she asked.

There was a chorus of no's.

"This is terrific just the way it is, Mom," said Melissa, sipping her first glass and wincing.

"A little strong for my taste," said Rod.

"Well," Meg explained. "It's been sitting out, you know, which makes it more tart." She smacked her lips as if giving evidence. "But let me see . . . the oven is on, the name tags—forget that—let me just check on the ice situation . . . and then we can play some games." Somewhat unsteadily, but again with short shuffling steps, she went into the kitchen.

"Games? What's she talking about?" asked Nigel.

"Lord knows, pay no attention," said Melissa. "I think the pressure of her daughter marrying is getting to her."

"Especially after all those false alarms," said Deirdre, realizing that the punch had calmed her lips disproportionately.

"What's that?" asked Rod.

"Nothing," said Melissa, flashing a look that could maim, if not kill, to her former sorority sister.

"Did I say that?" said Deirdre, taking another healthy mouthful of punch.

"You must have misunderstood, Rod," said Rebecca, coming to her defense. "Deirdre always gets taken wrong."

Deirdre fumed, and her previously insouciant lips began to quiver, the lower one especially. "I don't need anyone to make excuses for me, particularly you, Rebecca . . ."

"But you *do*, Deirdre, you really *do*," said Rebecca, begging to differ.

Simultaneous to this female interaction, a similarly antagonistic one was taking place between Milton and C.W., evidently precipitated by someone placing an unwanted hand in someone else's personal space.

"Get your paws off me!" said Milton.

"'Paws.' Now that's not very poetic!" C.W. protested.

"Be good, C.W.," said Rebecca, as Milton stormed off to the serving table to get more punch, which he badly needed.

Rod was slowly shaking his head, the dawn approaching, beginning to comprehend the underlying dynamics of the group. His face softened into a smile. "Everyone's so friendly and casual around one another," he said. "Like my old frat house. I think that's great! My family was always so stuffy!"

"Excuse me, but I think there's some real *sickness* here," said Milton, taking a very large swallow from his refilled glass.

Meg had returned from the kitchen, forgetting to bring more ice, and perked up at the mention of sickness.

"The hog flu!" she said. "I've never seen anything like it!"

"My head's beginning to ache," said Val. "Do you suppose that's how it starts?"

"Would you like a Tylenol, dear?" asked Meg, "The Pepto might be spoilt."

"This calls for more punch all round," said the gracious Nigel. "Val, your titer's down, get over to that bowl. And Mrs. Manning, you need a fill-up as well. Let me get that for you."

"Goodness, I do!" said Meg. "The room's hardly moving anymore!"

John, having finally decided to abandon Blair, made his re-appearance in the living room, intending to head straight for the punch bowl. But Deirdre was nearby at the table, picking at the most appealing slices of salami and ham. John warily kept his distance, immobile. Noting him in her peripheral vision, Deirdre met his eyes just long enough to transmit silent communication. Deirdre neither desired a rendevous with her ex at the punch bowl, nor cared to get in his way in a time of alcoholic craving. She hastily tossed a few more slices of meat onto her plate and moved away from the table, ceding the food and the punch bowl to John in a rare gesture of kindness and understanding.

Seeing that John had made his appearance and noting that the psychologist was still in the bedroom, Milton managed his way across the room and through the bedroom door as fast as he could safely execute without spilling his punch. C.W. came forward with open arms to detain him, but Milton brushed past, literally lowering a cold shoulder and figuratively leaving C.W. behind in the dust.

"What's wrong with her *now*?" Milton asked Blair. He entered the room just in time to see Candy, sobbing loudly, disappear into the bathroom and close the door behind her. A half-filled glass of punch in his hand, he looked around the room anxiously, as if someone hidden were about to jump out and attack him.

"Proabably just a virus of some sort, maybe an allergy," said Blair.

"Well, she should be grateful she's not in the other room. You too. The whole place is sick."

"Must be going around."

"You don't get my meaning. Not literally sick. I mean it ironically."

"Trust me, I get your meaning," said Blair.

"C.W. won't take his hands off me. I feel like I'm in a fish bowl with an octopus."

"So what's the problem? Everyone likes to be liked . . ."

"You don't get my meaning . . ."

Blair again attempted to reassure Milton that he did, in fact, get his meaning.

"No, you don't get what I'm saying. This is incredible. I'm a poet . . . words are my tools . . . and you don't get what I'm saying."

"Sure I do, Milton. I get your meaning precisely. Besides, I have some inside, privileged information." Blair paused before proceeding. "You see, most everyone here has been my client at one point or another, and unfortunately, as it happens to work out, this particular collection of people is—"

"—sick," Milton offered.

"—definitely dangerous," finished Blair.

"I still don't understand what's going on here," admitted Milton.

"Simple," said Blair, assuming a professorial demeanor. "The human character is not a unified entity. Rather, it's a collection of hundreds, even thousands, of facets, which glitter and reflect very much like a . . . like those reflecting balls that hang from the ceiling in discos and ballrooms."

"Reflecting balls?" asked Milton.

"You know," explained Blair, "they go around and around, and a light . . ."

"I don't get out much," said Milton, "I'm a poet."

Blair didn't want to lose the flow of his argument, perhaps he could use some of this material in his presentation later. But everyone had to be on the same page, understand what he was saying, especially the reflecting ball metaphor—was that what they were called?

"You know, the round balls with pieces of mirror . . . you know, they have a motor, and they rotate, and with the light shining directly . . ."

To Blair's dismay, Milton continued to manifest a blank look.

"Go ahead," the poet said, trying to be gracious as well as patient with one who clearly didn't possess his own verbal skills. "I'll pick it up out of context."

"Right," said Blair, pursing and unpursing his lips. "Anyway, the facets of ourselves that we project depend on whom we're with. Now, if the situation is so arranged such that there is a conflict—if a person must present different facets of himself to various people simultaneously, at a party, for instance—there can be real trouble."

"Like what? Examples, please."

"Okay . . . maybe a general feeling of discomfort, uneasiness, tension. Then again, maybe divorce . . . or murder."

"Holy smokes! Scary . . ."

"Indeed," said Blair.

"Well, I for one," said Milton warming to the conversation and taking a gulp from the punch in his glass, "would like to know more specifically what's going on. I've been trying to figure it out, but I'm an ousider. Of course, we poets are always the alienated observers of society, but still . . ."

"Uh-huh," said Blair, naturally easing into listening mode.

"You see, I came in here and Deirdre, my date, was in this bed with that . . . uh . . ."

"Dickie Rawlings."

"Him, yeah. Candy's husband. I'm not sure if you noticed . . . but if things had been totally innocent . . . well, I don't have to go into unneceesary detail, but let me just say there were certain indications that . . . but then . . . there's also something funny between Deirdre and her ex-husband."

"You think so?"

"Definitely. Very definitely. I sense it. But I think I understand what you were trying to say before. I think I have a personal example, if you don't mind listening."

Blair found it in himself to be sympathetic.

"I never mind listening," he said with a heavy sigh.

"Okay," Milton began. "I got this letter not too long ago; actually it was a birthday card. It was from a girl I met in Paris three years ago who lives in Argentina."

Blair nodded, encouraging him to continue.

"We met while touring Victor Hugo's place and did a few galleries together."

A particularly piercing wail, followed by a cluster of choked sobs, could be heard through the bathroom door.

Blair acted as if he had not heard anything and maintained uninterrupted eye contact with the poet. Milton, gamely fighting the temptation to look over to the bathroom door, continued.

"Very friendly, and nothing more than that. Not that I didn't want a little romance, though, just didn't come up. So three years later I get this birthday card and it's signed 'te deseo.' 'Te deseo, Gabriela.' You know what that means?"

Blair pretended he hadn't excelled in Spanish in high school, and shook his head while slowly flipping both of his palms upright.

"I *want* you," explained Milton, not skipping a beat. "'I *want* you. I *desire* you.' Ten thousand miles away and now she decided she's horny after my body. In Paris she just wanted to look at pictures."

Blair nodded, the kind of nod that threatens not to stop until someone starts saying something again.

Milton obliged. "Is that what you mean? About what's going on out there?" He indicated the other room with a contortion of his head.

"Not exactly," Blair replied.

"Well, it's a good story, anyway," said Milton.

"I think so too," agreed Blair. "And if I were you," he added, "I'd leave this party immediately and get on the next plane to Argentina. That's my professional opinion."

∽∞⊃

"I can't understand why he's in such a huff," said C.W., feigning hurt at Milton's abandonment to seek refuge in the bedroom.

"Honestly," said Deirdre, "have you no sense of decorum?"

"Now there's the pot calling the kettle black," said Rebecca.

"Calm down now, Rebecca, or I might be forced to play defender of the poor, hapless waif Deirdre," said an emboldened John Palopolus.

"That goes for you as well, Palopolus!" said Deirdre, more hotly.

"Now she calls me by my last name," said John, "which used to be *hers*, by the way."

Melissa, not sure the fuse could get much shorter, did the best she could to stomp on the rapidly moving flame. "People," she said, "I want to say again how great it is to see all of you . . . together in one place . . . at the same time . . ."

"I've heard so much about everyone," said Rod, unsolicited.

"Anyone care to discuss Margaret Thatcher?" asked Nigel, displaying British efforts at diplomacy. "Not that we need to change the subject, but . . ."

"Definitely not," C.W. dismissed him.

Nigel accepted diplomatic failure, at least with the interior decorator in the room, and gave up on détente. "Try as I might," he said, "C.W. Dexter never ceases to antagonize me."

"Boy, this punch is good," said Rod, a spurt in his blood alcohol level provoking a stream-of-consciousness phase.

"Tell me, Rod," said John, an impatience in his voice, "do you ever get bored with circuits?"

"Well," said Rod, clearing his throat, "I don't actually deal with the circuits per se. The engineering branch . . ."

"Circuit boards," said Melissa.

"Bored with circuits. That was a joke," said John.

"Bit of a pun," said Dickie.

"Always joking," said Deirdre, "but bad sex isn't everything."

The reference to manliness was designed to cut to the quick, but Deirdre didn't anticipate where John would be willing to go with it.

"Without a sense of humor," said John, "I never would have been able to live with Deirdre." He took a deep breath and dropped his bombshell as he exhaled. "By the way Dickie, what were the two of you doing together in Mrs. Manning's bed?"

The silence was deafening; even the ice cubes had the good sense to cease clattering in their glasses. John quietly waited for an answer or comment. He had cut an enormous verbal fart, and everyone was expecting a bad odor.

Predictably, Rebecca broke the trance.

"Jesus, where have I been?"

"I think," said C.W., "I'll get some punch before the bowl gets dumped on someone's head."

"You're entirely inappropriate, Palopolus," said Dickie, knowing he was not up to challenging the large Greek physically.

"Shove it up your ass, John," said Deirdre.

"Party talk just slays me," said Rod, chuckling.

"Me too," said Meg, "but I must admit I have trouble following. In my day we didn't joke so much."

"My head is beginning to hurt again," said Val, using potential sympathy as a possible distraction. "Anyone else getting a headache?"

"You're coming down with it," said Meg with assurity.

"Actually, Rebecca, it was like this . . ." All eyes in the room turned back to John. "I walked into the bedroom, and Dickie and Deirdre were under the coats together."

"Bit of a quick one?" Nigel couldn't resist, but was sorry the instant he spoke.

"Listen, people . . ." said Melissa, her voice becoming more plaintive with each passing minute.

"Americans! Fast food, fast everything," said Nigel, deciding to go with it.

"Does anyone smell anything funny?" asked Meg, as if John's verbal flatulance had not been a metaphor.

Melissa tried once more. "I would just like to repeat that I'm really, *really* happy that Rod has the opportunity to meet all of my—"

"I was just going to say that," said Rod. "More punch, anybody?"

"Did I tell you?" Val took a new tack, since apparently no one gave a shit about her headache. "The girl's basketball team I coach at Meadowbrook is going to State!"

"Why, that's wonderful, isn't it, everybody?" said Melissa.

"I didn't know you coached basketball!" said Rod.

"Don't be tedious, Val," Rebecca insisted. "I want to hear the dirt."

"Isn't there enough of it in your own filthy life?" said Deirdre.

"I think it's gone beyond trying to change the subject, Deirdre, dear . . ."

"Somebody must have left a cigarette somewhere," said Meg, sniffing the air like a bloodhound.

"What do you have to say, Dickie?" John was determined not to let anyone change the subject. There would be no diversions.

"I won't even dignify your accusations with a comment," said Dickie. "I'm a happily married man."

". . . maybe somewhere on the rug." Meg wandered around the room, nostrils flaring toward the carpet, stymied like the bloodhound confronting a large river.

"Now I smell it," said Val.

"Me too," said Melissa.

"I smell it as well!" said C.W., excited that he had not been left out of the discovery.

"The hors d'oeuvres!" cried Val, running into the kitchen, her mother trailing after her, setting the louvered doors scampering in their wake.

John was a patient man and had the single-mindedness of a very drunk one. He would not be deterred by the natural calamity of a fire, if there were one. He would simply wait for his opportunity. Similarly, Nigel saw his chance to make things right with Candy. With all attention focused on the swinging saloon doors, he stealthily made his way into the bedroom.

"I'd better help," said Melissa, who had been holding back, assuming Val would have things well under control, as she always seemed to.

"I bet they're burnt," said Rod.

"Marvelous perception," said John, refusing to be pleasant to anyone until he received the satisfaction due him.

"Uncanny grasp of the obvious," C.W. piled on, showing potential for becoming a fairly nasty drunk.

Val rushed out from the kitchen and opened an outside window, letting in chilled air but providing an outlet for the fumes, which were now accompanied by thick smoke.

Melissa came out from the kitchen next, having passively watched Val turn on the ventilation fan, turn off the oven, dump the plate of burnt hors d'oeuvres in the sink, run the cold water tap, and open up the window over the kitchen sink.

"Minor setback," announced Melissa to the group in the living room. "But there will be another batch, I've been assured of that."

"The suspense is killing me," said Rebecca, "How did they burn so quickly?"

"Mom set the oven set to broil instead of bake," explained Val, trying to find a compromise between keeping the room at a reasonable temperature while giving the smoke an extra escape route. She cranked the casement window to its midway point.

"It's not too chilly in here with the window open, is it?" asked Val. "I think we can all afford to cool off a bit."

⋘⋙

Milton was pleased that the psychologist was so receptive about his encounter with Gabriela from Argentina. Blair Brackman really seemed to be listening to him, something Milton wasn't accustomed to. It was a heady feeling. Milton finished off his punch, nodding enthusiastically at the notion of going to Argentina himself, when Candy pushed the bathroom door open quietly. Feigning dignity and composure as successfully as a drunk conveys sobriety, she dabbed at her swollen and red eyes with a crumpled Kleenex. She had discovered that multiple applications of mascara and eye shadow unfortunately could not camoflauge the whites of her eyes.

"Are you okay?" asked Milton in earnest.

Candy would have answered with some sort of Southern belle subterfuge, that it was nothing but a speck in her eye or that last drink of punch went down the wrong tube, had Nigel not entered the bedroom at that precise moment. Instead, her eyes fluttered, then rolled to the back of her head. She fainted again.

"Watch out!" shouted Milton, quick enough to catch her, or at least keep her from falling to the ground. He held her in an awkward dip, like a beginning dance partner, until Nigel and Blair came to his assistance. The three of them spontaneously managed to get her back on the bed.

"Long time no see, Nigel," said Blair. "You're really going to have to tone down your entrances."

"She was alright just a second ago!" exclaimed Milton. "Health is really a precarious thing! Should I get her any water or anything?"

Candy was coming to in characteristic fashion. "Oh, Dickie . . . oh . . . oh . . . oh . . . ." she moaned.

"She'll be alright," Blair reassured him. "She's fine. I don't think we need any more help. Why don't you join the party?"

Before doing as suggested, Milton grasped at a thought just occurring to him. "Is . . . is all this what you mean about reflecting balls?" he asked.

"Yeah. That's it. You got it," said Blair.

Milton Perkins strode out of the bedroom, feeling uncharacteristically positive, even reinvigorated. But he was quickly confused as he entered a smoke-filled room. Momentarily he stood like Lord Jim in the fog, and John pounced on his auspicious entrance.

"Here's the star witness for the prosecution!" he announced.

"Shut up, John!" shouted Deirdre.

"You're not going to back down now, are you, John?" said Rebecca.

"Rebecca! Don't provoke!" pleaded Val.

Melissa was almost too defeated to speak, but made the effort anyway. "I don't want to sound ungrateful for all the trouble you've gone to, Val, but this is a little too much."

"No problem at all," said Val. "Thank Mom."

John was steaming full speed ahead.

"You were there, Milton, in the bedroom. Is it my zany imagination, or were Dickie and Deirdre in bed together, playfully rummaging amongst the assorted wraps?"

"I don't think it was your imagination," said Milton, casting a rebellious look at his date.

"This is the last time I ever bring *you* to a party, Milton," said Deirdre.

"You never explained things to me, Deirdre," said Milton, hurt in his voice. "You said you were going to explain it and you didn't."

"I rest my case," said John.

"You're a contemptible bastard!" said Dickie. "No wonder she dumped you!"

Dickie made a threatening move toward John, but thinking better of it, and committed to going *somewhere*, he stomped off to the bedroom. He had a wife to care for, after all. She could be suffering from smoke inhalation, for all he knew.

"I really need this . . ." Melissa moaned.

"Somehow," said Rod, a look of concern beginning to settle on his face for the first time that evening, "no matter how much you've told me about your friends, I don't think I quite have the big picture."

"Don't look so downcast, Milton," said John. "You can get a poem out of this whole experience. Wait! Wait! It's coming to me!" He waved his hand in the air, as if conjuring a spirit. A thin layer of residual smoke, forced into a swirling motion, only added to the effect.

"You saw Paris . . . you saw France . . . you saw Deirdre's underpants!"

To show her appreciation of poetry, Deirdre threw the remainder of her punch into John's face, and Val rushed back into the kitchen for another wet towel.

"I feel dreadful about this," said Nigel. "It's never happened to me before. Not exactly like this, anyway."

"Uh-huh," said Blair.

"Of course, it's awkward enough for me just being here. You know, Melissa and I, at one time—well to be truthful several times—well, let me just say that we were very close. And leave it at that."

"Uh-huh," said Blair, realizing that Melissa had not exactly told him *everything* during her sessions.

"But, nevermind," continued Nigel, "I needn't burden you with my problems. Still, I just don't know what she sees in him."

"Maybe he's good in the sack," said Blair.

"Puh-leaze," said Nigel, discounting that as a possibility for obvious reasons.

"Well, there's no accounting for taste," said Blair. "Who can explain why one person finds another person attractive? Why someone feels they can't live their life without that person, that they can't go on without them? There's no rational explanation for it, is there? It doesn't make sense, it's just something that . . . happens."

"Perhaps," said Nigel, "we see in people what we need to see. It's always about us, I reckon, and someone just sort of stumbles in our way and we transfer the whole thing onto them, lock, stock, and barrel. Surely you must encounter that all the time . . ."

"Oh, Dickie! Oh, Dickie, oh Dickie, oh, oh . . ."

Both men looked at Candy, a case study, right before their eyes on the bed.

"Sit up slowly, Candy. And stay conscious," said Blair. "Deep breaths."

Nigel sat down beside her and took one of her hands in both of his own.

"Candy, darling . . . it was nothing. There's no reason for you to feel this way . . ."

"Oh, I knew this would happen . . . I knew I'd see you again!" Candy was trying to stifle her sobs, and she had given up dabbing at her eyes for wiping. Dark mascara streaked down both cheeks, and the semi-circles of iridescent blue eye shadow expanded its margins.

"I'm truly sorry . . . I had no idea," said Nigel.

"Just another casual affair. Two consenting adults. A night of unhassled, uninhibited, uncommitted, guiltless pleasure," said Blair. "I've read about that."

"Nearly two years ago," explained Nigel. "It was nothing, really."

"That's not what you said!" protested Candy. "And I was engaged to Dickie! I was going to break the engagement and move with you to your castle in England!"

"Actually," said Nigel, "it's more of a flat in Kensington."

"Liar!" shrieked Candy.

"A man in the throes of passion is incapable of lies," said Nigel, "only half-truths."

"Oh, Dickie . . ." said Candy, breaking down, pulling her hand free from Nigel's grasp to completely cover her face as she sobbed.

"Please don't cry," said Nigel.

"It's okay to cry," said Blair as a psychologist. "Just don't pass out again. Slow, deep breaths," he added, this time speaking non-professionally, as an asthmatic.

"You can't go on like this . . ." said Nigel helplessly.

Blair and Nigel, temporarily at a loss for words—explanatory, consolatory, or otherwise—had settled on watching Candy cry, unabated, and were doing so when Dickie Rawlings stalked through the door. His wife was sitting on the edge of the bed, head bowed, and weeping into her hands. Close beside her sat the Englishman; Blair Brackman stood by the bed on the opposite side.

"What's going on here?" demanded Dickie. "Candy? What's wrong? Speak to me, loved one . . ."

"Oh, Dickie, oh, Dickie . . ."

"If you're going to 'Oh Dickie' me," said Dickie, patience and charity quickly reaching their limits in his internal reservoir, "you can cry yourself into a stupor as far as I'm concerned!"

"I feel absolutely dreadful," said Nigel.

Dickie transferred his look from his distraught and repetitive wife to the eyes of the Englishman. Suspicious that the Brit had hurt his wife's feelings, perhaps with some careless remark about lip gloss, he squinted one eye in an aggressive fashion.

"I'm making a clean breast of it all," said Nigel, which he had decided for himself independently of Dickie's glaring.

"No!" Candy's protest was immediate and shrill.

"I repeat . . . what's going on here?" demanded Dickie.

"It's best for you," Nigel said to Candy softly.

"Oh, Dickie . . ." Candy began.

"Shut up!" snapped Dickie.

A renewed wail from Candy, then her shoulders began convulsing spasmodically as her sobbing reached a record level.

"I have a confession to make," said a resolute Nigel. "Your wife and I had a brief—a very brief—affair before the both of you were married."

"Pardon?" said Dickie, bewildered.

"I said . . ." Nigel prepared to repeat himself. "I simply said that your wife and I had an *interlude* together before your marriage."

"Oh, Dickie, Dickie, Dickie . . . I'm sorry, Dickie, sorry, sorry sorry . . ."

"Affair? Interlude? What are you saying, man?" Dickie had taken on the expression of incredulity combined with abject fear. "Are you trying to tell me that you *made it* with my wife?"

"Precisely," said Nigel, in the clipped tone of a senior regimental officer.

Dickie, uncomfortable with responding to one with such a seemingly unflappable military bearing, turned his attention to a more managable personage. "I'm sorely disappointed, Candy . . ."

"I'm sorry, sugar pie . . . oh, oh . . ."

"Don't hold her to blame," said Nigel. "I seduced her."

"And he's irresistible." Blair added his own two cents.

"More often than not," admitted Nigel, modestly. "And, it was, to be fair, before your marriage . . ."

"Very considerate timing," said Dickie, oozing sarcasm.

". . . though *after* your engagement," said Nigel. If he made a clear breast of things now, Candy would be spared the difficult task later on her own.

"You made it with my wife *during* our engagment?"

"In a word, yes," said Nigel. "I'm afraid so."

Dickie flicked the hair out of his eyes. Then he pushed the hair back with his hand, not bothering to try to tuck it behind his ear. Then he flicked again. He jutted his chin out and tilted his his head at a peculiar oblique angle, as if his necktie were tightening into a stranglehold on its own volition.

"Do you realize," he finally began breathlessly, "that *I* didn't make it with my wife during our engagement?" Disoriented, he flicked his head as if the hair were in his eyes, even though it wasn't. "I think that's awfully rude of you, and to protect my honor I shall have to kill you, or ruin you financially, or at least make sure you never get a decent table in a restaurant in this town ever again!"

"Oh, oh, oh, oh . . ." cried Candy.

"You don't frighten me," said a defiant Nigel.

"Just try to open up a charge account at Jack Henry's or Woolf Brothers! Blair, tell him! Tell him I know George Brett!"

"I don't want to get involved," said Blair.

"You *are* involved!" shouted Dickie.

"Oh, Dickie, Dickie, Dickie . . ."

Thus reminded, Dickie turned his attention back to his wife.

"And you! Harlot! How could you!"

"It was . . . an accident!" said Candy, not known for improvisational skills.

"An accident!" Dickie scoffed.

"What I mean . . . oh, Dickie . . ."

Nigel had reached his limit. "There was absolutely nothing between us, it's entirely over and done with, and your wife has since been one hundred percent faithful to you, which I might add, you don't in the least deserve. I have nothing further to say." Nigel strode out, by now comfortable with, and finding quite effective, a military demeanor.

∽

"Fag Englishman," said Dickie, as soon as Nigel was out of earshot. "Did I mention that I am sorely disappointed, Candy?"

"Yes, Dickie," said Candy.

"Disillusioned, dumbfounded, distraught?"

"Oh, Dickie, it will never, ever happen again. I swear to you, sugar pie. I . . . I . . . I . . ." Candy broke down yet again.

"Crocodile tears," said Dickie.

"I thought you had an understanding," said Blair.

"I don't understand a thing, do you?" asked Dickie.

"I'm not sure I try, anymore," said Blair. "I seem to spend most of my time listening. In fact, I've been listening for too—"

"Quit crying, dammit," snapped Dickie, turning his attention to his wife. "I won't forgive you any sooner!" He turned to Blair plaintively. "On top of everything I'm a cuckold. And all these months, I've been telling everyone how she wore white . . ."

"I *did* wear white!" screamed Candy.

"Mockery! Sham! Don't you understand that a Southern belle has nothing going for her besides her virtue? I can't cope!" His arms flew up in total resignation and he wheeled around, leaving the room a defeated man.

Confronted with a perennially sniffling woman, Blair tried to sound encouraging. "Don't worry," he said, "he'll get over it. He'll forget all about it."

"It was . . . it was such a deep, dark secret," Candy confessed after blowing her nose. "Now I actually feel better. I'm not afraid of him finding out anymore."

She gathered herself, stood up, and straightened her dress. Then she dabbed her eyes with the balled up Kleenex that had long out-lived its usefulness. Blair watched as she performed the final dabs, then reached out, and she handed him the Kleenex.

"How do I look?" she asked. Her eyes were even more red and swollen than before, and her black streaks of mascara marked both sides of her face like rain streaming down a window pane. But she gave him a game, honest smile, and her face lit up. Her eyes seemed to glisten, somehow reflected through the tears that hadn't escaped.

Blair, trying hard not to be jaded, knew that Candy still had a deep dark secret. She had liked it better with Nigel.

"You look beautiful, Candy, absolutely beautiful," he said.

John Palopolus dried off his face with a handful of cock-tail napkins and decided to take things in stride. Rebecca and Val were on their knees, wetting down the new stain on the carpet. Back at the punch bowl, John saw that Meg was back in the room, and appeared to have some-thing to say. He tapped the ladle against his glass, not completely successful in quieting the room.

"Everyone! Everyone!" Meg began, "I have an an-nouncement to make! Quiet, please!"

Val and Rebecca gave up on the stain and made their way to their feet. Val noted that her mother was slurring her words, but so was everyone else. And it wasn't as if she could make things any worse. At some point the night would end, and it couldn't be soon enough. Why hadn't anyone left? Were they all enjoying themselves that much, or were they just afraid they would miss out on something? Even Deirdre, after dousing John, acted as if nothing had happened and had immediately gone to get more punch. Milton was only staying on, Val rea-soned, since he had come with Deirdre and probably couldn't afford a taxi home.

"There has been a slight accident with the hors d'oeuvres," said Meg, after clearing her throat, and find-ing her audience obediently silent. "They are somewhat overdone. They are—to be honest—charred beyond rec-ognition. However, I have plenty more already made up and they're in the oven."

"Hear, hear!" said John.

"Shush!" said Rebecca.

"Thank you," said Meg, addressing John. "They should be ready in a few minutes, so if you'll just be patient . . . you see, my maid Ora Lee, who's been with me for years, came down with this damn—pardon my French—hog flu and . . ."

"Enough, Mother," said Melissa. "We can wait."

"Well put, Mom," said Val. "Have some punch."

"I swear that punch made me forget the hors d'oeuvres in the first place!" exclaimed Meg. "But it's delicious." From the look on her face, she was trying to gather her thoughts. Evidently she succeeded, her faced transformed from confused to happy. "But wait! I'm not done! What I want to say is . . . I hope everybody's noticed how beautiful the bride is and how handsome the groom is. That's my daughter!" Meg extended her arm straight out to point, which temporarily caused a loss of balance that was quickly restored with a few errant steps.

"Mother! I feel like such a child!" said Melissa, either blushing from embarrassment or flushing from the punch.

"And now I have another surprise," Meg went on, only to leave them hanging as she promptly turned and scurried back into the kitchen. Everyone in the room experienced the predictable, and now not entirely unpleasant effect of the swinging louvered doors, and assumed that Meg would either return with the surprise or had high tailed it into the kitchen to throw up. The former was correct, since within seconds Meg set the doors violently swinging again.

"Here it is!" she beamed, fortuitously stopping only inches away from being batted from behind by one of the doors. She held a grapefruit in each hand.

"Do those look like grapefruit to you, Rebecca, or is it the punch?" John asked.

"An alarming similarity," said Rebecca.

"Mother, no . . ." said Melissa.

"They're grapefruit," said Rod.

"Yes, grapefruit!" said Meg. "And do you know what we're going to do with them?"

"Mom, no . . ." said Val.

"I can't believe this," said Deirdre.

"I *love* party games," said C.W.

"I shudder to think," said John, "I've heard a lot about these kinky parties . . ."

"Mom, I really don't think anyone wants to . . ." began Melissa.

"I usually cut one in half in the morning for breakfast and sprinkle a little sugar on top," said Rod.

"We're going to *pass* them," said Meg. "Pass the Grapefruit! Okay, everybody line up in a straight line."

"Mother!" Melissa protested.

"Be quiet, Melissa, you're already acting like an old married lady! This game is so much fun! Okay, in a straight line, boy girl boy girl . . ."

Meg started herding them like cats, first grabbing the closest participant, who happened to be Milton Perkins. "I used to play this with your uncle, Milton," she said, dragging him by the hand to an arbitrary spot that seemed to offer the most room for two lines.

Val, in an inebriated blur, now made sense of her mother's earlier request of a few days before, to "pick up a couple of grapefruit" from the Safeway. She had inquired as to whether her Mom preferred pink or white, and Meg had replied "It doesn't matter, dear." She should have known, and would have kicked herself if she had known, or cared, which she actually didn't.

"Wait . . . we're not all here," said Meg, as Nigel entered from the bedroom. She grabbed the Englishman's hand and pulled insistently. At first he resisted, irritably, then relented, shrugging the padded shoulders of his suit jacket. Meg moved him to a position opposite Milton.

"There's two lines, one for each team," she explained.

"Last chance for punch," said John.

"Really!" said Rebecca. "I don't think so . . ."

"I thought you could never say 'no,'" said Deirdre.

"Go sit on a grapefruit!" said Rebecca.

"No, no . . . that's not how it's played at all," Meg corrected her. "You see, you put the grapefruit under your neck—like so—" she demonstrated, the rest of her sentence sounding as if it were coming from a bad ventriloquist, "and then you have to pass it down the line to the next person. Because it's a contest to see which team can win." She removed the grapefruit from under her neck, so as not to drop it. "It's so much fun, really!"

"What a great idea!" said Rod. "It's been a long time since I've been to a party where we played games!"

Rebecca was positioned next to Milton, and Deirdre, not to be outdone by Rebecca in any fashion, took a spot opposite, next to Nigel, before Meg had a chance to place her anywhere. They all stood rather listlessly, helpless but going with the flow.

Dickie Rawlings stormed in from the bedroom and immediately confronted Nigel, who didn't dare leave his place in line.

"I hope you're happy!" said Dickie. "You've ruined a wonderful marriage!"

"Piss off!" said Nigel.

"Goody, we have one more!" exclaimed Meg, clutching Dickie's arm.

"One more what?' asked Dickie, annoyed.

"For Pass the Grapefruit."

"You're joking."

"Now you just get on *this* team," said Meg, directing him next to Rebecca.

The lines were nearly formed when Candy entered, looking somewhat ghoulish.

"Oh, Dickie, I'm so sorry, honey bunch . . ."

Meg wasted no time in corralling her as well.

"This will be perfect. You're on the other team over here, Candy . . . and you've smeared your make-up a bit . . . but that can wait until later to fix up, dear . . ."

"But I . . ."

"This is Pass the Grapefruit," said Meg. "I haven't got time to catch you onto the rules, but I'm sure you'll pick it right up." Candy was directed next to Nigel, where she looked across at her husband.

"Melissa, it will be over soon," said Val.

"This is beyond surreal," said Melissa. "This isn't happening."

"Now keep your lines straight," ordered Meg, although no one seemed to be listening and order had already disintegrated. She, C.W., and Rod were the only ones with their hearts in the game. "Now, I'll start on this team," she said, "and Rod, you start on the other. Okay . . . grapefruit under your chin, ready . . . go!"

Val, Melissa, and John were already back at the punch bowl. Meg attempted to pass the fruit to C.W., which was coming across as rather lewd, due to physical improvisations from C.W. that involved more of his pelvis than his head and neck region. Meg herself, beyond tipsy, was having trouble just keeping her balance. Rod wasn't sure who to pass to, since Dickie was closest, and he thought that the fruit had to go to a person of the opposite sex. Besides, most people seemed to be wandering around instead of maintaining their lines.

"I'd like to take this moment," said Dickie, stepping boldly forward from his place, "to state to everyone concerned that my Southern Belle of a wife was unfaithful to me before our marriage."

"Dickie, how *could* you!" said Candy, one of the few guests remaining in her designated spot, the result of her extensive pageant experience.

"How could *YOU!*" shouted Dickie, wobbling from the force of his outburst.

"This is wonderful," said C.W., canoodling armlessly with Meg.

Rod, in the meantime, was still in search of a pairing and quickly noticed the proximity and direct path to Rebecca, now that Dickie had stepped out of the way. Rebecca acquiesced to his advances, more from sympathy than anything else. She felt embarrassed for Melissa, who otherwise would have to watch her fiancé waddling around in circles, with nary a friend to receive the grapefruit. Beyond sad, Rod was a charity case. Rebecca clasped both hands behind her back, jutted her neck out and to the side, then held the rest of her torso as far away as she could. Rod, meanwhile, had his face in her neck and was nuzzling ferociously without effect, a toothless vampire gumming his victim to death.

"We need to coordinate better," said Rod through clenched teeth.

"Then hold still for a second!" said Rebecca, also clenched.

"But your breasts are in the way, Rebecca," said Rod, turning his head more to the side, almost parallel to the ground.

His grip on the fruit loosened, and both the citrus and his chin began sliding downward. Rod was now only able to keep the grapefruit from falling by pressing it with a cheek against Rebecca's breastbone. The fruit slid further down, and the single-minded salesman doggedly determined to rescue it, burrowing in between Rebecca's breasts like a hungry infant unable to locate a nipple.

"Honestly, this is disgusting," said Rebecca jolting herself backwards to disengage. Remarkably, Rod still had possession of the grapefruit, although precariously, especially as he lurched forward with the sudden disappearance of the plush firmness he had been resting his weight against.

"Almost!" Meg shouted, still gyrating and wriggling with C.W. They had reached a stalemate of sorts, with the fruit still well secured under her neck. Meg was squeezing it hard, as if she did not intend to allow it to leave her possession, obviously her game strategy a conservative one.

"I don't have anyone to pass it to," complained Rod, staggering around. "Let's start over. Stop the game . . ." Everyone backed away from him, as if from a leper.

"Too late!" said Meg. "That's cheating!" She realized that with Rod unable to find a partner, she could be extra careful in surrendering her fruit to C.W.

"You're a bad sport, Rod," said C.W., becoming more assertive with his chin. Meg didn't seem to want to actually pass it to him, and he wanted to move on.

"Milton, you're next," he said.

"In your dreams," said Milton.

"I repeat," insisted Dickie, his hair well in his face now, "my wife made it with that fag Englishman!"

"Well, I don't blame her at all!" said Rebecca.

"What do you know, you bitch!" said Deirdre.

"Fuck off, whore!" countered Rebecca.

"What were you doing in the bedroom with him? That's all I want to know . . ." Milton asked.

"Who wants it? Who wants it?" said Rod, tiring of staggering around the room.

"Rebecca always wants it," said Deirdre.

"Rebecca? How about another try?" pleaded Rod.

"Stay away from me!" she shouted.

"I've almost got it!" shouted C.W.

"Almost!" agreed Meg.

Val and Melissa, both watching a train wreck in slow motion, found themselves unable to look away or intervene.

"Listen everyone . . ." Val finally said impotently. She realized she had to smooth things over between Rebecca and Deirdre—at least get them to opposite corners— before John got involved.

"Melissa? How about it, honey? My neck's getting stiff . . ."

"Maybe in a little while," Melissa stalled. She was too preoccupied to simply tell Rod to drop the damn fruit.

"Well?" Milton, courageous with punch, was not letting up on Deirdre.

"None of your damn business, you little pissant!" said Deirdre.

Milton contented himself with that answer for the moment. But as misfortune would have it, Candy, growing bored with standing in a line that no longer existed, had started to track the proceedings more carefully.

"Who was Deirdre in the bedroom with?" she asked, struggling to figure out what they were talking about and when such a thing happened. It occurred to her that she might have missed more of the party than she had thought when she passed out.

John was dispassionately viewing the proceedings through a fog of inebriation from his post at the punch bowl. But if clarification were needed, he would certainly provide it. After all, he had been known as the "Answer Man" at Princeton.

"Your husband," the Answer Man cogently replied to Candy.

"Dickie!" shouted Candy.

"John!" scolded Val.

"Candy," Melissa said, "maybe we should go powder our respective noses."

Candy, red-faced and tearing up, did not move.

Milton, now accepting that it was extremely unlikely that Deirdre would be having sex with him later that night, had nothing to lose.

"So what *were* you doing, huh, Deirdre?"

"Yes, what WERE you doing, sweetheart?" asked John.

"Stay out of my life, Palopolus!"

"Hey, come on," said Rod, "this game is no fun!"

"The name 'sugar pie' will always have a hollow ring to it," lamented Dickie, trying to change the subject back to Candy's infidelity with Nigel. But that was old news.

"Why don't you give your wife a break?" John's tone toward Dickie bordered on vicious.

"Stay out of it!" shouted Deirdre.

"Write some porn if you can't get laid, Palopolus," said Dickie.

"Better than fooling around with trash," said John.

"That wasn't nice to say," said Milton, proving that chivalry was not entirely dead in the room. Deirdre had her faults, in his estimation, but 'trash' was a fairly strong and pejorative word, and words were important things.

Rod was on the verge of giving up. But he had undergone hazing in his fraternity days and wasn't going to show weakness, even if he were tired and drunk and his neck was going into spasms. He needed to prove his spunk so everyone would like him.

"Somebody please take this," he said, trying not to sound too whiney. He would pass it along to anyone at this point, even a guy. He staggered over to Dickie Rawlings. "Please, my neck is killing—"

"For Christ's sake," said Dickie, "who the hell *is* this douchebag?"

And as if driven by an unknown force, Dickie Rawlings balled his right hand into a fist and punched Rod Schoenlieber solidly in the gut.

∽

Blair was relieved to have Candy finally out of the bedroom. He had been waiting patiently to get the valuable time he needed to be alone, but the distractions and interruptions had been endless.

Unexpectedly, though, his sense of relief was complicated by a definite tightening in his chest, an unusual combination. He cleared his throat and decided the sensation had to be his imagination. Ignoring the psychosomatic phantom, Blair began his rehearsal, approaching the mirror and looking himself in the eye. He saw a sincere, but definitely tired man.

"I've learned tonight that we are all desperate men. John . . . Dickie . . . Nigel . . . Milton . . . you all know what I mean when I say this."

He took a deep breath, which wasn't complete in coming. He took out his inhaler.

"Oh, this? Breath freshener. So I can get a fresh breath." He took a hit and calmly replaced the device in his jacket pocket, just as he might be forced to do in the real moment. Best to include it as stage business. He allowed himself another test breath, a large inhalation, which didn't quite seem to hit the maximum range, but he would allow the bronchodilators a bit more time to act.

"As I was saying, I have been listening too long," he went on, "and, as I have been gathering the pieces together, I have realized that only one person really matters to me. A very special person." Blair paused, let his eyes wander away from the mirror, and considered not wanting to hurt anyone's feelings. Then he began again.

"Yes, we are *all* special, but certain facets of some have a greater affinity for particular facets of others and . . . and . . . that's right, Milton, like those reflecting balls and . . . and the rest of you are wondering what I'm trying to say. Mrs. Manning, you look particularly perplexed. Please bear with me."

"One of us here is on the verge of making a grave mistake. And I feel it is my professional obligation to prevent such a disastrous event from occurring. The event is our reason for being here tonight . . . the proposed marriage of Melissa Manning and . . . and this *asshole* Rod Schoenlieber."

No, no, thought Blair, you can do better than that.

". . . and this *FLAMING ASSHOLE* . . . Rod Schoenlieber. Nothing personal, Rod." There would be stunned silence at this point, Blair knew. But he seriously doubted anyone would have the temerity to come to Rod's defense, even Melissa. He would have them all in the palm of his hand, crippled by his merciless honesty.

"Trust me," he continued. "Most of you are or have been clients of mine, and have faith in my judgement, even though the odds are you've never really heard me say much of anything. You see, I spend so much time listening to your issues that I—"

Not again! he thought, irritated as he turned to see who it was *this* time. None of these self-involved brats would give him a moment's peace . . .

But it was Val who stormed through the bedroom door. She looked frantic, and was holding a grapefruit.

"Blair! Quick! We need you!"

"Don't point that thing at me unless you intend to use it. That's a grapefruit."

"Dammit, I know! This is not the time to be flip, Blair. You're the only person who can salvage this disaster! Dickie Rawlings punched Rod in the stomach when we were passing the grapefruit . . ."

"That's normally not a very physical game," said Blair. "Is he hurt badly?" he added hopefully.

"I don't think so, but all hell's about to break loose!"

"Maybe he has severe internal injuries. Ruptured spleen. There's a chance."

"Look, Blair." Val's eyes were welling with tears. "I love my sister very much. I'm not thinking about myself. I don't want her to get hurt. I don't want this party to be ruined. And this means so much to Mom, Blair. Blair, please . . ."

"Val, I have a confession to make . . ."

"You love my sister."

"With all my heart."

Blair pulled out his inhaler and contemplated it as if it were Yorrick's skull.

"Then for her sake . . ." pleaded Val.

"The only reason I came here tonight was to break up this marriage."

Blair took a hit from the inhaler and gulped.

"Circumstances have worked into my hands perfectly," he went on.

He took another hit. He knew that one more would do it.

"It's fate, Val. This was meant to be. There's no stopping me. Don't try."

Val tried to grab him, but he pulled away from her roughly.

"Blair!" she shouted, running after him.

But Blair was already through the door and screaming Rod's name as if it were a battle cry.

Melissa knelt beside her grounded fiancé. She felt the wet on her right knee and realized she had placed it on the water-soaked towel on the carpet.

"Honey, are you alright?" she asked.

Rod had been writhing on the carpet, both hands clutching his midsection. But he had settled somewhat, and after a short preparatory grunt, managed to eke out, "Fine. I'll be okay."

"Dickie! How could you!" said Candy, who had finally left her spot in line and was also now kneeling on the carpet besides Melissa.

"A momentary fit of insanity from a jealous rage," said Dickie absently but not very regretfully.

John's thoughts were a muddle, but he could no longer contain the simmering of his emotional pot, now on an intense, blue-white flame. He bolted over to Dickie, grabbed him by the collar, and flung him up against the wall.

"If you so much as touch a hair on Deirdre's . . ." John snarled.

Dickie made a guttural sound and began to slobber.

"John!" screamed Deirdre.

"John!" yelled Rebecca.

The two women simultaneously rushed forward to pull John away, as did Milton, feeling the safety in numbers and happy to play back-up to a couple of fierce, front-line females.

"I've never seen Pass the Grapefruit induce so much hard feeling!" said Meg, wobbling and heading over to the sofa to sit down, resigned to letting the girls handle things for a change.

John didn't object to the women pulling at him so much as feel an unshaking animosity toward Milton, who could be sampling Deirdre's merchandise as well.

"Get your hands off me, you half-baked Rod McKuen," he said, refusing to release his grip on Dickie and fending the others off with violent twisting of his shoulders.

"Don't hurt Milton! Don't hurt him!" shouted C.W., even though Milton did not appear to be in immediate danger as John continued to manhandle Dickie. Nonetheless, C.W. entered the fray as well.

"Oh, my God, someone do something!" shouted Melissa, looking around the room for Val.

"Oh, Dickie, Dickie . . ." incanted Candy, as Nigel entered the brawl as well, intent on showing a more muscular diplomacy.

Nigel met with some success, as in concert with C.W. they were able to release John's grip from the now submissive Dickie. The generalized shouting and scuffling continued, however, and had taken on a new dimension, with Rebecca and Deirdre focusing their attentions on one another. They first pulled each other's hair and swung loosely gripped fists wildly, before settling into a gyrating clinch and falling on the floor together, entangled and trying to land meaningful punches while rolling around on one another. Rebecca, due to her superior size, was appearing to get the better of it. But Deirdre was feisty and had a personal trainer at her gym. Even though Pilates was not exactly preparation for street fighting, there appeared to be some benefits.

"Let go of me, you skank!" yelled Deirdre, contracting her core.

"Fuck you, whore!" yelled Rebecca.

And so on, as even Deidre's clanging bangles became nearly impossible to hear over the din.

Eventually, before much damage was done to the apartment or the Noguchi table overturned, the men diverted their attention to breaking up the women on the floor, who had shown themselves to be determined brawlers. Given the pandemonium, it was difficult to separate the fighters from the peacemakers, but all were involved in some fashion, either trying to mediate or perpetrate. Meg, in a safe zone on the sofa, had put her feet up and was lying back with her eyes closed, wishing the gathering hadn't gotten so noisy.

Needless to say, no one heard the doorbell or the knocking. The guest was late. Things had gotten hectic at the shop, as they frequently did on Friday afternoons. And he had to shower and change into his brown suit, which had a trace of mothball odor about it. With his bulky frame, he knew that suits never fit him quite right, so he didn't like wearing them. Nor did he like using hair gel, since the only time he plastered down his thick unruly curls was when he was going someplace special. This being infrequent, he looked strange and unfamiliar even to himself on these occasions, like a rube fresh off the farm and all slicked up for the county fair.

He waited patiently outside the door. The party was really loud, so it was no surprise they couldn't hear his persistent ringing and knocking. The real surprise was that he had been invited to the gathering in the first place. He had seriously considered declining, but felt confident his feelings of awkwardness would pass once he was socializing, chatting with the other guests. Still, standing there, ignored for the moment, he was as ill at ease as his suit was ill fitting. First thing, though, he would apologize for being late. The polite thing to do.

Mitch Harrington twisted the doorknob and gave a gentle push. Door open, he appraised the situation and realized that he might not bother apologizing for being late.

He was still standing in the doorway, motionlessly observing the brawl, when Blair Brackman barged into the room from the bedroom, clearly intent on bringing order from chaos. But why was he screaming, "Rod Schoenlieber" at the top of his lungs?

"ROD SCHOENLIEBER! I'M BREAKING THIS WHOLE THING UP!"

Blair Brackman made his entrance in dramatic fashion, the savior arrived. Val was at his heels, grapefruit in hand, breathing heavily.

"Thank God!" shouted Melissa.

"Wait . . . I didn't mean . . ." said Blair, his eyebrows furrowing and contorting like a snake under a blanket.

The fighting stopped. Everyone got up, except for Rod—still recuperating on the floor a bit away from the center of action—and carelessly adjusted their clothes and themselves. Damage assessment would come later. They had been fighting and it was over, just like that, everything resolved because of a distraction in the form of Blair Brackman, who now had all attention directed toward himself, all eyes glued on him, without needing to tap a spoon against a punch glass. He looked distressed.

He made an attempt to speak, but it was Melissa's voice that filled the room.

"My supposed friends," she said, sorrowfully, "at my party . . . at each other's throats—"

"Listen to me, people!" Blair interrupted, pulling out his inhaler. He pumped the device, and pumped again, but it was empty. "Damnation!" Blair flung the inhaler to the ground.

"Blair, please think . . ." said Rebecca, taking a tentative step toward him.

"How about another round of drinks, campers?" asked John cheerfully. He had his handkerchief out and was bleeding from his nose.

Meg, awakened by the sudden quiet, sat up on the sofa.

"Mustn't wrinkle your pants like that on the floor, Rod," she said.

Blair ignored the comment, as did everyone else, an insipid one because Rod was wearing jeans.

"I have had to piece things together," Blair said, "find some rational coherent whole amidst this rubble . . ."

"Look, everybody!" shouted Val, holding up her hand. "The other grapefruit!"

"Not again," said Rod. "I might throw up."

"Hold it back, Rod, honey," said Melissa. "Don't ruin things by vomiting at your own party."

"Let's line up again. Come on . . ." said Val.

"I'm game," said Rebecca, "and I promise to keep my tits out of the way this time, Rod. Come on . . . John . . . Deirdre . . ."

"Not until I've finished!" shouted Blair.

"The kitchen, Mom," said Val. She couldn't stop the inevitable from happening, but at least she could keep her mother from witnessing it.

"What?" asked Meg.

"Check the hors d'oeuvres. Remember?"

"Thanks for reminding me, dear. I knew there was something . . ." She hoisted her body off the couch with difficulty and stumbled to the kitchen. The louvered doors clattered, then quieted, granting permission for things to proceed.

"Punch, anyone?" asked John.

"No more for me," said Rod, now sitting cross-legged on the floor.

"Shut up, John," said Blair. "I've been listening too long. And because I've been listening so long, now I can't even . . . even . . . *breathe* any more." He was in bronchospasm, and there was nothing he could do about it, other than panic, which he did. Getting in air was like grabbing a handful of sand and trying to hold it intact. The grains escaped from his fist, and he had no air left.

"Blair, are you alright?" asked Melissa. Blair hunched over like a sprinter at the end of a race, hungry for air.

"I'll take you to the hospital," said Val, putting an arm on his shoulder.

"My car's in front . . ." said Rebecca.

"What about an ambulance?" asked Milton.

"Somebody call 911," said C.W.

"I'm scared, Dickie," said Candy, huddling up into her husband's arms like a frightened child.

"Nobody move! I'm fine!" Blair managed to gasp, pushing himself upright for a moment. "Just a little asthma!" He quickly bent back down, resting his forearms on his thighs.

Rod managed to get himself to his feet and come over. He patted Blair on the back tenderly.

"Take it easy, Blair," he said. "Both me and my brother had asthma when we were small. Just relax and don't fight it. There are probably some cat hairs or something in this room. And how about this? We can share an ambulance to the hospital and they can check me out too. My stomach's killing me . . ."

Blair, still hunched over, twisted his head and looked directly into Rod's eyes.

"I . . . love . . . Melissa. I love Melissa." he said.

The room was still.

"Blair, I don't understand what you're saying." Melissa's lips were quavering.

"Everybody loves my Melissa," said Rod. "Who can help it, you know? But nobody in the world loves her as much as I do."

"It was never like that, Blair," said Melissa, tearing up. "It was never like that."

"But . . ." gasped Blair, "but . . ." Shaking his head and staring blankly through blinking eyes, he was a fighter knocked to the canvas, disoriented and insensible. He closed his eyes. "Shit, I can't breathe," he finished.

"Let's get that ambulance," said Milton.

"I'll call them," said Dickie.

"Just call 911!" insisted C.W.

"Right," agreed Dickie.

"A taxi might be quicker," said Nigel.

"My car's right out in front," said Rebecca.

"Give me the keys," said Val.

"I can take him," said John.

"I'm taking him," said Val.

Rebecca ran into the bedroom for her purse. She had set it on the bed with her coat, but things were a jumble. She haphazardly rummaged through the coats until she found it and retrieved her keys. She also found what she thought was Blair's coat, and easily recognized Val's.

Val and Blair were waiting near the door, Blair still bent over. Val grabbed the coats and keys from Rebecca.

"If there's anything I can do . . ." offered Dickie.

"I'm taking care of him. He'll be fine," said Val. John held the door open for them.

Mitch Harrington had decided to step back into the hallway before anyone had seen him. He needed to think things through. Once out of the apartment and heading to the elevator, Val passed him with a look of surprise. Mitch, ever thoughtful, ran ahead of them and pressed the "Down" button.

"Thanks," said Val. "Mom invited you too?" she managed to ask needlessly.

Mitch stood awkwardly with them in the hallway, still wearing his coat. He looked sweaty. The elevator rang and the door opened.

"I've got the invitation," said Mitch, reaching into his coat pocket.

"Jesus fucking Christ," Val said, stepping into the elevator with Blair.

"Sorry I'm late, Val," Mitch called after her as the door closed.

Mitch Harrington spent a couple more minutes in the hallway summoning the courage to attempt another entrance into the party. The apartment door had been shut behind the departing Val and Blair, and he decided that he would ring the doorbell again. Things had quieted, and he assumed someone inside would hear it this time.

Indeed, all was quiet inside. No one was saying a word.

John was at the punch bowl, refilling glasses for Deirdre and Milton. Candy was sitting on the sofa between Nigel and Dickie. Dickie had an arm draped over her shoulder. He pushed his hair back being the ear, where it belonged. C.W. had arranged a plate of cheese and cold cuts for Rebecca, and he was making another platter for himself. Rod Schoenlieber was near the Noguchi table, consoling Melissa, who had her face in her hands and was quietly weeping.

Meg entered from the kitchen, carrying a tray of hors d'ouvres. They were of assorted, even bizarre shapes and size, but all appeared to be a uniform golden brown. Meg was smiling broadly.

"Everyone . . . they're perfect!" she exclaimed.

As the louvered doors stopped swinging, and all was quiet once more, the doorbell rang.

PART THREE

Aftermath

Saturday, March 14, 1981, 1:00 A.M.
Baptist Hospital, Room 401

Val offered to hang around until Blair was discharged, but he insisted that he would call a cab when the time came. She had brought him to the emergency room, after all, and hung around far longer than any friend reasonably should have, but when the ER staff decided to admit him overnight—just to be on the safe side—he told her enough was enough. Val nonetheless accompanied him and the orderly as he was gurneyed to a private room on the fourth floor. She waited as a nurse helped him with the transfer to bed, switching the oxygen tubing from the tank to the regulator and flow meter on the wall, dealing with the IV fluid bag, propping his head up with a couple of pillows, and covering him with a sheet and light polyester blanket. Val sat and watched silently from the orange vinyl visitor's chair in the room.

When some time had passed with Blair's eyes closed and no words spoken, Val got up to leave. She walked to the head of his bed and leaned down to kiss him, choosing forehead rather than nearest cheek to avoid the green tubing that connected to the nasal prongs. She held her lips there for a moment and felt his body relax, or possibly she was just imagining that.

So it would have been fine if she had simply inched her way backward out of the room, pretending he was asleep. But Blair, like Sleeping Beauty, opened his eyes with the kiss.

Val felt awkward, Blair could see it in her eyes, that she yearned not to end the evening with one of those "things left unsaid" moments. Substantive events of recent memory—the unspeakable scene he had made earlier with her sister in front of a number of friends and clients—had not been broached. He preferred it that way, trying to force the incident from his mind lest it affect his breathing, and comforting himself with the optimistic belief that he was too pathetic to be a laughing stock. But Val would not oblige him, at least not entirely.

"Some party, huh, Blair?" she said, her mouth in a forced smile.

"Sorry I didn't get to try the punch."

His parrying response missed the mark, perhaps because he was avoiding eye contact. He tried again.

"I suppose I made a scene." He looked her straight in the eyes, attempting a plaintive facial expression, but hard to say a successful one without him checking in a mirror. He could only assume that a breathing tubing helped one achieve a plaintive look.

"Just one of those things," she replied. "Your asthma, I mean."

Blair tried to read her expression, to no avail. Fleetingly he was conscious of the disconcerting sensation of having known Val for over twenty years without ever having gone past just seeing her. She would let things go for now, he hoped, not aggravate a sick man.

"Bad time for an attack, I suppose," he said, appreciating the safe zone that the topic of sickness provided.

"No." She paused and Blair noted that her jaw had clenched. "I'd say the timing was just about perfect."

And so it had been.

Val turned and walked out of his hospital room.

Blair forgot to thank her.

◠◦◦◠

Saturday, March 14, 10:30 A.M.
Baptist Hospital, Room 401

Blair, long finished with his hospital breakfast, was waiting for his discharge orders to be processsed before bothering to shower and change into his street clothes, or more accurately, into his party clothes from the night before. He was in no hurry. No one seemed to be rushing him, so the hospital census was likely down. He absently flicked through the channels on the TV; the sound was off and nothing tempted him to linger and raise the volume, so he let the screen settle on muted Saturday morning cartoons. The rapid scenes flashing before him, designed to avert the boredom of a six-year-old, were undeniably soothing.

Three floating red heart-shaped balloons appeared in the doorway, tethered by red ribbons to a small package held by a perky blonde candy striper. She walked in confidently, confirmed Blair's identity, and left the parcel and its attached card on the tray table next to him. Having acquited her duty, she flashed a wide smile through metal-armoured teeth and left.

The package sat benignly on the edge of the tray table, next to the empty orange juice container. Blair stared at it, shooting daggers. What he should have done—and he was kicking himself for not thinking of it a moment earlier—was refuse to accept the damn thing.

"I don't know what this is or who it's from, but I'd really like you to have it. Please. Take it. I'm serious."

That's what he should have said. Because, dammit, he really didn't want whatever it was. And he didn't want to know who it was from, either.

Finally, Blair relented, jerking the tray closer and ripping at the surface of the package so that the three balloon hearts fled heavenwards, bobbling for several seconds against the ceiling, protesting gallantly before settling into stillness. Tapping the unopened envelope against his open palm, Blair wondered who could possibly be cruel enough to send him heart-shaped helium balloons. Certainly his friends wouldn't—at least, not Rebecca or John, if only for the fact that heart-shaped helium balloons were corny, even contemptible. But who would mock him so? He felt his chest tighten. He squeezed his eyes shut and willed himself to relax, taking slow, deep breaths.

Before his anxiety could crescendo again, he rapidly tore open the envelope and removed the floral-themed card. He didn't bother reading the canned Hallmark text, an italicized sans serif font that had been undoubtedly group-tested and shown to convey heartfelt personal emotion more than any other font. The sentiment terminated with an exclamation point.

But he did decipher the messy script beneath it and the signature, from a blue Bic that was a running low on ink:

Dear Blair—

Just a brief note to tell you how pleasureable it was to meet you last night, and to express my thanks for the kindness and consideration you showed me. As a token of my appreciation, I'm enclosing a copy of my latest book. Hope you enjoy it! And hope you're on the mend soon!

Best personal regards,
Milton Perkins

Blair allowed himself a smile. He had listened sympathetically to an extremely short and, he had to be honest, completely irrelevant story about Gabriela from Argentina. Such had been the extent of his reduced-fat milk of human kindness to Milton Perkins.

And now, with a friend for life, Blair found himself tearing off the wrapping paper from the present in his hands, a token of appreciation from a grateful poet.

Blair turned the book over. It was thin and soft bound. The front cover said:

"Castration: A collection of love poems"
by Milton Perkins

As cartoon explosions continued silently on the televison set overhead, and a slight draft from somewhere caused the balloons to shift on the ceiling ever so slightly, Blair thumbed through the book, then went to the table of contents.

He ran his left index finger down the side of the page and found what he was looking for, what he knew would be there. And then he turned to page fourteen, to the poem entitled "Te deseo, Gabriela."

Blair started to read.

∽∞∾

Saturday, March 14, 11:30 A.M.
Baptist Hospital, Room 401

According to hospital policy, all patients had to be wheeled to the lobby by staff to meet their rides home, which for Blair would be one of the yellow cabs dependably loitering outside of the hospital entrance. Now dressed and waiting for transport, he was in the bathroom for a parting shot urination. In the meantime, an unexpected visitor had entered his hospital room. Giving the empty room the once over, and figuring Blair was in the john, Rebecca Harvey decided against the beat up vinyl chair that looked like a possible carrier of disease. She pushed the rolled-up johnny aside and and hopped up backwards to sit on the edge of the bed, legs crossed immodestly, though comfortably, at the ankles. Impatiently, she rocked her calves back and forth, causing one of her shoes to drop off.

Make-up was unusual for a Saturday morning, and Rebecca rarely bothered when she met John at the New Stanley. Today was different. Her face was fully made-up, an attempt to hide the fatigue that did unpleasant things to her face, so noticeable that morning. And she hadn't slept a wink after that damn party. A quick glance at her watch reassured her that she had plenty of time. She had come to the Baptist right after dropping off Bea at her dance class—earlier than usual—instructing her daughter not to get worried if she were a bit late picking her up. Mommie had an errand to run for a friend, she explained.

Blair was zipping up his pants when he emerged from the bathroom, gaze downward, and didn't see Rebecca until he was nearly on top of her. He jumped and made a small sound of surprise. She was sitting on his bed, and looking pretty good for eleven o'clock in the morning, especially after a night of intense partying. Or more accurately, after a night of an intense party.

"What are you doing here?" Blair's tone of voice, non-accusatory, expressed only genuine curiosity. Under normal circumstances, he might have been pleased to see her, and for an instant, given the sudden surprise, he forgot that he had ample reason to feel embarrassed, even mortified. The instant he remembered, he felt a queasiness in his stomach, then a tightness in his chest. He took a deep breath, and the sensations abated. Blair wasn't sure if he were ready to face people yet, but if anyone were to intrude on his planned, impending isolation, Rebecca was probably the best choice, second only to Milton Perkins.

"I'm giving you a ride home," Rebecca answered.

"That's really nice of you, Rebecca, but I'm planning to take a cab."

"I need to talk to you about something," she said. Her expression was one of absolute seriousness.

"I guess I kinda blew things," Blair said, sitting beside her on the bed. There would be no beating around the bush with Rebecca. He began to swing his dangling legs, as she had, but she had stopped; her legs were now still.

"You're a mess, Blair," she said.

"I know. I'm a psychologist." His attempt at humor fell flat.

She took a deep breath. "I can't believe you kept those feelings for her all these years. It never would have worked . . ."

"What do you mean by that?"

"Christ, Blair, I love Melissa, but damn, you know as well as I do . . . if you could just be honest with yourself for a minute . . . that she's not all that bright. And she . . . she's shallow!"

Blair bit his lip. Maybe, he thought, this is helping . . .

"Look at the men she chooses. Rod Schoenlieber . . . and Mitch Harrington! Doesn't that tell you anything? Do you need her so badly to fill some hole in your life that has absolutely nothing to do with her?"

Blair heard himself say something, that he couldn't believe himself, even as he was saying it. "I . . . I guess I hadn't really thought that much about it." He squirmed on the bed, a movement, transmitted to Rebecca, that momentarily broke her stillness.

"You're so self-absorbed that you can't even see what's in front of you," she said, shaking her head.

"Everyone's self-absorbed," Blair responded defensively, "the whole crew, the whole group of us. And desperate. All of us, not knowing what we want, not knowing where to look for it."

"Speak for yourself, Blair."

He looked at her, blinking back tears. "I don't think I'm as self-aborbed as everybody else because . . . because I'm always listening to them. If I listen all the time to other people, how could I be self-involved?"

Rebecca hadn't stopped shaking her head.

"I'm not sure you've been really listening to anyone, Blair."

"I need to take some time off."

"You do. You should."

"I've lost nearly all my clients anyway." Another failed attempt at self-deprecating levity.

"You've saved some money, right? You're okay financially?" Rebecca asked.

He nodded.

"You could find something else, some other line of work. Go to back to school. Or teach. You could teach."

Blair sat silently, looking down at his lap.

"I'm going back to school," Rebecca said, a little proudly. "Night classes at U.M.K.C. to finish up my bachelor's. And then I think I may go on to grad school."

"Rebecca! Wow! That's fabulous!"

Both of them glowed in smiles for a moment, than Rebecca let her smile escape.

"It hasn't been easy, trying to balance work with being a mom, and trying to get those credits at night. The babysitting costs have been a killer, but sometimes my sister helps."

Blair gave her a sympathetic look.

"Good for you."

Rebecca inhaled deeply. "And a great aunt of mine died. Left me a little money. Not much in the grand scheme of things, but for me it's going to make a big difference."

"That's really good. Sorry about your aunt, though."

They both sat, sharing the awkward silence. Rebecca finally broke it.

"About last night . . ."

"I'm over her . . . I'll get over it . . . I just made such a fool out of myself. In front of everybody."

"They broke up."

"What?"

"They broke up. The engagement is off."

"What?" Blair was incredulous. "When?"

"After you left. We could have used a group session. You provoked it, then split the scene. You kind of caused a 'Come to Jesus' moment. Not in the way you intended, of course. But it shook people up. Brought people to their senses. Maybe everyone was a bit less self-involved for a moment." She paused. "And all because you took a crap in the middle of their reception."

"They were listening to me for a change," Blair said, still processing. He tried to visualize the scene, wondering what Melissa had said, what she had done . . .

"How did it . . . where is she?"

"I thought you were over her, Blair."

"I am. I will be."

"You need to be over her, Blair. It isn't what you think."

"*What* isn't what I think?"

Rebecca placed her hand on Blair's thigh and gave it a gentle squeeze before returning it to her lap.

"Melissa is getting back together with Mitch." She unconsciously brought her knees together. Hands in lap, knees together, Rebecca could have been in Sunday school.

Blair blinked heavily, as if he had a tic. He started to say something but stopped himself, instead stifling a grunt at the back of his throat.

"How did that happen?" It felt odd, him asking questions like that about Melissa, when he usually would only have had to wait until their Thursday session to hear all about it first-hand. No more Thursdays.

Rebecca sighed.

"Who the fuck knows? Melissa has issues, you know that. But evidently she still loves the guy, or thinks she does. Maybe your little confession made her think about what she was doing and why. Gave her some insight, for once. That long sought catharsis."

"Right. Well, I was always shooting more for transference than catharsis," Blair said, not attempting to deflect with humor, just being truthful.

"Maybe you just can't help yourself, Blair. You're the best fucking therapist in the world. Even when you don't want to be."

"Oh my God . . ."

"It was quite a scene. In any case, your St. Augustine confessions sure as hell gave Mitch the courage to speak up and express his feelings. That and the fucking non-alcohoic rhubarb punch. Unlike you, Harrington had the staying power to get through the whole thing. Told her how much he still loved her, how he knew they could make it work, that he had 'grown up.' Poor Rod. I really felt for him. He took it like a man." Rebecca considered. "Actually, not at *all* like a man. He was understanding, empathetic, compassionate. Despite his broken heart. Guess he isn't as narcissistic as most of us."

"I can't believe—"

"Well, you fucking better. And be thankful, Your own little escapade pales in comparison to what went on . . ."

Blair now had both hands covering his eyes. He wasn't really sure what he was feeling, and he had no urge to articulate his emotions. His emotions, whatever they were, were real, and his analysis was bound to be bullshit.

Rebecca continued.

"The absolute worst of it was Meg. Worse than you can possibly imagine. She was absolutely devastated. Hysterical doesn't begin to describe . . . screaming for Ora Lee. It broke my heart."

Blair looked up at Rebecca, eyes red.

"And Val wasn't there to calm her down. She was bringing you here, remember? We thought we were going to have to call an ambulance . . . thought she might have a heart attack or stroke out."

"Is she alright?"

"Well, you can guess who calmed her down . . ."

"Rod."

"You bet. Everybody was completely freaked out, Mitch and Melissa hugging and crying, everybody else in the room with so much baggage in their lives, so overwhelmed by their own selfishness. It wouldn't have done the Marines proud, I'll tell you that."

"Except for Rod."

"Yep. Good guy, that Rod. Has a heart, even if he is kind of a dork. Rod and a handful of Xanax that Meg had lying around in the bathroom cabinet. And—oh yeah, that little poet guy was pretty helpful as well."

"Milton. Milton Perkins," said Blair, and feeling ridiculous after he said it, added, "He gave me these balloons."

Rebecca, feeling ridiculous herself, couldn't help but look up at the red, heart-shaped balloons.

"What the fuck," she said.

"Not important," said Blair.

They sat silently for a while, both looking down, with their hands in their laps.

Blair sniffled and wiped away a tear with the back of his hand.

"So that's why you came to pick me up. That's what you needed to tell me."

Rebecca looked at him, then down into her lap, then up at him again. She wiped her own tear aside, not minding that she smeared her make-up. She pushed her hair aside first with the right hand, then with the left. Then she bit down on her lower lip and held her teeth there for a few seconds, composing herself. Her newly found resolve was rock solid.

"Yes, that's it, Blair. That's what I needed to tell you. And now you know. Listen, I need to pick up Bea." She looked at her watch.

"I was going to take a cab anyway," Blair said.

"Call Val."

"What?"

"Have Val pick you up. She's crazy about you. God knows why, but she has a thing for you. Carrying a torch. You, of all people, should know what that's like."

"I don't think—" Blair began.

"She's the pick of the litter, Blair. Smarter than her sister, nicer than her sister, and under those school marm clothes, she has a terrific little body. She could do a lot better for herself, so I don't understand why she bothers with *you* . . ."

"I wasn't really aware. Just thought we were friends."

"You don't know what's in front of your face, Blair." She stood up to leave. "You're such a fucking project. So much work."

"I don't think Val can deal with . . . it's a terrible position for her to be in. To feel like she's second fiddle, that I'm with her because I can't get over her sister . . ."

"You're over her sister."

"Right. I am."

"And it's her choice to deal with it or not, she's a big girl. Maybe you should give it a try. Or not. I don't really care. I gotta go."

He stood up with her.

"Maybe I'll call her. For the ride. Thanks, Rebecca."

She moved close to him and pressed both of his cheeks with the palms of her hands. She put her face right in front of his, their noses practically touching.

"You do that, Blair Brackman," she said. "You need to learn to see what's right in front of your face." She kept pressing for a couple of seconds, squinting with one eye. Finally, when she finally released the pressure, he said, weakly, "I will."

She turned to stride away, but before doing so, she reached up and grabbed at the red ribbons floating nearby, at eye level. She pulled the three balloons down and towards her. They bobbled by her head, like frisky puppies.

"You don't need these, do you Blair? Bea will like them," she said, not waiting for his answer. And she was gone.

∞

Rebecca had plenty of time before dance class ended; enough, at least, to have a quick cup of coffee while John drank his Scotch at the New Stanley. She knew he'd be there, waiting, nursing his Saturday morning breakfast of Johnny Walker Black and wondering where she was. It wasn't like him to worry much, though. He knew she could always take care of herself.

The helium balloons were a nuisance in the car, blocking her view out the passenger window and obstructing part of the front windshield when she turned. At the first stoplight, she anchored them down in the passenger seat with her purse. Why did that dweeby poet send Blair heart-shaped balloons? she allowed herself to wonder, but only once. Men were crazy.

She'd had her chance to tell the truth and passed it by. She was too naturally guarded to be the confession type, especially in the bright daylight without Meg Manning's rhubarb punch. A secret African recipe that had undoubtedly been responsible for much inter-tribal discord on the continent. Rebecca knew she'd have other chances, other opportunities if she wanted, and none would ever be at a good time. Besides, she had made her decision years earlier, and her instincts had been right. Her life hadn't been easy, but things were looking up. A degree, a better job, a bigger apartment in a better school district for Bea. And Bea was a great, well-adjusted kid. She had asked about her father on a couple of occasions, and certainly she would ask in the future, but Rebecca had so far been able to deflect the questions. When she couldn't deflect any longer . . . well, she'd worry about it when the time came.

It wasn't that she didn't want to dump the load on Blair. She just couldn't deal with the drama, the emotional cost of a full time, complicated project when her life was only now coming into its own. It was selfish, she knew. She had waited in line, the queue for the self-involved, and now her turn had finally come. She'd be damned if she were going to step out of line just to tell Blair that Bea was actually his daughter.

If he had loved her, or if there had been any possibility that he might ever love her, she might have viewed things differently. But Blair didn't love her. He would just overthink, overcompensate, be guilt-ridden. He would try to become a part of Bea's life, and it would never work. Already an emotional basket case, he would become a complete pain in the ass. Never expect a man to change, she reminded herself. They never do. So she could live with depriving Blair of his daughter.

In any case, it was all hypothetical. She would keep her secret for as long as possible. The question of fairness was relevant, though, but only insofar as Bea was concerned. Was it fair to keep the identity of her father a secret? How would she react when she found out the truth? Would she hate Rebecca? Feel betrayed? Would it jeopardise their relationship, and perhaps screw Bea up for the rest of her life? Would a teen-age Bea someday scream at her: "You bitch! You're so selfish and self-absorbed! How could you do this to me? You've ruined my fucking life!"

It was always a possibility. But maybe, after getting her degree, Rebecca would be offered a job out of town, get out of Dodge. She could start a new life on the coast—either coast would do. And with a couple thousand miles between Bea and Blair, she could just begin by saying: "There was this guy, when I was young and stupid, and he really never loved me. He's married to someone else now and lives in Kansas City . . ."

The car parked, she headed toward the bar, knowing she looked pretty good and it showed in that confident walk of hers. She sensed a trio of passing men turning to watch her. A mother of an eight-year-old and she still had it, even if no real purpose were served. She slowed and ran her free hand through her hair, exposing her forehead. The other hand held the balloons.

A male arm reached in front of her to grab the oversized brass door handle and pull the door open for her. She didn't say thanks, but stepped over the threshold and searched the tables for John. He sat by himself at a table in back, looking into a coffee mug. Coffee?

Rebecca stood in place, smiling to herself. The man who had opened the door for her, cologne-emitting but otherwise a spectre, brushed by her. She felt particularly free and optimistic about the future. Bea might get screwed up over the whole mess, she thought, but damn it anyway, she'd get over it and be a survivor like her mom. And if need be, by then her mom would be able to afford a good therapist for both of them. Anyone but Blair Brackman, of course.

John Palopolus looked up and saw Rebecca standing just inside the doorway, smiling and holding three heart-shaped helium balloons. He sat up straight, eyes acquiring a sparkle. He pointedly looked at the balloons, flapped a limp hand against his chest, and mouthed, "Por *moi*?"

Rebecca brushed the hair away from the left side of her face and yanked the ribbons up and down, tantalizingly, jostling the balloons. John Palopolus, God love him, had a goofy smile on his face.

Rebecca Harvey strode over to his table.

THE END

ACKNOWLEDGMENTS

Art Suskin, John Bruce, Joe Leahy, and Dr. Charles Porter were present at the beginning of this process, and helped me in both tangible and mysterious ways. I am also grateful to several readers who contributed more than they probably realize, including Michael Beiriger, Keith Raffel, Deborah Victoroff, Sarah Payne Stuart, and Robert N. Reeves III. Sara Mannarelli Durfee filled in my knowledge gaps about Princeton, and Drs. Carol Benson and Peter Doubilet graciously lent me their apartment to complete the final touches. The Levitt family also has my heartfelt gratitude.

As always, I've heavily relied on the support of my wife, Sharon Tyers, and our daughters Jordan Vincent and Caitlin Vincent. As she has in the past, Caitlin served throughout as a patient and accommodating sounding board and my go-to editor, a task made more difficult given my obstinacy. And again, Jim Cunningham has provided exemplary service as a designer.

Although this novel takes place in Kansas City, I wrote it entirely in Melbourne, Australia, which I highly recommend for other authors setting their books in Kansas City. I rate the State Library of Victoria, the City Library of Melbourne, and the Journal Café as my favorite spots for writing, ever. And to get me in the proper frame of mind for my efforts, I must credit walks on DeGraves Street, coffee from Addis Café and Roastery, and Olympic Donuts.

If you enjoyed this novel by L.M. Vincent, you might want to check out some of his other books:

SAVING DR. BLOCK

"An entertaining coming-of-age story . . . The historical setting provides a rich backdrop to the action, and the spy capers keep the story moving along at a quick pace. Humorous touches and a likeable protagonist make this heartwarming tale a treat."

—Kirkus Reviews

IN SEARCH OF MOTIF NO. 1
(A Non-fiction "Must Read," 2012 Mass Book Awards!)

"Like all good tales it begins with a question and tracks through some pretty interesting turf to get an answer . . . As he [Vincent] unravels the tale, he takes the reader through a delicious amount of local art history populated by some pretty colorful characters . . . It all makes for a quirky, personable read."

—Patricia Harris, BOSTON.COM

PAS DE DEATH

"Pas de Death has wit, intelligence, esoteric information, and a wildly inventive (yet plausible) murder method that is surely unparalleled in all of detective fiction. How much more could anyone want in a mystery?"

—Aaron Elkins

"Great stuff, carefully written and thoughtfully conceived."

—Adam Woog, Seattle Times

". . . the season's most original reason for not telling the police what you know about an unusually clever murder."

—Kirkus Reviews

FINAL DICTATION

"Final Dictation is the most absorbing mystery yet from Seattle's large stable of crime authors."

—The Seattle Times

"Vincent's first novel is a surprisingly ingenious whodunit with a hospital setting and a radiologist hero . . . a wry, well-plotted entry in a pleasantly old-fashioned mode."

—Kirkus Reviews

"Fascinating medical detail, an ingenious plot, and a surprisingly mature style . . . all contribute to a fine whodunit."

—Booklist

ABOUT THE AUTHOR

A native of Kansas City and former editor of the Harvard Lampoon, L.M. Vincent has published both fiction and non-fiction, and his plays have been produced regionally and Off-off Broadway. He and his wife have two grown daughters and divide their time between Seattle and Melbourne, Australia.